I Know You, Joanna

'Does it excite you when I ask you intimate questions?' asked Adam.

'Yes.' I swallowed nervously, awaiting his next question.

'In what way are you excited? I want you to describe to me how you feel.'

I burned with shame but managed to answer him. I revelled in the shame and humiliation he was subjecting me to.

'Sexually. Your questions are exciting me sexually,' I told him.

'Tell me, Joanna. Describe to me how your body is responding to my questioning of you.'

I looked up at him then, straight into his eyes. I had to know just why he was doing this to me. Never before had I felt so completely helpless and I had to know his motives. I had already lost my will and my control, but even more powerful was my real fear of losing my soul to him. I just had to know why. His eyes smouldered as he waited for my answer. However hard he tried – and I knew he was trying – he couldn't hide the glaring fact that he was just as turned on as I was. I glanced down at his crotch and he fidgeted, unable to disguise the powerful bulge that threatened to burst his zip.

Other books by the Author:

King's Pawn

I Know You, Joanna
Ruth Fox

BLACK Lace

Black Lace books contain sexual fantasies.
In real life, always practise safe sex.

First published in 2002 by
Black Lace
Thames Wharf Studios
Rainville Road
London W6 9HA

Design by Smith & Gilmour, London
Printed and bound by Mackays of Chatham PLC

ISBN 0 352 33727 3

1

I am a little ashamed, in a delicious sort of way, to admit that all the following words apply to me: tease, nymphomaniac, loose, wanton, immoral and debauched. Over the past year or so I have been called all those things and more, usually by a man with a smile on his face and an erection in his trousers.

I suggest you judge for yourselves whether or not those terms apply to me once you have read my story.

As an admin assistant, which is really just an upmarket term for gofer/computer inputter, I was reasonably well paid by Jacamann Publishing. Everyone in our office had known each other for years, and they found to their delight after only a few months that I had an insatiable need to write horny stories. My close group of colleagues would hand them around the office and then beg me for more. But they teased me incessantly, suggesting that I only wrote about sex because I wasn't getting any. The sad fact was that it was true.

I had finished a long-term relationship two years before and hadn't been able to get back into the swing of things again. I still tended to do just what George and I had done almost every night for five years – stay in and watch the telly. I had even found myself looking forward to getting into work so I could discuss the latest episode of *EastEnders* with Stacy, one of the girls. I was desperate for a bit of excitement, preferably sexual, so I poured out my longings in stories.

When *Leather and Lace* was launched it was quite a

step away from the usual stuff the company published. It wasn't long before I was summoned to the top floor to meet Mr A Jacamann, or AJ as everyone called him. I had no idea why.

Everyone speculated about why Jacamanns had decided to launch a pornographic magazine to add to their range of publications and decided it had been a whim of Adam Jacamann, our illustrious boss. It had been launched, according to one of my more fanciful friends, as a dare or a tax dodge but, to be honest, I didn't give a damn about all the stuffy politics upstairs.

I had sat in stunned silence, in total awe of AJ and his office, as he informed me that my writing abilities had come to his notice. He asked if I would be interested in trying my hand at writing full time. Of course I agreed but I was mortified that he knew about my stories.

The interview lasted no more than five minutes and, at the end of it, not only did I get this amazing new job where I could spend all day doing the thing I enjoyed most, but I was offered the option of staying at my usual desk or utilising a small room that had once been a walk-in store cupboard. I opted for the store cupboard – mainly because I couldn't imagine myself writing all my rudest thoughts in a room full of friends. Letting them read my stories was one thing but I did tend to get rather overexcited when I wrote. It seemed to help me write convincingly.

So, within days, I had my own tiny office at the end of the corridor on the fourth floor of the office block that housed Jacamann Publishing. I kept myself to myself as much as I could. As long as I had my job writing rude stories and articles they could keep all their meetings and other projects. Much of the time I got the distinct feeling that only a handful of people actually remembered I was there so I kept my head down. I made sure I always produced my work on time and, so far, it had worked well. The only fly in the ointment was that from the moment I had been summoned to Mr Jacamann's office and stood outside the door trembling, I had been having fantasies about him. If only he knew just how often my stories were written with him in mind.

I was living in the small garden flat of a beautiful old Victorian semi that housed me and three other singles and was set in the slightly seedy end of a thriving town on the east coast. The whole flat consisted of a largish lounge with a kitchenette hidden behind a screen in one corner. I had made my little home cosy with a deep old squidgy settee and a couple of floor cushions to take the overspill if I had friends round. The bedroom was a bit larger with a shower cubicle that had been built into a large alcove off to one side. With my large brass bed and Victorian washstand that I used as a bedside table it was almost full. The small square of courtyard garden was just about big enough for a washing line and a sun lounger. If I laid out starkers to top up my tan I was almost in private. Apart from the single man in the flat above me, that is.

Alex. Tall, blond, quiet Alex was only about thirty and appeared to enjoy my sunbathing. He would watch for hours from his upstairs window, sitting on a chair in the bay, alternately reading and gawping. I would stretch languidly and turn over often to give him a good eyeful, or put my bed as far out of sight as possible so he had to crane his neck. A bit naughty, I know, but harmless all the same and he obviously enjoyed the game. My attitude was this: I knew he had to stretch some way to see me properly, so if he was prepared to make so much effort then who was I to spoil his fun? I had lain there when it was sunny for a whole year unobserved before he took the empty room, so I was damned if I was going to change when he moved in. For the first few months after he moved in above me he would avoid my eyes if we passed in the doorway but, as he settled in, he started blatantly gazing at my breasts when I saw him, then he would grin at me a little sheepishly. Then we progressed to 'Morning', and 'Nice day, isn't it?'

One Saturday, while I was locking up my bike in the lobby of the house, Alex squeezed past me quite unnecessarily, brushing against my bottom as he passed. He stopped behind me. 'Nice enough for sun-bathing is it, Jo?' he asked. I stayed looking down at my padlock while I desperately thought of a fitting answer. Instead of the witty retort I searched for, I stuttered, embarrassed at being confronted by my wantonness. Flaunting in the garden is one thing, but being con-fronted with it was different. Then it came to me. I stood up and turned to face him with a definite invita-tion in my eyes.

'I was thinking of lying out for an hour this after-noon. Are you free? You could always join me instead of just watching.' I was convinced he would be ashamed to have his voyeurism pointed out but he grinned wickedly and promised me that he wouldn't miss it for the world.

True to his word, there he was that afternoon, stand-ing above me less than five minutes after I had unfolded my bed and stretched out on it. He had a brand new sun lounger still in the polythene tucked under his arm and the biggest grin on his face when he saw that I had put a bikini on. However much I enjoyed winding him up I couldn't be brazen enough just to lie there naked knowing he was coming, so I had put on the flimsiest sunwear I could find. It was bright butter-cup yellow, very brief with a low-cut top and thong bottom.

'Sexy, but I must say I prefer the one you usually wear. I am a little embarrassed now because I didn't bring anything to put on.' He laughed at me as I looked up at him. The sun was behind him and all I could make out was his very sexy grin. Without another word he unpacked his bed and laid it out so close to mine it was almost touching. Then Alex shucked off his clothes as if he stripped for a living. I was so glad I had my sunglasses on because I could watch his every move without him knowing and, believe me, his moves were poetry to a sex-starved girl like me. His body was strong and muscular with the small waist and broad chest of a bodybuilder, but not too many bulging muscles. He was eminently watchable.

I am sure Alex knew I was watching him because he posed as each piece of clothing came off. He strutted a little as he walked around the end of the bed to lay his clothes neatly on the wooden bench tucked away in the corner, milking every moment to show off. Eventually, when he had taken off everything but his boxer shorts, I taunted him, convinced he wouldn't have the courage to strip completely. But he turned to face me then slowly pulled down his shorts. He stepped out of them then stretched up to the sun. He ran his hand over his tackle with a hint of promise then sat down on his bed and casually challenged me, 'Your turn now! You can't lie there week after week tantalising me, you bad girl, then leave your clothes on when you finally invite me to join you. That really isn't fair!'

He was beautiful, and his bronzed body stretching out on the bed so close to mine was very distracting. I tried surreptitiously to look at his parts but it was impossible without craning my neck – and that would have been rather obvious. I enjoyed a fleeting glance before he lay down but it was too brief; just a flash really. I didn't have to think for long. After seeing him strip so provocatively I was very horny. Sunbathing always made me horny anyway so this was unbelievably exciting. I rose to the challenge and, before any second thoughts deterred me, I quickly wriggled out of my thong while still sitting down and then struggled to undo the hooks of my bra.

'Here, let me help,' he offered with a definite huskiness to his voice. 'Turn over.'

In for a penny, I thought, and turned as directed. His deft hands unhooked the clasp then eased the straps off my shoulders so I could work it out from under me. Before I knew what was happening he had picked up my bottle of oil and squirted some into the hollow at the base of my spine. I squealed at the shock and the ice was truly broken. As he very adeptly massaged the cool viscous liquid into my flesh we talked and got to know each other. When he asked what it was I did for a living that allowed me to spend long hours out in the garden, I told him that I wrote for a magazine. I tried to change the subject but he was having none of it. He kept asking what mag I wrote for but I evaded the question for at least five minutes as his knowing hands smoothed the oil into increasingly intimate places.

I jumped out of my skin when he slapped me on the bottom and insisted, 'Answer the question, Jo.' The sting of the slap on my bare oily flesh tingled through my body and snaked up my spine as I wriggled my pleasure and involuntarily raised my bottom from the bed.

Alex had already offered the information that he was a mature student at the local university and that he was taking a degree in biology. His continued onslaught of slaps on my rear finally persuaded me to tell him about *Leather and Lace*. I looked sideways at him from under my hair as I explained that I wrote erotica. He sat on the side of his sun lounger, leaning over me, transfixed by what I was telling him and he made me giggle when he suggested that our interests were a bit alike – bodies and all that.

The smooth practised action of his hands became very hypnotic as he asked me how I felt about writing erotica. 'Do you get turned on when you write?' he asked, as his hands slid further down until they were delving between my thighs. The slipperiness of the lotion so close to my pussy was sending me crazy and I bucked upwards to invite him in, wriggling and writhing shamelessly.

'Of course I do,' I groaned.

'What about the one you wrote about Tamsin, the girl who had sex in the park, open to the elements? Did you get turned on when you wrote that one?'

I started to jump up to protest that he had tricked me, but he just pushed his fingers further into the hot slippery gap between my legs. As his magical hands explored me he explained that he had known for ages what I did. The other tenants couldn't wait to tell him that they had a porno writer living in their midst.

His fingers had taken on a life of their own and were insinuating their way between my sex lips, teasing my clitoris and working their way inside me. I strained upward to gain more intensity, so grateful that no one could witness my debauchery. He withdrew his probing fingers slightly and teased some more. His fingers tugged gently on my pubic hairs, creating a very exciting shivery feeling that swamped me. I didn't care any more – all reservation flew out the window as I raised my bottom as far as I could and spread my legs apart to entice his fingers back, back to the exquisite game they had been playing a minute before.

'You can do better than that, Jo,' he cajoled, enticing me further into the game.

I groaned loudly as I stretched myself up as far as I could and he kept pushing until I was on all fours with my naked bottom rudely on display. His fingers rewarded my disgusting behaviour and buried themselves deep inside me. His other hand cupped my breast, which was no longer crushed beneath me but dangling, the invitation obvious. He tantalised my nipple. He was pulling and rolling it between his fingers until I thought I would go crazy if I didn't get to come soon. I thrust down onto his hand, my breast in his palm, and begged for release with my moans.

'What's the matter, Jo? Do you want to come?' he asked softly, bending close to my ear.

'Please, please make me come,' I pleaded. 'Just touch me there and I will come. Please, Alex.' I wiggled, hoping I could move his attention to my clit, but his devious hands continued their play; just enough to keep me on the boil but not enough to tip me over, and he knew it. His thumb started to twirl around the nerves surrounding my clit but deliberately avoided what I needed to give me the relief I desperately wanted.

'Alex,' I wailed. 'I need it now.'

'Do it then, Jo. Show me what you want. I want you to play with yourself.'

'I can't,' I cried. 'It's far too personal. I can't do it here in the garden in front of a stranger.' I think we both realised the stupidity of that sentence at the same time. There I was, naked in the garden with this 'stranger's' hand sunk deep inside my pussy but I was too embarrassed to touch myself. I laughed out loud as I slipped my own hand between my thighs and sought my slippery clit. He actually bent over to look, and then got frustrated because he couldn't see properly. He pushed me over onto my back but kept his busy fingers right where they were. My legs got tangled with his arm for a moment but a bit of amateur yoga did the trick and then we were where we wanted to be. I was on my back, legs akimbo, with his fingers as far into my greedy sex as they would go and his other hand exploring my heavy breasts. His eyes greedily took in the whole scene before him. He picked up my hand and put it on my clitoris for me, persuading me by his actions that it was OK. I rubbed frantically as his fingers pushed and probed my insides and his free hand pulled and tugged on my nipples one at a time.

Less than a minute later I exploded into a sweaty heap as his hand slowed to a stop and his blitz on my nipples gradually relaxed. I lay for a minute or two with my arm across my eyes to protect them from his knowing look, then tentatively removed it and glanced over at him. Talk about a wide-mouthed frog ... he was grinning from ear to ear as if he had just won the lottery. My eyes travelled down his torso, now glistening with sweat, to his hard throbbing cock that looked about to burst. I wanted to touch him so badly. I sat up and pushed him backwards until his hands went behind him to balance and he was leaning back, exposing his gorgeous cock and tight straining balls.

I pushed the bed away and knelt in front of him, no longer bothered by my nakedness, and pushed his legs apart. I shuffled forward until I was right between his spread thighs and cupped his cock between my large breasts. I grabbed the bottle of oil and dribbled a little over my breasts until it trickled down my cleavage to his cock. He gasped as the slippery substance coated his now-straining hard-on, and I cupped my breasts together to enclose him just as I had in a story I had written a week or two before.

As I slowly moved backwards and forwards, rocking on my heels, his purple cock slid out of sight then pushed its way up in the hot slick tunnel between the mounds of my breasts. By this time his face was almost as purple as his knob, and he was panting rapidly with his eyes rolled back in rapture as I wanked him with my breasts.

'Oh fuck, that's good,' he groaned. 'Christ, you're amazing. Where did you learn to do that?'

I was born for this, I thought, as I murmured a non-committal answer, knowing I had never done anything like it in my life. I longed to take him in my mouth so I slipped further down onto my haunches and first kissed then licked his balls, tight now with sperm. I could see his cock, dark and throbbing, dancing before my eyes. I broadened my tongue and took one long wet lick from his balls to the tip of his cock then teased the end with the tip. More than anything I just wanted to devour him, but I had to tease him as he had me so I just tantalised the shiny bulbous end, swirling my tongue around and grazing my teeth gently across the end.

Alex obviously couldn't stand any more because he took his weight on one hand and grabbed the back of my head with the other, forcing my lips down over his length. He tasted strongly of oil but I was past caring. An overwhelming feeling of peace and acceptance came over me as he took charge and fucked my mouth. His cock filled my mouth to capacity and caused me to retch occasionally when he became overkeen, but his hips gyrated upward just the right amount to fill me with cock. I cupped his balls in my hand and rolled them gently in my palm as they tightened, ready to explode. Then dribble dripped off my chin and his smell filled my nostrils as his hand held me in his control and his desperate cock pumped salty spurts down my throat. I gulped furiously and kept my mouth latched onto him until his spasms stopped and his erection subsided.

Oh yes, I loved my little flat. I was self-sufficient and very happy. I was even reasonably sure of my sexuality: middle of the road, hungry, but definitely adventurous which, in hindsight, seems unbelievable. Alex had made me realise just how much I longed not only to have some sex of any kind but also to experiment.

I knew everyone felt that, at 32, I should have settled down long ago with a 'nice' man, a couple of kids and probably even a dog. I can't decide which image put me off most. The 'nice' bit probably. I never have gone for 'nice'. Even when I was younger and my sisters met and married just the type of men that everyone approves of I didn't ever dream of anything but sex. Lots of sex! I wanted sex of every description known to woman. I always wanted more. Even when I had been with George I had been unsatisfied. I didn't necessarily want more in quantity but certainly more in variety and exploration. I longed to experience everything my body and mind was capable of.

I yearned to put my adventurous spirit into sex but had never met the right man. Alex remained a contender but he only lived above me during the week in term time; the rest of the time he lived on a farm somewhere in Shropshire with his parents.

After our vulgar fun in the garden we drifted into a friendship that was pleasurable but had definite sexual overtones. So I remained titillated but unfulfilled – not a good combination. Not if you are impatient like me.

As I sat in my tiny office the day this all started I

was writing a fantasy story by 'Sandra from Basildon'. It was about an adventurous young lady (Sandra from Basildon, of course) having sex with three men at the same time. I sat pounding away at my keyboard with my legs crossed tightly under my desk to stave off the tingling sensation in my crotch that a particular description had aroused. I had no idea what it would be like to have sex with more than one man but my imagination did all the work. My stories were good and, according to the letters we received in response, they were very popular. At the last staff meeting it had been suggested that I be given more to do in response to my 'fans', but nothing had materialised as yet. That's the problem with working for a largish company – too many promises.

I was gazing out of my window across the rooftops trying to imagine how it would feel to be in my heroine's position when my computer pinged to let me know I had an e-mail.

Joanna
I'm sure you are busy this morning but could you do a reshuffle and come to see me at 10 a.m. I have a proposition for you.
Adam

To begin with I couldn't even think who Adam was. Then, when I eventually realised that I had been summoned by *the* Adam, the Adam who set my heart racing, I was surprised to say the least. Adam was very rarely that polite – he was gorgeous but not often polite. Usually any summons from on high was an order, not a polite request. He also probably guessed that I was never *really* busy, so my female intuition was very confused straight away.

'Come on in, Joanna. Thanks for coming at such short notice,' he said as he smiled his welcome.

'That's OK, Mr Jacamann, I didn't have much on anyway,' I answered tentatively, my curiosity making it almost impossible to stay relaxed.

'Call me Adam, please. If you accept my proposition we will be seeing a lot more of each other and I hope we can be friends. I am convinced that my proposal is perfect for you. I just hope you agree.'

As Adam was going against everything I had heard about him and was behaving in a most amenable way, I decided to do the same.

'Go on, I'm all ears,' I said as I settled my bum into the squidgy leather chair he had indicated. He sat opposite me and I met his gaze across the highly polished coffee table in the little oasis that was the area of his office set aside for informal meetings. How could any visitor possibly be at ease in this cosy setting, with their knees almost up around their ears? Oh well, I thought. Here goes.

'Good. I was hoping you would be open to suggestions. I enjoy your work for us on *Leather and Lace* and I would like you to start a new project. It will be an agony aunt page but with a difference. I want you to meet the readers. You – and we are offering this to you first – will be responsible for the whole project. I see it perhaps like this: they write to you, we publish their letters and you meet one of them and do a feature on their specific type of sexuality. You are at liberty just to meet and interview the readers but I get a gut feeling about your enthusiasm for the subject and I would be very surprised if you wouldn't enjoy this on a more intimate level. I know I am asking a lot of you, but this would really be ground-breaking stuff and I am sure I have picked the right girl for the job.'

He didn't actually ask for an answer. He just looked at me and raised his eyebrows. I was absolutely gob-smacked and found it very difficult to take in at first. I wasn't quite sure what he was suggesting but he quickly made it very clear as he continued: 'If you agree, and once we iron out a few facts, I would be happy to let you call the shots that would ensure that you were never in a position you didn't want to be in. So to speak.' The look on his face as he grinned at the end of his sentence was decidedly suggestive. I did a double take, questioning what my eyes were seeing. Adam had never, even though I fancied him like mad, ever shown anything but professional interest in me. Unless you counted the Christmas party the year before when we had a very rude drunken slow dance. As I couldn't remember what we had talked about and even though Stacy had said we were giggling and chatting for about ten minutes, I had just put it out of my mind. Apart from that one lapse in my memory I had only seen him a few times.

Adam was a bit of a dark horse really and all the girls had been really cross with me when I'd told them that, even though we had danced very intimately, apparently, I had no more information about our sexy enigmatic boss than they had. We all spent hours gossiping about him. He was far too discreet about his private life for our liking. No specific information to talk about, just speculation, so we made a lot up. Most of the girls agreed that he was a pompous arse who thought he was better than us – but I had a different image of him. Perhaps it was based on things that were said between us while we were dancing, I don't know. But I had a completely different idea about Adam Jacamann. Yes, he was powerful and arrogant, but something about him appealed to me deep down inside my sexuality. There was an untouchable quality about him, an aloofness that sent my insides into meltdown. He had a controlled, confident air about him that set off all sorts of fantasies in my head, and elsewhere. I caught him looking at me in the lift once. It was a day or two after our little dance and he gazed at me very boldly and suggestively and then the next day ignored me as if he had no idea who I was. When he looked at me with that way of his I felt as if he knew everything about me, from my thoughts and needs to my under-wear choice and my body parts. He managed to give this impression without actually doing anything apart from giving the occasional knowing half-smile. Very disconcerting to a horny, hungry single like me.

I mentally shook off my thoughts. I didn't have to think about it. I knew instantly that this was for me. My heart was pounding and my head racing with ideas already. Even before I had any of the details, I longed to slide my hand between my thighs and rub. Already it was a very exciting prospect.

It is so shameful how easily I get aroused. All it takes is a meaningful look from a horny-looking man on the bus or a rude passage in a book and I am oozing from all orifices. Only that morning, as I rode to work on my bike with my cotton skirt riding up with each turn of the pedals, I had imagined a hard dildo fixed to the seat. I pictured myself with no knickers on, the sun burning down on my naked thighs and my sex-lips gripping the solid protuberance as it was sucked into me with every move of my body. I shuddered as I stopped at the lights with my clit aching, and winked at the hunky-looking man in the car next to me. I knew I looked very flushed and wanton just by the leering way he looked at me with amused interest. He jerked his head in the direction of the pavement, silently suggesting that I pull over to meet him, but I just whizzed off, the breeze catching the hem of my skirt and revealing far too much tanned leg.

I snapped my thoughts back to the present and tried to gauge just how much extra time I would have to spend with Adam if I took on this extra work. Even the thought of another few hours was enough to sway me – not that I needed much swaying.

'When do we start?'

'Think about it over the weekend and try to come up with some proposals for me. We can get together again on Monday and sort out some details with a bit of luck. What do you say, Joanna? Are you game?'

'I certainly am.' I grinned. Without a second thought I added, 'Lead me to the men,' then cringed at my overactive mouth.

I tentatively looked for his reaction to my sleazy reply, expecting disdain, but he was looking closely at my face. He smiled back at me and explained, 'I didn't say it had to just be men. Did I? Any and every variety of sex is OK. Just make it sexy and at least bordering on legal. Oh, and Joanna ... don't forget I am always here if you need any advice or ... well, anything.'

I took a hard look at my boss then to balance the little I knew about him with the way he was flirting with me. He was almost criminally attractive, with a tall hard lean body, wearing a severe business suit. I guessed he was in his late thirties or early forties, so the discreetly expensive charcoal-grey suit and the crisp plain white shirt and sombre tie were a little out of place. All his staff wore smart casual clothes and he appeared to be quite happy about that. Perhaps that was his way of setting himself apart from the crowd – to give him the air of authority he needed. It certainly had an effect on me: his overall image of powerful success with his gold cufflinks and slim gold watch worked for me every time I saw him.

As I struggled out of the low chair, his deep brown eyes travelled down my expanse of bare thigh. I got to my feet without, I hope, showing my knickers. I tried to understand how the almost non-existent relationship I had previously had with him compared to the new slightly suggestive spark between us now. Adam was definitely going beyond the usual boss–staff thing.

I stuttered a little with embarrassment but decided it would be safer not to say anything. I turned to leave. But, just before I opened the door, I was stopped in my tracks by his voice, husky and sure of himself now with something that sounded far too much like amusement to me.

'Joanna?'

'Mmm?' I mumbled, keeping my eyes on the door and trying to sound casual; something was affecting me badly here.

'You will have to try and be a bit braver than that if you are going to live up to my expectations of you. If you can't even look me in the eye, how will you cope with your new brief?'

I didn't answer. I had no idea how to answer. I knew that I would be able to face any punter I chose without a second thought; it was him that was making me go all fluffy. But I couldn't tell him that, could I? So I paused, facing the door, and tried to pull myself together when he shocked me again.

'Look at me, Joanna.'

My pulse thumped its reaction to the steely control in his voice as I turned and slowly met his gaze. I felt a trickle of sweat start its irritating journey through my hairline and longed to brush it away but I was transfixed; caught in his web like a fly. And he knew it.

'Are you up to this, Joanna?' His voice caressed me.

Something stirred in my belly. A runny warm feeling like melted toffee swirled around in my stomach and clenched my abdomen in a vice-like fist. I wanted something sexual so badly that I felt like crying but I had no idea what it was. I knew without a doubt that it was connected to the way Adam had been talking to me and that he knew exactly how I was feeling. It was as if I were pre-programmed to respond to him in this way. I could see that knowledge in his eyes.

I stood motionless as Adam rose from his chair, walked around the table and then over to me. He walked around me until he faced me, standing between me and the closed door. He crooked his finger under my chin and raised my face to look at him. I almost groaned.

'Do you think you are the right girl for this, Joanna? Did I choose correctly, or was I wrong about you?'

I tore my eyes away from his hold, pulled my head away from his control, and lifted my own chin to an arrogant jaunty angle and shook off the thoughts in my head.

'You just watch me. I will put everything I've got into this and I promise I won't let you down.'

'Good girl! I'll speak to you again after the weekend,' was his parting shot as he turned back into the room. It was as if nothing had occurred between us and, as I let myself out of the room, I began to wonder if I had imagined it all.

I was going to chat over the events of the past few hours with Stacy but she had already gone from her desk. Anyway, on reflection, what had happened between Adam and me was beginning to take on an intimate feel so I decided to have a good think before I discussed it with anyone.

I cycled home in an absolute daze with my head full of my new assignment and very discourteous thoughts about Adam. I was convinced that I hadn't imagined the electricity in the room when I had met with him but, when I tried to remember anything tangible that had happened to make me feel the way I did, I couldn't think of one single thing.

I sat at my small dining table with the door open to the garden and relived the fun I had had with Alex. I found myself wishing he was going to be there for the weekend. The sun streamed through onto my bare arms and I decided that I had to put it all out of my mind and get on with the project in hand or I really would be letting Adam down. There was a need inside me to avoid ever letting Adam down and only to please him in every way I could. When he had said the words 'Good girl' to me my sex had contracted deliciously, sending shivers of need up my spine. I am not sure why I wasn't annoyed when he called me 'girl'. From anyone else I would have found it so patronising, but from Adam it had an undertone, a suggestion of power that I found very intoxicating.

I was so excited about the prospect of his proposal that I tossed ideas about until I realised that the sun was going down, my bin was full of screwed-up paper and my Pot Noodle had gone cold and congealed. Yuk! I was convinced that the package I had come up with was sure to please Adam. I ran over and over the finer points until I knew I could go to him with confidence, then hopefully I wouldn't feel at such a disadvantage. Perhaps I could put my ideas to him without his completely taking control of me and my thoughts the way he had at our previous meeting. Some of the proposals I came up with were scary on a personal level, but I knew once I got started that I was game for anything. I knew I would enjoy most of it, if not all. I also knew that I would enjoy the extra time I would have to spend with Adam and that would hopefully outweigh the scarier bits.

After I had tidied up the details and sat down in my armchair with a cup of tea, I wondered how Adam had known I would be prepared to carry out his preposterous suggestion. I ran through a mental checklist of what he knew about me, hopefully to shed light on his demeanour. All he could possibly know were the facts – Joanna Anderson, 32 years old, tall and a bit too shapely to be taken seriously. I knew I had a wanton look about me with my olive complexion, and the tumble of light brown wavy hair that fell over my shoulders. My lips are too full and that makes me look as if I am pouting all the time. Men seem to be attracted to that look but I felt it was a recipe for being taken the wrong way. Adam should not have noticed any of this because I always tried to disguise the shapely and wanton look by tying back my hair and holding back on the make-up. I also played down my embarrassingly full breasts by wearing loose jackets and attempted to distract the eye from them by wearing skintight jeans that enhanced my long legs. Or I would wear soft floaty skirts like the one I had been wearing for my first meeting with Adam.

Anyway, I am sure you have the picture. I think about sex all the time. I look as if I am begging for it. I write about it for a living and I am very frustrated. Perhaps Adam actually saw through the voluptuous but toned-down me that he would have seen at the office. And, of course, whatever went on between us at the Christmas dance might well have been a factor.

2

On Monday morning I waited two hours for him to summon me, going over my proposals in my mind and trying to convince myself that, in the cold light of day, I could go through with them.

When he did call, his voice sent shivers through me. Again there was nothing I could really put my finger on but when he said, 'Good morning, Joanna, are you ready for me?' I just wanted to blurt out, 'Oh God, yes!'

I tapped on his door and waited for his invitation to enter. I had decided to go in all guns blazing hopefully to redress the balance between us. In my fluffy haste that morning I had tried on and discarded at least four outfits. The jeans were too casual by far. The floaty, flirty skirts that I love were too girly, so that left me with the power-woman look. I thought that image might give me confidence so I picked a dark blue suit that usually just sat at the back of my wardrobe to be dressed up for weddings and down for funerals. I remembered that I had worn it when I applied for the job and now I was sort of applying for another. I teamed it with a soft creamy yellow blouse left open at the throat to complete the image I was trying to portray. I put on horny underwear because, let's face it, we all know just how good that can make you feel. Adam the macho man would have no idea that under my rather formal clothes my heavy breasts were tucked into a wickedly expensive French lace half-cup bra and my bottom was hanging shamelessly out of the matching very tiny thong. I thought adding to my height might intimidate him a little, so I slipped my naked feet into high court shoes. I toyed with the idea of stockings. That would floor him if he caught a glimpse, but then I remembered the low seating and the expanse of thigh and chose not to be quite that obvious. Anyway, there was a tiny ladder in the only pair I had and Sod's Law said that the second I sat down it would spread into a gaping hole, and that wouldn't do. Far too many of my holes were metaphorically gaping already.

As I walked through his office door I was so excited I could have burst, partly about the proposed new game I was about to play, but mainly just because I was about to spend time with Adam.

'Thanks for coming, Joanna. I hope you are going to please me with these ideas of yours.' He said this as he looked up from his desk and stripped me with his eyes. 'Sit down,' he added, indicating the chairs around the low table we had sat at before. 'Would you like a coffee?'

'Mmm, black, one sugar, thanks.'

He stayed at his desk to order the coffee, watching me very closely as I tried very hard to lower myself into the soft chair as demurely as I could. I caught the appreciative look in his eyes and, as before, it was definitely tinged with the amused arrogance that I found so disconcerting. I stared at him defiantly, determined to wipe the amused look off his face.

While he was on the phone to his PA I had a chance to straighten my skirt and look around his quietly opulent office. Everywhere was black leather and dark wood. The desk was obviously an expensive antique with a tooled leather top and carved legs. The smell of leather and wax oozed age and class and was a very intoxicating mix to my already heightened senses.

He got up and walked over to me, smiling enigmatically. It was so frustrating how he managed to do everything enigmatically. I laid out my proposal just as Glynis, his PA, brought in the coffees. I deliberately waited until she was gone and then broke the silence when he nodded to me.

'I thought we could have one or two pages dedicated to Joanna's Journal. I would ask the readers to write and tell me about their sexuality, suggesting that I have no preconceived ideas about any of the variations available.'

'And have you, Joanna? Any preconceived notions about sexuality?' he questioned, blatantly expecting an answer and trying to look as if the answer meant nothing to him. I had a feeling it could end up meaning quite a lot. I felt a little less intimidated by him by this time, probably because he was listening to me and so far taking me seriously. So I had a sip of my drink to give me a chance to compose myself and put previous thoughts aside. I tried to approach the question at a business level. After all, if I were to do this, I would have to discuss sex openly with a lot more people than Adam.

As I hesitated Adam added, 'Please be as open as you can with me, otherwise this will never get off the ground. I will need to know how you feel and how you are likely to react in any given situation.' I wasn't totally sure that he needed to know how I felt but I liked the idea that he wanted to so I thought before I answered.

'Well, I suppose what I just said is true,' I told him tentatively. 'I don't really have any preconceived ideas. I feel passionately that we should all feel free to do whatever takes our fancy as long as all parties concerned are consenting. I read a lot of books about sex.

Not only fiction, but factual books about how people feel relating to their own sexuality, what they do with each other and what turns them on.' I blushed profusely but Adam didn't bat an eyelid, so I felt confident enough to carry on. There was something divinely exquisite about talking to him in this way. I wasn't sure why but it was exciting me immensely.

'I know I am not prejudiced about what many people may look on as deviances – in fact reading about bizarre practices thrills me. The more bizarre the better.' I finished, already slightly regretting the last bit.

He stared at me with an expression akin to delight at my awkwardness but then, like all his lapses into normal reactions, it had gone in a flash and I wondered if I had been mistaken.

'That must have been very embarrassing for you, but if we are going to work together on this we will need to talk about everything and anything. Won't we? I know it will get easier for you as we go along.'

I carried on with my ideas, very conscious of the fact that it was only me who was doing the sharing. Adam still looked very cool and collected but I was squirming in my seat. It was like the old truth or dare games I used to play with my friends at school. Even then it was always me who had to tell all.

'I thought we could offer a liaison with me as an incentive for readers to write to me.' Even though this had in part been his suggestion, I felt very silly talking about myself as a sort of prize and must have reddened again because Adam stopped me.

'Don't feel self-conscious, Joanna. I can assure you there will be thousands of people out there who would fall over themselves to have a liaison with you, especially if you hint at a sexual encounter. Let's be honest, everyone who wants to meet you has to buy a copy of *Leather and Lace*. How would you feel about that? Would you be prepared to have a sexual encounter with one or more of our readers as part of this experiment? Or is that asking too much of you? Only you know how you will feel. I am not going to try to push you into something that is beyond you, unless you want to be pushed, that is. I am fully aware that everyone has his or her limits and I am sure that over the next few months we will find yours. You never know, once we have found your limits you might want to extend them.' He held my gaze as if everything hung on my answer.

'I haven't been particularly adventurous up till now,' I replied, 'but this idea really excites me on a sexual level and as a writer. I'll just have to see where things take us, won't I? I suppose the best way would be to treat this just like my personal life. I am quite gutsy and liberated so if I meet someone I fancy and the feeling is right, then I am not averse to a quick roll in the hay. I enjoy one-night stands as long as the arousal is mutual and no one is being hurt. The only place I draw the line is if I don't find the person attractive and then I am sure nothing, not even a large raise, would persuade me even to contemplate having sex with them.'

He hung on my every word and, as I got to the end of my little speech, there was a definite look of satisfaction on his face, which turned to intrigue.

'Tell me this then, Joanna,' he asked, leaning forward and picking his words carefully. 'If you were in a position where a reader was trying to persuade you to try, say, a type of sexuality that you weren't sure about and I particularly asked you to go ahead with it to please me – as your editor, of course – how would you feel then?'

I had a fleeting, totally unbidden image of myself kneeling in the middle of a large empty hall with a black silk blindfold tied around my eyes and my hands clasped on my head. I knew there was a man in front of me because I could feel the hard end of his cock nudging against my tightly closed lips. Adam was standing behind me dressed all in black leather and his arrogant controlling voice was saying, 'Open your mouth, Joanna. I want you to do this for me.'

I had an instant reaction to the brief fantasy. My insides lurched into freefall as I stuttered and stammered, trying to think where I'd dredged the image up. Up until that moment I don't think I had ever had sexual thoughts about being dominated, but I sure as hell did after that. And it made more sense of the effect Adam was having on me. He watched my reaction intently.

'I ... I'm not sure. I guess it would all depend on what you wanted me to do,' I stammered, but when I clocked his intense interest I got a bit cocky. 'Of course it would also depend on just how persuasive you were. Wouldn't it?' Our eyes met and held for a good ten seconds before Adam cleared his throat and we got back to business.

I continued with my ideas and tried to put aside not only my fleeting fantasy but also the way he had looked at me. I was very confused indeed. I could have sworn that I had seen flirtation, satisfaction and intrigue all fighting to hide themselves from me. But then, I'm fanciful.

'I propose that we print three or four suggestions from the punters,' I suggested, 'and then let the readers decide who wins. Obviously, even though that is what they are told, if someone wins who is totally unsuitable then we can use a little artistic licence to pick a winner that I am prepared to meet. We would have to fill a bit on the first issue, but after the meeting not only do we have the next few offers, we also have my account of the meeting. Joanna's Journal ... I could set it out like a diary and share with everyone what happened at my meeting with the winner. Maybe even tell them the gory details. I would probably need quite clear guidelines so I don't overstep them. I also thought it would be a good gimmick if I was quite ruthless and honest.'

'I like it so far, Joanna. As far as I am concerned you can write what you like. We have to take the legal side into consideration but go for it. And I agree it would be good to tell the truth and shame the devil. Go and write your first intro and bring it back to me. If possible I want it to go in this issue so you only have four days to wow me. Do you think you can do that?'

There he goes again, I thought. I wished he wouldn't use my name so much because there was something so horny about the way he said it and the way he ended every sentence with a question – usually a leading one. He always seemed to be demanding that I give away yet another secret with each answer. It was very disconcerting. I found the only way to treat him was to try and be as suggestive and arrogant as him so I answered, 'Can I do what, Adam? Wow you or meet the deadline?'

Adam threw back his head and laughed openly at my brazen answer. It was the first time I had ever seen him let his guard down and, even though I was delighted, it wasn't as sexy to me as his usual untouchable stance, but I at least felt more in control.

'Good girl! I can see that you are going to be a bit of a challenge. Luckily there is nothing I find more stimulating.'

Adam stood then, leaned across the table and pushed out his hand for me to shake. I grasped it as firmly as I could but his warm dry strong grip held me just a little longer than was necessary. He might just as well have grabbed me between the legs because that was the effect it had and I left his office convinced that we had started something. I had no idea what it was that we had started, but I was more turned on than I could ever remember.

3

This is a challenge to all you readers out there who like something a little different. We are looking for one special reader who thinks he or she can shock or interest the rest of us with his or her personal story. Tell us about what makes you tick sexually in not more than a thousand words and each month the rest of you get to pick a winner. That winner will spend an intimate evening with Joanna trying to persuade her that he or she could show her a good time. If the persuasion works then Joanna will tell us all about it in our new Joanna's Journal the following month. If the persuasion doesn't work, then Joanna will tell us all about it in Joanna's Journal just the same. Make sure it's good.

COME ON, TELL US ALL ABOUT IT

My invitation went to print in the next issue, just as he asked, and all I could do was sit back and wait for the responses, if there were any, while I stuck to my usual fantasy writing – which seemed tame by comparison.

I sat in my office day after day, wondering if it was a non-starter and trying to think of ways we could fake it all if we didn't get any replies. I hoped Adam would summon me and I dreaded the thought of going back to my old life without this new excitement. Then the first one arrived. I couldn't believe it. It was a good job I did have an office on my own because I danced about like a loon, I was so excited. I checked the door was shut, put my feet up on the corner of my desk, and read the first letter.

Dear Joanna

My husband Steve and I are both swingers. We enjoy a very exciting sex life when we are alone but then once a month we meet a group of about twenty like-minded people to have fun. We would be honoured if you would join us on one of our club nights, then we could show you what we are about. There is never any pressure on any of our members to 'swap' if they don't feel inclined and that of course would apply to you too.

Why don't you come and join us for an evening's entertainment? If nothing else, you will probably enjoy watching the couples and groups who get their kicks performing for the rest of us.

I particularly love to watch Steve's cock as it slides into the pussy or mouth of one of the other club members. He likes to watch me being fucked from behind as I suck off another man. It all makes for a very sexy and exciting evening. Why don't you join us?

We meet on the first Saturday every month at a private address. Sometimes the party will trail over into Sunday, but please feel free to 'gatecrash' at any time for as long as you like – we would be so pleased to see you.

Steve and I saw a picture of you in your magazine a few months ago and we both think you have a very sexy body; you stimulated a rather exciting fantasy for us that night. We will keep our fingers crossed that your readers like the idea of hearing about you swinging with us.

Keep swinging

Rosie and Steve

By the time I had read Rosie's letter for the third time I was as nervous as hell but hoping that our readers chose this letter for me to follow up. I loved the idea of their club and their flattery of me. The thought of a couple working on me together was steamy stuff indeed.

I longed to phone Adam and see what his reaction would be to this initial offer but decided it would be much more professional if I e-mailed him. And it wouldn't look so obvious that I just wanted to see him.

> Adam
> We have received the first answer to my proposal for Joanna's Journal. It sounds like a very exciting prospect. I'll keep you informed of the progress.
> Joanna

I decided that titillation was the best form of aphrodisiac and it worked its charm. Within half an hour the reply came from my supposedly cool and collected boss.

> Joanna
> Thanks for keeping me up to date. As I need to keep abreast of progress I would find it advantageous to read the first letter. I'm due in a meeting straight after lunch so perhaps you could spare me a few minutes now?
> Adam

I was torn. The relationship between us was beginning to take on a gamelike quality. I knew there was something in the dynamic between us but I couldn't swear that Adam knew what he was doing to me with his subtle suggestions. All the little innuendos that I picked up on could be perfectly innocent if analysed. But if it was all innocent, why was my heart beating so hard as I took a deep breath outside his office door? I had toyed with the idea of pretending that I hadn't received his message just to keep him waiting and to prove that I too could be dominant. My resolve had lasted all of three minutes before I ran my hands through my hair, checked in the loos just how flushed I was – far too much – and rubbed on a little lip gloss. I disgusted myself by being so weak.

The closed door muffled Adam's 'come in'. I stepped in the room to find Adam sitting at his desk engrossed in a file. I found it very frustrating when he didn't even look up at me. He instructed me to sit. So I went and sat in the usual place. I was blowed if I was going to sit across the desk from him like a naughty schoolgirl. I took the chance to look at him more intently: the expensive cut of his dark navy suit, the way his hair just rested on his white collar, and his strong hands, so horny, carrying out such routine tasks. I found myself imagining what his body would look like without clothes. Would his naked form be as exciting as his clothed one? I didn't doubt it for one moment.

Just for a second I took my eyes from him to take off my jacket and rearrange my T-shirt to show a little more of my cleavage – well, a girl has to use her best assets, doesn't she? When I looked up again Adam was turned toward me and was staring at my breasts with that infuriating amused look that he had perfected too well. I felt like a teenager being caught behind the bike sheds. His eyes captured mine and would not release them.

'While I tidy these away, why don't you read the letter to me?' He watched my reaction as if it was of the utmost importance to him. I stuttered, flustered and embarrassed at being caught flaunting myself.

The idea of reading Rosie and Steve's erotic suggestions out loud to this arrogant, domineering man was both exciting and terrifying. I knew I would get aroused, not only because it was so sexy, but also because he would be listening.

I began reading and, when I got to the bit about watching them perform, Adam interrupted me. 'Sorry to interrupt, Joanna, but I can't hear you properly. Could you read that last bit again and speak up?' While he spoke he carried on shuffling papers about and sliding files into drawers.

As I read the sentence again Adam stopped what he was doing and watched me intently. By the time I got to the bit about Rosie watching Steve's cock disappear into a waiting pussy or mouth, Adam had joined me at the table and was sitting far too close to me. Only the small table separated us but I felt as if Adam was inside my head. I carried on to the part where Rosie is fucked from behind and my mouth started to dry up. I swallowed nervously, recrossed my legs and forced myself to carry on. I couldn't bring myself to look up at him.

'We think you have a very sexy body,' I read. Rosie's words made me tremble from head to foot but I tried desperately to control myself. I thought I heard a soft murmur at that sentence but within a second was unsure. When I had finished I still couldn't bring myself to look at him so I continued to look at the letter, waiting for him to comment, but the bastard didn't. He waited until I became uncomfortable and tentatively looked up at him. He was leaning back in his chair totally relaxed and calm but with a wicked sparkle in his eyes that I had glimpsed before. He usually made that face when he had succeeded in embarrassing me.

'How do you feel about that, Joanna?' he queried, while his gaze brazenly roamed my body, from my flushed face, my nipples that stood rock hard and horny poking through the soft material of my T-shirt, down to my naked legs. I became paranoid that I was showing my knickers but I knew that if I rectified my position it would only make matters worse.

'Feel about what, the letter or the suggestions?' I asked before I made a complete fool of myself.

'Well, for instance, how do you feel about Rosie having an audience while she is not only being taken from behind but she is also having a rampant cock slid into her willing mouth? How does that make you feel, Joanna? It is obvious to me that something has aroused you to fever pitch.'

'Oh, I don't know,' I groaned miserably, remembering the fantasy I had conjured up the last time I had been in his office and wondering if his question was completely professional. 'I find the whole thing exciting. The watching, the sharing, the compliments and the idea of being part of it all.' I longed to blurt out that the thing I found more sexy than anything else was him and his way of making me feel like a dissected insect staked out on a board to be inspected. That image in my head was my undoing. I felt my insides melt, ooze out and soak my knickers. It was so shameful. My breasts felt twice their size and my mouth seemed to slacken at the thought of a cock, especially Adam's.

'So, you would consider meeting this couple and going to one of their parties, would you?'

'To be honest, Adam, I want to anyway, even if it isn't for the magazine. I really hope that if we get more letters this one will be chosen, because I am beginning to get into the swing of it all.' I giggled at the pun. Adam didn't.

'I am sure that if this is the one you want to experiment with, as long as you promise to come and tell me how you got on, then I will work my persuasion. And believe me, it will win. I can't disappoint my protégée, can I?' He rose from his seat. 'Well, best get on.' As before he cut off the conversation before I had a chance to think about what he had said and, more importantly, what he had meant. I never could remember afterwards. I started to walk back towards the door, across the expanse of his very businesslike domain, over the expensive carpet. He walked alongside me and draped his arm casually over my shoulder, muttering platitudes. His relaxed hand was dangling far too near my breast as I fluttered at his touch.

'Let me know if you get any more. If not, you might have to write one or two yourself just this first time.'

Back at my office I slumped in my seat, my head spinning with the turn of events and my pussy eager for attention. I hated the necessity of waiting until I got home but I knew that sitting on my bike seat, with the hard and intrusive saddle nestled up into my crotch, would be wonderful titillation and a perfect intro to what I intended to do when I got there. I shut up my office and left for the day.

As expected, the bike did the trick. Not only did it tone my legs beautifully but it did all sorts of other things. By the time I got to my front door I was desperate for an orgasm but I was determined to prolong the pleasure. Sometimes if I got horny I would just lie on my bed and tease my clitoris for a few minutes imagining having something rude done to me. Then I would nestle my finger between my sex-lips and rub in a continuous circular movement until the object of the exercise was achieved: a shuddering orgasm. But this was special. Adam's words still filled my head as I started the exciting fantasy images in my brain.

I strolled into the bedroom, imagining Adam behind

me. The late afternoon sun was shining on my bed, turning it into a soft golden sexual stage just right for me to lose reality for a while. I remembered the fantasy of kneeling in a large hall with a black silk blindfold heightening my senses and I went to my cupboard and pulled out a scarf. It was deep blue but it really didn't matter by that stage. I tied it around my eyes and drank in the feel of the fantasy taking over. I could actually feel Adam's presence behind my right shoulder.

'Face the window and take off your T-shirt and panties for me, Joanna.' His imagined words spoken in my ear made me tremble with all the pent-up needs he had provoked in me. I did as the voice requested, taking my T-shirt off to reveal my bra, then fumbling up under my skirt to remove the lacy wisp of G-string. I imagined him smiling his approval as he looked me up and down and I expected him to instruct me to remove my skirt, but the voice told me to climb on the bed and kneel. I groaned loudly and imagined Rosie on her bed with her audience.

I clambered onto the bed, slightly disorientated by the dark world behind the silk, and carried out his request. My heart was pounding as I awaited the next instructions. When they came I didn't feel for one second that I had produced them.

'Spread your legs, Joanna, and put your hands on your head with your elbows out in line with your body. I want you to thrust out those gorgeous ripe breasts until you can stretch no more. I want you to hold that position for a while so I can look at you.'

For a brief second I lost the fantasy as reality tried to break through, but I obeyed the inner voice anyway. As soon as I took up the position and forced my arms out to my sides I could feel what the stretching did to my breasts. They rose proudly and thrust forward, no longer being hidden and subdued under clothes that were designed to reduce them. My already hard nipples, grazed by the lace of my bra, engorged with more hot blood. I moaned my pleasure and remembered the legs instruction. I spread my legs as far apart as I could until my skirt was tight across my thighs and my sex felt naked and exposed. The thrill of that exposure trickled like water over me. I was completely lost in my fantasy world, actually hearing Adam's instructions and feeling his eyes like hot burning coals on my breasts.

I am not sure how long I just knelt there revelling in my debauched submission, but my passion grew until I longed for the next instruction. Somewhere my subconscious came up with it.

'Take your brassiere off and kneel down on all fours please, Joanna.' I don't know where that came from but it ceased to matter. The fantasy was all that mattered. I imagined Rosie and Steve entering the room just to stand and watch my performance. I obeyed the forceful thoughts, by this time totally incapable of disobeying. I flushed with shame as I felt a dribble of my excitement gather within the sticky cup of my sex then drip away from me onto the bed, oblivious to the fact that there was no one there to witness my abandonment. As I bent forward my heavy breasts fell away from my body and dangled downward.

I heard whispered comments in the far corners of my mind.

'I want to fuck her from behind.'

'Tell her to masturbate.'

'Christ, just look at that mouth just begging to suck my cock.'

Then a female voice dragged up from my imagination somewhere.

'I wonder if her other lips are pouting just as much.

Pull up your skirt, Jo. We all want to see what you have got for us.'

It was the word 'all' that elicited the ragged cry from my throat as I knelt up and pulled my skirt up around my waist then returned to the wonderful, terrible position I had left. I could still feel Adam's influence on the periphery of the proceedings but his next imagined instruction came from close in front of me. My imagination was in full swing.

'Open your mouth for me, Joanna. Open it as wide as you can.'

My pussy flooded as I opened my mouth wide and then wider, wishing he were there to fill it. My puffy sex-lips fell open, exposing my hole for all to see. I swear I felt the bed move as someone took position behind me and thrust a hard cock up against me, threatening a forced entry but not quite entering me. My sex became a desperate hungry sucking hole to my body, and nothing else. Images raced through my brain taking my arousal to exploding level. I almost tangibly felt a hot body lie along my back and a pair of unseen hands grab my pendulous breasts and grip hold of the nipples. I could actually feel the heat of a groin by my face; the tickle of pubic hairs and the velvet heated flesh of a penis as a beautiful sex smell filled my flaring nostrils. I stretched forward, straining for a taste, but when I moved too far the cock nudging between my legs disappeared. So then I strained backward again to rekindle the image but the cock at my mouth was lost to me.

I groaned out loud with frustration, my head almost igniting with need, the imagined touches no longer enough. I rolled on my back, still sightless, and pushed one hand between my thighs and the other in my mouth. I sucked my fingers in desperation as if they really were Adam's cock and fucked myself hard with my bunched-up hand. The base of my thumb rasped my throbbing clit until the powerful throes of need overpowered me. I thrashed about boldly as I came with all my fantasy lovers watching my every move.

The sun had moved across the room leaving me in partial shadow as I lay exhausted in a pool of cool damp on the quilt. I was totally satisfied and sated. My breathing slowed and my pulse rate quietened as I dozed away with a smile on my face, my fingers still buried inside me.

4

When I walked into my office the next morning there was a pile of post that brought a wide grin to my face. I felt slightly silly about the fantasy I had enacted the day before and hoped fervently that I wouldn't have to meet Adam. I knew I would be unable to face him until the vivid memories of my rudeness had faded a little. I reread the letter from Rosie and Steve and still it managed to excite me, so I wondered how I would react to the others. I couldn't wait to find out.

A few of the letters were just invitations from single men to go out on a date with them; my article inviting suggestions appeared to have brought all sorts out of the woodwork. One or two were rather inventive but not what the project was all about and certainly not a patch on the swinging couple's invitation. John from Bolton even went to the extraordinary lengths of sending a portfolio of pictures of his unexceptional member.

I managed to pick out three others that could be judged with the original one I received, arranged and rearranged the page in my mind with the original idea printed again across the top, and guidelines as to what we were looking for along the bottom. I arranged with our admin department to do their best to set up a phone-voting system. It worked wonders and, by the deadline, we had over a thousand votes. Over 60 per cent were in favour of me meeting Rosie and Steve with their group of friends, so I got down to business.

The readers must have had the same ideas as me

because the other 40 per cent favoured the only other response that had caught my imagination. It had actually excited me even more than Rosie's. Sent anonymously on a plain white sheet of paper with just one paragraph of writing and a mobile phone number at the bottom, it had caused hot prickles to break out all over my body. In retrospect I am not sure if I was more amused by it than turned on, but I was intrigued to the point of obsession. I reread it at least twenty times and each time it had the same effect. In the end I just had to put it away because, even after examining it and reading it so often, the need in me to know more was undiminished.

I KNOW YOU, JOANNA

You are a very naughty provocative young lady. You deserve to be thoroughly punished for your enticing thoughts and inviting suggestions.

Agree to meet me, Joanna, and I will introduce you to extremes of pleasure I know you have only dreamed or fantasised about.

Believe me when I tell you that I know you right to the depths of your sexuality. I know your fantasies and your needs.

I KNOW YOU, JOANNA

I put Mr Mysterious out of my mind, relieved that he hadn't been chosen. His suggestion had brought to mind my adventure with Alex and my bottom twitched at the memory. I wondered what it would be like really to be spanked. What did he mean about pleasure I only fantasised about? I played with ideas and thoughts that his letter provoked but my mind just went round in circles. I knew I would love to know what he was like but something about his letter nudged feelings that were a little disturbing, so I put them aside and phoned Rosie.

I wondered if I would ever be capable of doing this assignment to Adam's satisfaction when it took all my courage just to phone her. My heart was hammering as I waited for someone to pick up, so when a rather sexy male voice said 'Hello' in my ear, I was thrown.

'Hi, is that Steve?' I asked, trying to stop my voice from trembling.

'Uh huh. How can I help you?'

'My name is Joanna Anders –' but I didn't get any further before I heard Steve screaming to Rosie.

'It's her! It's Joanna from the magazine! Quick, Rosie, it's her!'

I think he must have gone completely to pieces because the next thing I heard was an excited female voice admonishing Steve for being so rude and infantile.

'Hi, Joanna. Please forgive Steve, he's rather excited. Have we won? Do we get the prize?'

My confidence blossomed in response to their excited voices, enabling me to answer in a more casual voice. 'Well, I'm not sure if you could call it a prize but yes, your letter was chosen with a majority vote of 60 per cent.'

'And does that mean you are really going to come and meet us all? It wasn't just a publicity wind-up?'

'It definitely wasn't a wind-up but I will warn you that this is the first time I have done anything like this. Perhaps we could meet and discuss some arrangements?'

'Why don't you come and meet us all? We don't bite.' At that Rosie yelped and burst into fits of giggles. 'Sorry, I lied,' she spluttered down the phone. 'Steve just bit me on the bum.'

I laughed too at their infectious enthusiasm and, against my better judgement, I agreed to visit them the following evening when they would call an 'extraordinary meeting' in my honour. Rosie assured me that it wasn't too short notice and that she was convinced everyone would manage to be there. She offered to put me up for the night as they lived in Cheshire – six hours' drive away – but I declined. I tried my best to sound as if it was a professional decision but really I was far too nervous to commit myself to staying that long. Rosie was obviously disappointed but she suggested the name of a good country inn. She warned that it was a little on the expensive side, but I decided that my expenses would cover it. I reminded myself that I needed to discuss expenses with Adam, but if he got cross with me so be it. I tried to ignore the knowledge that I quite liked the idea of having to make it up to him somehow.

I was petrified.

I booked the room then sent an e-mail to Adam to keep him informed of my arrangements. Before he had a chance to return my message I left the office with my pulse racing and an excited knot growing in my belly. I couldn't bear having to face him again, not in my present state of arousal. The last thing I needed was another interrogation about how horny I was. Anyway, he confused me far too much.

I pedalled home leisurely to give myself time to think about what I was planning to do. I thought about what I would take with me and tried to decide what one wears at a swingers' party. I decided the answer was not a lot.

I spent the best part of the evening sorting out the things I wanted to take with me. Anyone who didn't know would have thought I was going away for a week. I went upstairs to Alex's flat hoping he was there. I longed to tell someone what was going on and he was about the only one I could talk to about it. He made us a coffee then sat next to me on his couch – far too close for comfort. He swivelled his body round so he was facing me intimately and asked for all the details.

I could see the bulge grow in his jeans as I told him about Rosie and Steve and their club. I also told him about the letter I had received from Mr Mysterious. In those brief minutes Alex personified all the classic arousal symptoms. His breathing noticeably quickened. His pupils dilated and he fidgeted like a two-year-old, alternately staring into my eyes then looking away nervously. He made me promise to tell him all about it after I got home and, as I went back downstairs, I realised he would have to get in line; there were all my readers and, of course, Adam before him.

I leaped out of bed the next morning, which was totally out of character. I was pleased to see that the day was bright and sunny, just right for my adventure. I rushed my breakfast, eager to be on my way, and went to take my pride and joy from my garage around the corner. Baby, my beautiful, sexy, MG Roadster in British Racing Green winked at me as I opened the door and slid my hand along her sleek bonnet, caressing the cool metal and removing the light layer of dust. I carefully rolled the leather top back, knowing that I would probably get cold, but I didn't care. Baby was my one luxury; she was why I rode to work on a bike each day and one of the reasons why I was still in a tiny rented flat. Basically, I had her instead of a mortgage. I promised myself that one day I would grow up and be responsible. But not yet, hey?

Baby coughed and spluttered as I coaxed her to life,

then purred beneath me raring to go. I patted the wheel whispering to myself, 'Me too, Baby.'

As usual, the journey flew by. Baby and I raced up the motorway, blowing away the cobwebs, ready for a new adventure. I could have sworn Baby basked in the admiring glances we got, just as I did. I could never decide which mode of transport afforded me more attention. Riding a pushbike in a short skirt can be very distracting to passing motorists, but Baby and I make a dynamic team when we are on an adventure.

The inn that Rosie had recommended was wonderful. The Grange was an old coaching house just outside the village. I was shown to a spacious sunny room with a big double bed all to myself. The French windows to my room opened out onto a tiny lawn, then the car park, which meant I could keep an eye on Baby. Then the tarmac tapered away to rose beds, then rolling hills. Perfection! I felt very important and very spoilt as I lay back on the crisp cotton bedcover trying to imagine what was in store for me. I dozed and fantasised until it was time to get ready.

After I had showered I sprayed my body with a musky body spray that I loved. I made sure I didn't have any fluffy bits that wouldn't be welcome at the party, then dressed in sexy underwear made of stretchy black shiny Lycra. The style of the bra and briefs set combined sexy with sporty, which I decided would be a good image to portray. After all, Rosie had said that I was just to meet these raunchy friends of hers and that might be as far as it went, but a girl had to be prepared. I sat at the old-fashioned dressing table trembling with excitement and nerves. I put on just a touch of eye make-up and a bit of lipgloss; I was almost ready for anything.

Casual, Rosie had said, so I slipped on my black T-shirt and wriggled it down to a place just above my navel. My boobs looked enormous as they fought the constrictions of the clothing and I kind of liked it. Then I pulled on my soft black and turquoise skirt with the beaded trim that swirled just above my knees. The two garments left a gap of six inches of tanned tummy. I added a jet necklace that complemented the low-necked T-shirt and a matching bracelet. Strappy black sandals completed my ensemble and I twirled in front of the mirror, very pleased with the finished article. Eat your heart out, Adam, I thought as I slung my glitzy bag on my shoulder and wondered what he would make of this Joanna. I felt so good that I wished to myself that he could be there to see me now, at my best with my eyes sparkling, a tantalising array of sun-kissed flesh on show and my wicked pussy hungry enough to eat him for breakfast.

As I left the inn I even found myself thinking about Mr Mysterious and arrogantly decided that there was no way he would know me now; I didn't even know me at that moment.

It only took me ten minutes to find the house. I was pleasantly surprised to find that Rosie and Steve's house was just an ordinary village semi with flowerpots on the front doorstep and a very innocent overall image. There were four cars in the narrow drive at the side of the house and, while I plucked up the courage to go in, I worked out that there could be as many as ten people in there or as few as four. I knew that however many there were they would all be looking at me as I walked in. I was also very aware that they would all be expecting me to be the high-flying journalist, not an occasional writer who just happened to have a job on a pervy magazine with an even pervier boss – well, it was beginning to look that way, wasn't it?

I checked in my mirror for the third time, ran my fingers through my hair, rearranged my clothes for no other reason than to kill a few moments, left the comfort and safety of Baby and walked up to the front door.

Rosie was just as I had imagined her. Her smile enveloped me into her warmth from the second she opened the door. She reached out and took my hand, pulled me inside and gave me a big hug as if she had known me all her life.

'I am so thrilled you have come. Well, we all are. We wondered if it was all a bit of fun by your magazine, but then when I spoke to you I really wanted to meet you anyway. You sounded just like the rest of us – fun.'

She looked me up and down as boldly as any man, making my stomach, much against its better judgement, flutter on cue. Her startling blue eyes were crinkled around the edges, and her lips were so horny I couldn't take my eyes from her mouth as she talked to me. I didn't even notice she was still holding my hand, not until she clasped both of mine with hers and pulled them into her body. She drew me into that warm intimate inviting space between her exceptionally pretty breasts. The tight purple bodice held her torso firmly and pushed her perfectly sized bust delightfully over the top. Rosie was so overtly sexy that I adored her immediately.

'Pretty,' she whispered as she touched my chest and rearranged the tiny jet beads on my necklace so they lay flat. The delicate network of beads fell like a cobweb almost to my cleavage. I felt goosebumps break out all over as her cool fingers touched me, tracing the strings of black.

'You are just as beautiful as your pictures. Come and meet the others – they are dying to meet you. Can we call you Jo? Joanna is so formal and we are hoping you will want to be anything but formal tonight. In fact, we are all rather hoping you will want to be intimate friends with us.' With that she turned on her pretty bare feet. A gypsy skirt swirled around her legs as she dragged me behind her into the spacious lounge before I had a chance to object.

Would I have objected, given the chance at that stage to turn back? I don't think so. Rosie was the most infectiously gorgeous woman I had ever met and already I felt at home in her house. As we moved into the lounge I heard a tinkling sound and realised Rosie wore an ankle bracelet covered in bells that signalled our approach.

The sight that greeted me took my breath away. Picture this: the room had been decorated for the evening as a sort of harem with soft white draped curtains falling from the ceiling in swathes. Each bundle as it fell from the centre of the room was caught in a bunch with red satin ribbons and then fed to the sidewalls to drop to the floor. The floor was covered with cushions and pillows of every shape and size, from large floor cushions that sat two people to gaudy little bright ones with beads and braid that gave a hint of the Orient.

In the corner sat the largest beanbag I had ever seen. At least six people had fallen into a heap in the middle and appeared to be rather enjoying the struggle.

The subdued lighting was provided by at least one hundred flickering candles. They covered every surface and filled numerous shelves and sconces around the room. There was a heady perfumed smell reminiscent of patchouli, which contributed to the overall ambience.

Around the edges of the room were placed three or four sofas. The room had obviously originally been two rooms knocked into one, and the result was perfect for a large party. There were people everywhere. At least twenty of them and, just as I had imagined, they were all looking at me, but it didn't seem to matter. Every face looked thrilled to see me. A few of the people dotted about the room jumped up and came over to introduce themselves but the names faded as soon as they were spoken. Nerves, I expect!

I was specifically introduced to Steve, who was just as lovely as Rosie but for some reason didn't intrigue me as she did. I found myself taking sideways glances at her but told myself that it was just because she was my hostess.

I was encouraged down onto a large soft cushion by Rosie, who kept close by my side. Someone offered me a drink. I thought maybe the punch on offer wasn't a good idea until I felt more at ease, so I asked for anything long and cold but non-alcoholic because I had brought Baby. Everyone laughed just as we would have at school about the 'long and cold' reference and I found myself joining in and explaining who Baby was.

A rather hunky young man sitting on his own in the corner almost squealed when I told them I had an MG, and he rather pointedly asked if he could have a ride. Again everyone laughed and I guessed they were well into the punch already. I looked him up and down, openly admiring his young firm body, nowhere near disguised by his stone-coloured trousers and white T-shirt. I flirted back that I would be more than pleased to give him a ride any time he liked. Everyone cheered at my bravado. The sexy guy jumped to his feet but Rosie told him to wait until I had relaxed a little.

'I'm sure Jo isn't ready to give anyone a ride quite yet and, anyway, you would probably frighten her off. You are far too enthusiastic for a beginner, Mark.'

Mark, a young man in his twenties with blond hair

bleached by the sun took it all in good spirit and sat down again grinning at me, completely unaffected by the catcalls from the others. There was no mistaking the promise in his look as he stared straight at me. He whispered something to the guy next to him who nodded enthusiastically and grinned, looking at me with a glint of true mischief in his eye. In fact there was obvious flirtation and mischief in the eyes of every single person there. I was in heaven. The whole room sizzled with excited anticipation. For the first time in my life I felt that I wasn't the only girl on the planet who was obsessed with sex. I made a mental note to keep an eye on Mark for the rest of the evening because, if things did get personal, I wanted a taste of this beautiful young man.

We talked for about an hour. Occasionally we got rude but mostly they all wanted to know about my job, the competition and Adam. I found myself telling them everything. I wasn't used to having that many people hanging on my every word and it went to my head. I told them all about the feelings I got when Adam and I were together but that there was nothing I could actually put my finger on.

Rosie laughed at my description. 'What you have there is a dominant. I thought you would be a little worldlier than that, Jo, doing the work that you do. You manage to write all those horny stories that we read to each other every time we meet, but you don't even recognise a dom when you meet one. He is playing sexual games with you, sweetheart. Remind me to introduce you to Nick later,' she said, tossing her head in the direction of a rather ordinary-looking man sitting in the corner by himself. I hadn't actually noticed him before, but when I looked over his grin was just like Adam's – knowing and slightly amused but completely in control. That's two I want to get to know better, I thought, as I realised what Rosie had said. The moment passed, then I thought of what she had said about my stories.

'What do you mean, you read my stories to each other?' I questioned.

'It's the highlight of every meeting. We take it in turns to read out sexy stories and yours are always the most popular. That's why we were so excited when we read about the competition and at the thought of getting a chance to invite you to meet us all. A different person reads a story of their choice then discusses whether or not we can reproduce them. This gives each of us a chance to introduce an element of their fantasy that they would like to share with the rest of us. If there is some reason we can't reproduce it then it never matters because by then we are so turned on anyway, we don't care. We have saved the latest one hoping you would read it to us. It's one I was going to read this week but I know everyone would rather you did. If you don't mind?'

I racked my brains trying to remember what the latest one was about but I knew sometimes we ran two or three months behind so I had no idea. I blushed at the idea of reading to this already very excited group of people. Rosie had by now managed to get into a position where she was leaning her thigh against me, and the heat from her leg was intruding on my concentration. Perhaps that was the intention.

'Which one was it?' I asked, distracted by her neat toes with deep rose-coloured nail polish and the tinkling anklet. I hoped the story wouldn't be one I was too embarrassed about.

'Well, you called yourself Sandra from Basildon but we would know your work anywhere. I have read it but the rest haven't. I saved it for you.' With that she gave me a very knowing look and winked at me. The tip of her tongue ran around the edge of her reddened lips in a most provocative way.

'Down, Rosie,' Steve ordered from the back of the room where he was lying on a cushion made for three. There was a man on one side of him and a youngish attractive woman on the other. They were both leaning into him with obvious intimacy in mind. I gulped at the blatancy of their relationship. 'Remember what you told Mark. Well that goes for you, too.' He chuckled as he reminded her of her earlier words and they all joined him in his teasing of her.

Oh, God, my heart was pounding. For the past hour I had found myself glancing at Rosie over and over again. Every time I looked her way it was to find she too was looking at me, issuing a clear invitation. For a while I was able to tell myself it was a general invitation, but all of a sudden my thick brain registered that she was really chatting me up, and the rest loved it. Stop being such a tart, Joanna! Just go with the flow, I told myself.

I took the magazine from her with shaking fingers and opened to my page. There I was at the top with the silly insipid grin that I hated. I hated the position the photographer had insisted on, with me sitting at my desk but leaning forward showing a hint of what was down below the buttons of my blouse. I began reading and the room went silent:

Dear Joanna

I want to tell you and your readers about an evening I spent with my bloke and his two mates. It all started so innocently one night at the pub with John, that's my bloke's best mate. He was pressing his leg against mine under the table and somehow he managed to turn the conversation to women who talk about shagging more than one fella. He insisted that they didn't really mean it. He looked at me so pointedly that I knew straight away that Ben, my fella, had been talking to him about a conversation we had had the night before in bed. I looked over at Ben to see him and his other mate Paul grinning like Cheshire cats.

I'd already had far too many drinks and found myself answering like a slut. 'And who says we don't really mean it. Clever arse.' I knew I was teasing them.

Before I knew where I was I was being carried into John's flat with Ben and Paul following behind egging him on.

I knew every eye was on me as I continued to read about Sandra being taken into the bedroom where all three men rapidly undressed her until she was naked. She ended up lying between Ben's legs as John and Paul nibbled on a nipple each with their fingers exploring her most intimate places. As usual I had written graphic details that my readers appeared to love, but reading them out loud was a different thing entirely.

Ben's fingers were exploring my mouth as I sucked desperately, imagining it was his prick that invaded me. The playful fingers at my tits were driving me to distraction, as was the hand that explored between my thighs. I gripped my thighs together, still far too nervous to give myself over to these men completely. But the mismatched pair of hands, one John's and the other Paul's, one large and rough and the other more delicate, forced my legs open.

Further and further they stretched them apart until my pussy was exposed and completely sopping wet. I groaned deeply into Ben's hand and up into his face, looking for the go ahead I needed to let myself go. He was obviously very pleased with what was happening.

I was getting so turned on reading those words. The images in my mind as I had written them had excited me but that was nothing compared to reading them now to this room full of horny people hanging on my every word. I stopped for a moment to have a drink; my mouth was dry with nerves. Or maybe it was with excitement. I glanced up and realised that at least three couples were lying on their cushions rather than sitting and there were flashes of bare flesh wherever I looked. As I drank I glanced over my glass at Mark, who immediately took up the unspoken offer and came slowly across the room towards me, picking his way carefully through the limbs that were stretching into almost every available floor space. He sat down beside me, holding my gaze the whole time.

Rosie's warmth still invaded my thoughts but as Mark sat down and leaned over to kiss me openly on the lips I moaned my invitation. I longed just to sink into the cushions like the others but Mark pulled away and begged me to carry on. All around the room there were muffled breathless murmurs of agreement. Rosie on the other side of me began tantalisingly to stroke my bare shoulder, sending shivers through me from my hair to my toes.

I read on with an obvious quiver to my voice; the anticipation was sending me crazy, but I don't think anyone noticed. I read of John and Paul getting Sandra so horny that she begged them to fuck her. All the time I read, Mark was distracting me by staring at me intently as if he were delving into my soul. His finger trailed up my bare leg until it almost did naughty things but not quite. The room was filled with the smell of sex and the couple immediately in front of me had stripped each other to their underwear and were enthusiastically exploring each other. His hand disappearing into her knickers transfixed me, and I longed to stop what I was doing and just watch them and concentrate on what was happening to me. By the time I got to the end of the story and read the last paragraph I knew my own knickers were soaking wet. Rosie's hand was lazily circling my nipple through my T-shirt and Mark's hand had reached the top of my inner thigh. They spurred me on.

I knelt on the bed doggy style and sucked hard on Ben's rock-hard cock, trying my best to swallow it all. One of the boys had their cock buried so far up inside me that I felt as if I would burst, but they shuffled about making me wonder what new invention they would come up with. We had tried every position known to man. We had sucked and fucked and fingered each other almost to oblivion. I had come at least six times and I knew each of the boys had ejaculated until they were coming dry, but still we carried on. We were hot and running with sweat but it all added to the sexy smell that filled the room. I felt a second cock start to nudge at my bumhole but had no idea how he had managed it. I felt totally disgusting as I thrust back onto it until I felt my muscles relax and my hole stretch to capacity. Paul's cock was inside my arse while John's cock was inside my twat. My throat was full of Ben and his hands were gripping my tits as they hung in front of him. I was choking from all holes, stuffed full and still begging for more. All three of my lovers took up a single rhythm, forcing their tired cocks into me as far as my abused body would allow. I was invaded, violated, full and grunting my pleasure as they fucked me and fucked me.

We just about managed it. The combined thrusts, the grunts and the groans all built into one almighty orgasm that shook the house. Well, it felt like it did. We all fell into a heap panting and whining that we were knackered.

Afterwards we agreed that it had been fun and we were going to meet the following week. Ben laughed and said perhaps next time he could have a go at his own girl. The boys said he could as long as they could watch. I will let you know how we get on.

5

I was a little embarrassed by the time I breathlessly finished the last sentence. I had forgotten that I had written the story in such a crude way; so reading it had been bizarre to say the least.

Even though I had written it and enjoyed every word, 'Sandra's' description of her exploits was far from the way I felt about sex, a bit too raw and basic for my taste. I was more into the subtle approach. It seemed as if Rosie and Mark were feeling the same way. Just before I slid down into the soft cushions between them I looked around the dimly lit room. Someone had blown some of the candles out. I found it hard to make out the shapes in the corners but there were at least two groups of two or three close enough for me to hear their appreciative noises and see their writhing bodies.

As far as I could see no one was left out, apart from one pretty blonde girl who was sitting propped up on the far wall with her knees up and her skirt bunched around her open thighs. The damp crotch of her knickers was pulled over to one side and her busy fingers disappeared from view. The satisfied smile on her face said it all. She was exactly where she wanted to be. Her eyes were half closed in arousal as she dreamily glanced about the room fuelling her play.

I blocked out all distractions and let myself get lost in what was happening to me. I felt as if Mark and Rosie had a prearranged signal because the second I relaxed they went to work on me. In perfect synchronisation they gently and persuasively stripped me of my clothes. I was so naked I wriggled further into the cushions trying to disappear, but I had no second thoughts whatsoever.

Rosie snuggled down beside me and stroked my breasts, softly squeezing my nipples until I gasped with the pleasure of it all. Her devious fingers played with the nerve endings under the skin by cupping her splayed fingers then raking the nails down my breasts until they met at my raging nipple. Mark had curled into my back and I felt his hard groin pressing against my bottom. The zip on his jeans was cold on the hot cheeks of my bottom so I wriggled more to encourage him. I don't think either of them needed encouragement. Rosie's face was buried in my hair when I noticed her mouth getting nearer to mine. I felt a pang of nerves – I had never even thought of kissing a girl, let alone tried to – but I didn't hesitate for a second as I let her lips explore mine. She nibbled and probed with the tip of her tongue until I lay gasping and begging with my mouth agape and hungry for more. I panted, sighing as she kissed me more thoroughly than I had ever experienced. I drowned under her mouth, breathing deeply through my nose. I longed to taste every inch of her.

From somewhere deep inside I found the adventurer in me and moved down her body until I reached the top of her tight bodice. Her breasts were hot to my lips as I buried my face in her heat. Touching her with my lips and face and hands felt so natural, so right. I unhooked the row of fasteners that held the front of her bodice until her breasts lay exposed before me. Her breasts were swollen, their pink nipples crinkled and hard, inviting me to play. I lowered my mouth to the nearest teat and tested its reaction by kissing the very tip. Rosie and I both moaned at the intensity of that first touch so I drew it hard into my mouth, sucking until I felt its shape against my tongue. I cupped her breast in my hands and suckled like a baby at its mother while her hands cradled my head, encouraging me.

From lying beside her and wanting her to make love to me, almost unnoticed my feelings did a complete about-face. All I could think of was how much I wanted to give this horny girl pleasure. I wanted to do all the things to her with my mouth that I always wished a man would do to me. Now was my chance.

Rosie's eyes danced fire as I looked up and smiled at her. I slid further down, not quite oblivious to Mark's hardness behind me, but far more interested at this stage in how Rosie's legs, without any encouragement from me, dropped open. I ran my hand up under her long skirt as it draped around her white thighs in a most enticing way. I was apprehensive about my ability to please her but I was determined to try, if only this once. I told myself that I didn't have to answer to anyone and if I wanted to make love to this sexy girl who so obviously wanted me to, then sod 'em all. Rosie whimpered quiet little mewling noises like a kitten as my trembling hand explored her inner thighs intimately. Her flesh was so soft, smooth and fragrant, quite unlike the solid hairy muskiness of men. Rosie smelled of flowers and, at this close range, her sex smelled wonderfully inviting. I wanted to bury my head in her but chose to explore first.

I leaned up on one elbow to get a good look at Rosie. Obviously, doing the job I do, I had seen pictures of many, many pussies in my time. From tiny neat little-girl pussies with no inner lips at all to the voluptuous hairy puffy-lipped opposites. Rosie was delicately in the middle of those two. The soft brown curly hair had been trimmed until it just framed her sexy slit, making it more of a temptation, if that were possible. Her inner sex lips teased from between the fleshy outer set, glistening with her juices. I just gazed for a moment or two, drinking in the differences between the two of us, and revelling in them.

I touched her gently at first and drew one fingertip around the halo of hair, then moved closer to touch the bits she really wanted me to explore. I knew this was sending her wild because, just like mine would have done, her hips bucked up, straining toward my searching hand. She grasped my head and bent forward from her cushion to kiss me again. My fingers became far more adventurous as they explored her. I cupped my whole hand over her mound and played my fingers in between her wet sticky lips while she kissed me hard and horny. The experimental feelings had all gone; all I wanted to do was enjoy. Mark's now naked body was curling around my back as his rampant cock thrust its way between my legs. It was almost impossible to concentrate on both experiences at once so I just let Mark carry on while I moved between Rosie's legs and put my head where it wanted to be ... buried in Rosie.

Rosie tasted just as good as she smelled as I took her tiny lips into my mouth and gently sucked. She writhed and moaned but remained lying back, relaxed, as I played to my heart's content. Mark's hand was sliding deliciously over my brazen bottom that stuck up in the air. His fingers teased and tormented, first my pussy then my bottom as he trailed my wetness from one hole to the other, sending me berserk with hunger for him but keeping me at the level of arousal we all needed to keep up this marathon.

Rosie's hands clutched frantically at my hair, taking

it in her fists and gripping hard as my tongue jabbed at her clit. I had been so worried that I wouldn't be able to find it but, as soon as the tip of my tongue travelled up the slick slit, her clit jumped and begged for attention. There was no mistaking it. It throbbed small and hard in my mouth until I slackened my whole mouth and covered her with it. Encompassing as much of Rosie's pussy as I could, I drew her into my mouth and bit gently. She filled the space in my mouth exquisitely, her furry, crinkly flesh, her hot sticky copious juices all melted together as I bit and sucked. Her body shuddered violently as she groaned out loud. Well, I assumed that if I loved the thought of it she would love it too.

'Christ, Jo, what are you doing to me? Please make me come now.'

Not on your life, I thought. I have too many things I want to try before I finish with you. I crouched back on my haunches to free my hands but this gave even more access to Mark behind me. He dipped his fingers into my pussy and I just had to push back onto him. Part of me wanted to forget Rosie and turn around to Mark to continue his exploration of me but she was far too tantalising. I mirrored Mark and slid a finger into Rosie as my tongue continued abusing her clit. That tiny hard little bud had pushed its way out of its surrounding folds, swollen and throbbing, begging for more.

I was writhing and gyrating my hips to convey to Mark that I wanted more. Like me, Rosie wanted more too, so I removed my finger, bunched three fingers together and pushed them sharply into the sucking heat inside her. I could feel all her internal muscles pulsate around my fingers as her body attempted to grasp an orgasm but I relaxed and removed my mouth for a few seconds. I wanted to force her to calm down a little.

The walls of my sex were by now stretched to capacity as Mark forced his fingers right inside me. I could feel his knuckles rasping my lips as they were stretched apart to make way for this immense intrusion. It felt so disgustingly debauched to be knelt over this gorgeous girl's body while being impaled so perfectly by a man I had not known two hours before. I turned my head slightly to look up at him as he knelt by my side and all I could see was his impressively large cock bobbing wildly, actually quite close to my face. I looked up past it to Mark's face and he grinned manically at me, wormed his hand into me a further few centimetres and mouthed 'nice'. Still latched onto Rosie, I nodded my agreement, which sent Rosie into another frenzy as my lips were firmly holding her clitoris. She pulled my head back to its task and I obliged with greed. Mark was forgotten for a few minutes.

I heated up the pace with Rosie by pushing my fingers into her as far as they would go then removing them until just the tips teased her dripping entrance. Next, I pushed them in again, then as her body rose to beg for more, I pulled them out until she cried out in frustration. I kept up a slow rhythm that kept her on the brink of coming but sent her mad for the finish she craved.

Mark bent close to me until his head was close to my ear. 'I want to fuck you so badly, Jo. This is sending me crazy. Please say I can fuck you.' While he persuaded me to let him do exactly what I wanted him to do anyway, his free hand had wormed its way between my legs to search for my clitoris. It was at least ten seconds before I gave in and spread my legs as far apart as I could to help. He had no trouble finding the spot. His gentle knowing fingers massaged until I begged him to squeeze it gently. That sent me as crazy as Rosie under my mouth and Mark in my ear. I nodded frantically.

Mark didn't hesitate to take his place behind me. Rosie scooted up her pillow a little and drew up her knees until her bells tinkled as she wantonly spread her thighs apart. My fingers continued the onslaught as I explored her reactions to being nibbled. She loved it so much that she wriggled frantically until I found it difficult to stay latched on to her. I stepped up the speed, pushing my fingers inside her and spreading them wide each time they were in her depths, only to withdraw them teasingly. Rosie was panting hard, groaning loudly now with each thrust of my hand. Mark slid his cock so far in me with one thrust that I grunted like the animal I had become. I groaned deeply with Rosie's clit between my teasing teeth and worried it until it swelled large in my mouth.

Mark fucked me hard, ramming his cock in me as forcefully as he could, his frustration obvious. I loved it like that. His hands were gripping my hips and his balls bashing the backs of my thighs. I longed to finish myself off but I had no hands free so I wriggled hard trying to rub my clit with my thighs, but it was frustratingly impossible. It didn't matter too much because just the wriggling felt wonderful with Mark so deep inside me. I glanced up to find people surrounding us watching.

Steve slid in behind Rosie to cradle her in his lap; he took hold of her nipples and rolled them hard between thumb and forefinger. Her clit started to pulsate in my mouth and I longed for attention to mine.

I was vaguely aware of Nick slightly to my left watching everything intently. When I glanced up at him he didn't look quite so ordinary. His eyes were blazing and, even though every one else was just about naked, Nick was still clothed. I could just about see the bulge in his jeans but, apart from that, he was still in complete control. He held my gaze and moved into cross-legged position close beside me. I either had to tear my eyes away or let go of Rosie, and I think she would have killed me if I stopped. She was so close to coming.

For a brief second I imagined what we looked like to the watchers.

Steve was sitting against the wall on Rosie's cushion with her cradled between his legs on her back. Her hands were holding her knees up and spread wide and his were tantalising her breasts. By this time her nipples looked red and angry as she grunted with each soft nip of my teeth on her clit. Her pussy was throbbing rhythmically around my hand, moving her rapidly towards her goal. I was kneeling naked on all fours between her legs. Mark knelt up behind me, fucking me for all he was worth, grunting just like Rosie, and just as close as Rosie to ending the game. At least ten people surrounded us just watching and stroking each other, enjoying the show. Nick sat to my left and I couldn't take my eyes off him. It was almost impossible to carry on pleasuring Rosie and helping her achieve her mind-blower while craning my neck to see Nick. I was hypnotised, so I managed it. He leaned down towards me until his face was so close to mine that it rested on Rosie's sweaty trembling thigh.

Nick devastated me with his words. 'You are going to come for me, Joanna. I want you to feel that enormous cock buried up to its hilt in your cunt stretching you and filling you. I want you to taste what you have done to Rosie and savour her flavour in your mouth – you created that flavour. Don't stop any of what you are doing but it will be me that makes you come. Open you legs for me, Joanna. There's a good girl.'

My head screamed its helpless acknowledgement and I feared it would burst with tension. I knew without a doubt he was right. I knew he could do it. Somehow I knew that my wicked body would obey him. I longed to obey him.

I did as he ordered and experienced every inch of Mark's stiff cock, the smell and taste of Rosie and the sounds around me. I cried out my desperation into the hot wet folds of Rosie's pussy. I thrust hard backward, swallowing Mark into me as far as I could. I tried hard to get there without Nick's intervention. But I knew he was right. The thrill of whatever it was he intended to do was exactly what I needed to tip me over the edge. I looked in his face as he very slowly and deliberately took the tip of his middle finger and slipped it between his lips and sucked it pointedly. My stomach lurched.

'Are you ready now, Jo? Do you want it?' he whispered as he removed it from his mouth, glistening wet. I nodded again. 'Are you sure?'

I screamed, 'Yes!' but my desperation was lost between Rosie's thighs. Everyone in the room knew I was begging. They cheered their approval.

Nick bent closer to me and, still holding my gaze, slid his hand between my dangling breasts. It travelled agonisingly slowly down my hot torso until just that one arrogant finger rested and waited above my clitoris. He raised an eyebrow in question, smiled and touched his finger to the hood of my clit and slowly drew it back to expose the hard nub of engorged flesh.

I felt Rosie buck under my mouth and her pussy flood its juice into my mouth. Mark's cock twitched and spat its sperm inside me to the renewed cheers of the group and he collapsed along my back. That one finger, now slippery from me, touched my aching straining clitoris. 'Now, sweetheart! You can come now.' Just as he had promised I exploded under his fingertip as it ran just once over my raging clitoris.

The pounding of my orgasm took my breath away. His finger remained in place, touching firmly but gently as the spasms gripped my belly and thighs. My back arched as each wave of pleasure thrilled through me. Nick removed the object of my explosion and the contractions softened but they were re-ignited by little fresh squeezes and touches and softening thrusts. From being totally absorbed by his control I was again aware of everyone else.

The powerful memory of his one finger on my clit was like a touch all in itself and it continued to send wonderful shock waves right through me as I collapsed into Rosie's lap. I had not taken my eyes from Nick. He bent down to me and said, for all to hear:

'Good girl.'

6

When our floorshow had finished, everyone gathered round our naked bodies and chatted as if we were doing nothing unusual. I suppose to them we weren't. Steve raved about how horny it was for him to watch me between his wife's legs giving her a good seeing-to. I wasn't quite sure about his turn of phrase but I knew exactly what he meant. Rosie kept looking at me with smouldering encouragement. Her breasts were still soft and swollen by her arousal; the nipples still hard and crinkly. Within minutes I was ready to begin again, but I desperately needed to stand back a bit and take stock.

There were hands all over me, attempting to persuade me to stay, but I began to feel a little claustrophobic and tried hard to express the need I had to take time out to think. The last thing I wanted to do was insult anyone because I had just experienced the most amazing night of my life. So I let them down as gently as I could and made my escape, promising them faithfully that I would visit again. Very soon!

I walked out of the door into the darkness and looked back into all the friendly faces, feeling sad that I was different. This was part of their lives, but for me it was an assignment. I had to go back to my life, my office, and of course, to Adam. Thinking of Adam reminded me of Nick, and I searched the sea of faces for his. I looked right into the hallway, beyond Rosie's flushed face and Steve's rampant cock that threatened to burst out of his hastily pulled-on trousers. I looked past

Mark's pleading eyes to the back of the group and there he was. Nick was standing right at the back of the hall, leaning casually against the wall with his arms folded across his chest, watching the proceedings. His eyes met mine and he smiled, but it was the most quirky, knowing smile imaginable, and in response my chest fluttered and I felt my pussy ooze shamelessly. I knew without a doubt just from that one look that he knew exactly what I was feeling. I was instantly reminded of the letter I had received, that up until then I hadn't really understood. The message, 'I know you, Joanna', took on a whole new meaning. I felt undeniably that Nick knew me inside and out and we hadn't even spoken. I shook off those unwanted scary thoughts and waved my goodbyes.

As I fired up Baby and reversed out of the driveway I felt an overwhelming sense of relief and freedom.

By the time I had got back to The Grange I was feeling very confused. There were so many new experiences to think about. I had known right from the start that this proposal of Adam's would be different and therefore exciting to me. But in no way was I prepared for the churning in my stomach and the sweet fluttering that was still making itself felt in my lower regions. I could still feel Mark inside me, and still taste Rosie on my lips and fingers.

Rosie had totally blown me away. I was shocked to the core, not by what I had done – after all I had enjoyed every second – but by how much I had gloried in her femininity and my enjoyment of her. I lay in the big double bed remembering how soft her skin was and how I had loved the smell of her. But, above all, the one thought that kept coming back to my mind with a sharp pang of feeling deep inside me, was Nick. Nick, who had, after all, only touched me with a finger. It was Rosie and Mark who had wooed me, aroused me and then amazed me with their finesse, but Nick wormed his way into every thought I had.

Nothing could persuade me to sleep, even though it was four o'clock in the morning. I even found myself wishing I had taken up their very tempting offer to stay. Rosie and Steve particularly made a point of explaining in great sexual detail what they would like to do to me if I stayed. Mark, like the young puppy he was, enthusiastically agreed that I should explore them further. I think what he really meant was that he would like to explore me further, if the look on his face was anything to go by.

Eventually I must have dozed off after a frantic desperate masturbation session, which lasted all of five minutes and left me just as frustrated as I had been before.

The following morning I rang Rosie to thank her 'for having me' and she laughed. She assured me she would be happy to have me again any time. She also expressed a wish to see me again on my own and I found myself agreeing. I explained that I would need to get the rest of this competition out of the way but yes, I would like to see her again and yes, I would really like to visit their group again. We left it at that.

When I went back to work the day after my return from Cheshire, I was even more nervous than when I had sat outside Rosie's. The knowledge that I would have to go and see Adam to keep him up to date was playing very serious tricks with my brain – and other distinctive parts of my anatomy. I decided that the best policy was to write the article first, then e-mail it to him. That way he would know exactly what had gone on without me having to go through that mortifying routine we had drifted into – where I told him all my sexual thoughts and he just watched and listened, revelling in my discomfort.

It didn't actually take long to write my piece. The words flowed from my keyboard. I experienced every touch and feeling all over again, from how my tongue felt as it first touched Rosie's clitoris and the stuffed feeling I had as Mark rammed first his hand and then his cock hard into my pussy. I remembered too the touch of Nick's finger on me, and the complete control he had over me for those few short moments. I put that to the back of my mind, perhaps to dissect later. I knew the way Nick had made me come would be a little hard to believe so I left it out. Anyway, the way I felt about my experience of him was so personal I wanted to keep it to myself. Plus, if I was honest, it was a tad unbeliev-able. I could almost imagine my readers' comments. 'Oh, yeah, course she did. She came with just one man touching her clitoris.' I tried to write it like it was but it wouldn't come out right and I felt it would be detrimental to the credibility factor. I had to make the readers believe I really had done these things, otherwise there was no point. So I took the easy option and ended my piece as if I had been taken to orgasm by the administrations of Rosie and Mark.

I am not sure if the article I wrote just felt bland because I couldn't put into words exactly how they had all made me feel so special, or that trying to relive a fantastic experience in words can never be wholly adequate. The other thing I realised at that very early stage was that you cannot 'tell' a whole evening properly in the limited number of words I was allowed for my article. I could have gone on for ever describing each little innuendo and movement, each sight and sound, each taste and experience, but I was restricted to one double page. I did my best and sent the unsatis-factory piece to Adam.

While I waited for his response I turned to other things to take my mind off the waiting. I had known that this whole idea was bizarre to say the least, but I'd had no inkling that I would feel so involved and con-fused. Neither had I any notion that after just one encounter I would want to pull out; not because I wasn't enjoying it, but because I was – too much. I thought about it at length and decided that I wanted the new position and prestige more than I liked to admit so I would carry on unless it became too difficult.

In my absence I had received another batch of replies to the challenge, so I began to wade through them. There was the usual dross that every magazine gets in response to any request and a few that had no oomph about them. I weeded them out and narrowed down my next search to five that were possibilities.

Again one stood out from the crowd. Kevin, a trans-vestite, longed for a woman to take him in hand, so to speak. Up until the day he wrote to me he had never had the courage to 'come out' to anyone. He begged me to meet him in his female persona, then tell the world that he wasn't a freak but a man who loved to give up his responsibilities occasionally and enjoy the freedom that wearing female clothes gave him. He explained that he had completely conflicting thoughts and needs and I immediately related to him. I so wanted to take away the pain I could read between his words, if only for one night, but I had no idea how my readers would feel about that. I decided the best thing was to put my idea to Adam when we next met and see what he said. I knew there would be more replies before I had to write the next issue so there would be a lot more competition, but Kevin had touched on something that made me want to help him.

Adam made me wait two days and I was on tenterhooks the whole time. I went through the motions of writing and sorting. I even rewrote parts of my Rosie and Steve article in the hopes of feeling better about it. Then I got his summons.

Joanna
We need to talk about your article. I have scheduled a meeting in my office for Friday at 10a.m. Please bring any correspondence you have received.
Set aside at least two hours. That will give us the opportunity to go through your proposal for the next issue too.
Adam

I sent a brief message to let him know that the time was OK for me but, I was a little worried about what he meant by 'We need to talk about your article'. I fluffed around waiting for the meeting, shuffling what I had to show him and going over and over my account of my meeting with the swinging group. I became convinced that he hated it, so by the time Friday came I was a wreck. I toyed again with the idea of power dressing or sexy dressing, but in the end I was so convinced that it would go badly I didn't really care. I just slipped on a skirt and shirt.

'Come in, Joanna.'

As usual my heart pounded as I walked through the door.

Adam was already seated at the little oasis of coffee table and comfy chairs with my article laid out in front of him. 'Come and join me.'

I couldn't quite make out the expression on his face but he certainly wasn't the Adam I had met before.

'I don't understand.' He started in on me before I even had a chance to settle. 'I thought we understood each other and where this project was going.'

'I'm sorry, but I don't know what you mean,' I said quickly.

'We agreed, and correct me if I'm wrong, that you were actually going to meet these people and write a true account of that meeting. So what changed your mind? Or was I wrong about you and you were just not up to the challenge?'

His face was expressionless. At that stage I had no idea what he was feeling but I knew without a doubt that he was disappointed. Stuttering and stumbling over my words, I infuriated myself as I tried to persuade him that, as far as I knew, I had carried out my part of the agreement.

'So are you telling me that this is a true account of your meeting with this Rosie character?' He picked up my article and stared at it.

'Of course it is. Why would I lie?'

'I don't know, Joanna. Why don't you tell me? Perhaps because you got cold feet but didn't know how to tell me,' he added with sadness tinging his words.

I stared at him dumbfounded. I had no idea what he was getting at.

'So, you are trying to tell me and your readers that not only did you walk into this couple's house and have sex with a group of strangers – which I can just about believe – but you also are one of the tiny percentage of women who can orgasm just because she is being fucked? Forgive me, Joanna, if I am sceptical, but believe it or not I have had the occasional relationship. In my experience, even though most magazines would have us believe otherwise, most women need clitoral stimulation to orgasm. Since *Leather and Lace* was launched I have prided myself on the fact that we tell sex like it is. We don't have women swooning at the sight of a cock and then having multiple orgasms. We have got to steer away from the fallacy far too many men believe in; that all women need is a good hard fuck and they will orgasm to order and consequently be grateful to them for ever.'

Adam paused for breath just long enough for me to get a word in. Up until that moment Adam had read me so well. He had played with my emotions and my sexuality until I was ready to kneel on the floor at his feet. Part of me was still worried that he was *just playing* with my emotions. For all I knew he kept every woman in his life on a sexual string to be jerked into place on a whim.

I wanted to explain what had happened, to tell him that every word I had said was the truth, but far too big a part of me was annoyed with him for not believing me. I wanted to shout that, apart from leaving out Nick, everything I wrote was exactly what happened ... but that would mean telling him about Nick. I guessed that if he didn't believe what I had already written there was no way he would believe that Nick made me come with one touch of a finger. I wasn't sure if I believed it myself.

Confused, not only by his attitude but also by my reaction, I felt the best thing I could do was leave. Without a word I got up from my seat and began the walk to the door.

'Stop, Joanna! Come back, please. We need to talk about this.'

I stopped halfway to the door and waited with my back still towards him, fighting with myself. I wanted to explain about Nick but I knew I wasn't ready to tell him about the way I had been controlled, in the same way I felt *he* controlled me every time I was with him.

My chest was heaving with suppressed hurt, but something in me wanted to turn around and go back – go back and face him. I asked myself why I always had these mixed feelings when I was with him. Part of me was inclined to shout at him, tell him to stuff his job and the rise that went with it. But the side of me that he had awakened, the side that Nick had tapped into so knowingly, longed for him to take complete control. And I mean complete control.

There was silence for a minute or two while I stood still with my back to him. I have no idea what he was doing or thinking but I could almost hear him struggling with the same difficulties I had. Eventually the silence softened and the tension went from the room. My shoulders relaxed but still I was unable to turn around. I was so relieved when Adam broke the silence. His voice was calm; in fact his whole demeanour had changed, so I assumed he had come to terms with whatever he had been fighting with. I knew I hadn't.

'Joanna, come here . . . Please?'

I returned to the table but refused to look at him. I sat on my chair, chin to my chest, and waited for him to speak.

'I'm sorry.' He explained gently, 'I was determined to let you explain before I had a go at you but I had such high expectations of our little project and as soon as I saw you looking so innocent I just snapped.'

'You didn't even give me a chance –'

'I know,' he interrupted. 'But please can we start again?'

'Anyway, why shouldn't I look innocent? I haven't done anything wrong. I am a single woman, and if I choose to sleep with five hundred people of mixed gender then I will. And –' I was almost shouting by this time '– who the hell are you to judge me? It was you who put me up to it in the first place.' I stopped, breathing hard but glad I had got it out.

'You silly girl. I didn't mean sexually innocent. I meant that I assumed you would come in looking sheepish because you had felt that for whatever reason you had been unable to go through with our plan. Do you honestly think I could be interested in a girl who is *sexually* innocent?' he added. 'Don't get me wrong, this –' he picked up my article and pretended to skim through it '– is one of the best bits of erotic writing I have ever seen and you can trust me when I say I'm jaded. Perhaps you should just try to explain to me what happened. What went wrong?'

'I still don't understand what you're on about. I did exactly as we agreed I should do. The only thing that wasn't a part of my brief was the level to which I enjoyed it. I had the most amazing, horny, erotic, mind-blowing experience of my life, I wrote it down to the best of my ability and all you can do is doubt me.' Defiantly I stared straight at him. 'You're right, perhaps you did choose the wrong person. Perhaps you were looking for someone who could stay completely detached from the whole thing, then come back and write an explosive report of the proceedings. Well, I am sorry to disappoint you ... sir!' I added sarcastically. 'Whatever you think, and frankly I don't care what that is, I did go, I did do everything I wrote about, and I fucking well enjoyed every sweaty second.'

I thought I had better stop then. I couldn't believe what I had said but I didn't really care. I was so upset but my heart was thumping. I wanted him to be proud of me. But more than that I wanted him to feel the connection between us that I felt. Just being in the same room as him was so disconcerting and sometimes I felt that he was experiencing the same feelings as me, but then he would act like a boss again. It was a bewildering experience to realise that each of his personas was as exciting as the other. I couldn't decide which was the hornier.

'Whoa, OK, point taken. Tell me then, Joanna, if you are being so honest about everything, am I right in assuming you are one of those lucky few women? The few who don't need more than a thrusting cock for them to climax? Because, if so, why are your other stories so explicit about the range of titillation and attention that leads your heroines up to their moments of glory?'

I sat still, unable to answer him; not knowing how. Struggling with myself, I looked up at him and my stomach jolted with a need I couldn't begin to describe.

'All right, something else did happen. But I don't feel comfortable telling you about it.' I stood up again and put my hand out to him. 'Give me my article back and I will write you the climax that you obviously need to satisfy your ethics.' I stood trembling as he looked into my face.

'Sit down, Joanna.'

'I can't.' I was almost in tears when he grabbed my wrist. I tried to pull away. 'Let me go. I don't want to tell you,' I cried, but his psychological pull on me was stronger. I sat. My heart constricted into a knot at his hold on me. I crumpled inside, totally incapable of breaking that exquisite pull I was feeling, the pull that produced the liquid toffee feeling in my guts. What was happening to me? Was I helpless to deny him this power over me? Confident in the knowledge that he had me where he wanted me, he released my wrist.

'Please tell me, Joanna. I need to know what happened. You can trust me, I promise. I'm sorry I didn't believe you. I'm sorry I have upset you and I promise just to listen without interrupting. Please, Joanna?' His voice had become the liquid toffee of my guts. My head was spinning. I longed to tell him everything but I knew that if I told him about Nick and how he had made me melt inside we would never have the same relationship again. I wasn't quite sure how he would react, but I had a pretty good idea. I knew exactly what telling him my secret would do to me. I knew that as soon as he realised I was susceptible to that kind of mind game I would never be able to look at him in the same way again.

'OK, OK. I'll tell you but don't say a word. I don't want to know what you think about it. All right?'

'Agreed,' Adam answered, smiling softly. He sat back in his chair, his gaze almost hypnotic as I tried to find the right words.

'It was probably just the tension of the moment, or the desperation I felt for an orgasm, but while I was exploring Rosie and while Mark was doing what he was doing behind me . . .'

'Fucking you, Joanna. He was fucking you.' Adam had a friendly smirk on his face.

'OK, when Mark was fucking me from behind, there was a man there who up until that moment had just stayed in the corner still dressed, watching all that was going on. It appeared that he got all his kicks from voyeurism. At the time that didn't surprise me; there was a young girl in another corner doing exactly the same thing and obviously having a ball with her own thoughts. But then, just as I was desperate for release, and wondering how I was going to free a hand to help it along a little – both my hands were rather busy with

Rosie – I caught his eye. He walked across the room and sat down beside us, then, after a few minutes of watching intently, he whispered in my ear. He told me he was going to make me come with just one of his fingers. And he was right, he did. He held some sort of control over me, and had done ever since I'd entered the room. It was probably just the way the whole group of them managed to form one seducing entity . . . well, that was what I tried to tell myself at the time. Nick, the man I'm talking about, had a way of appearing to control the whole event even while not being involved. Well, not until the very end anyway. I found his presence beside me compelling. I began to believe his claim. Anyway, it sounds silly now, which is why I didn't put it in my article. He just leaned over, held my gaze and touched one finger to my clitoris and I came. Amazingly.'

As I always did when talking about sex to Adam, I sat for a moment or two with my head still bowed, stumbling over my explanations as to how it could have happened. Eventually I looked up to see his reaction, expecting derision. Adam, my enigmatic boss, was yet again staring at me with an indefinable expression on his face. God, he was frustrating.

'What?' I almost shouted when he said nothing in response to my confession.

The emotions that flitted briefly across Adam's face were confusing. I definitely saw the ever-present amusement. That was closely followed by fascination. I watched intently at the slight grin at the corners of his mouth and his dilating pupils softening his face. This whole new image of him flustered me intently. I became shamelessly aroused.

'How did that make you feel, Joanna? Did you enjoy his control over you?' He leaned towards me then, waiting for my answer, and for the first time I felt almost in control. No longer was he boss and I employee. For the first time he was just a man talking to a woman that he so obviously found exciting. I knew my answer was very important to him and therefore probably to me too. My chest was fluttering as I returned his enquiring gaze. Without a doubt I knew that he would read my answer, not only in my words but also in my body language and my eyes.

I thought for a second, completely aware that if I wanted anything more between Adam and myself then I had to get this right. It wasn't until that moment that the enormity of this exchange really hit me. All that time we had battled back and forth with words and power struggles but I knew then that Adam was asking me more than 'How did it make you feel?' and 'Did you enjoy it?'

I answered carefully. 'I absolutely loved it. It was as if everyone else in the room faded into oblivion, leaving just me and Nick's finger. Even more important than that was the incredible way he took over my will. He held my mind in a vice of my own making. Well, that's how I felt anyway. Right from the moment I first looked at him I felt compelled to, not necessarily *obey* him, but to be under his control. Having said that, I do know that I would have happily obeyed him.'

My breathing was ragged and erratic as I paused for his reaction. His eyes roamed my face, and then roamed my body with an arrogant glint. There was a tangible shifting of control back to him. I brazened it out and carried on looking into his eyes as I waited for what was to come. My pulse was racing, hoping I was reading him right. I felt I would shatter if he were just playing with me.

'Have you ever felt that way before, Joanna? Please be honest with me.'

Oh, God, this is it, I thought, as I chose to tell the truth. There was something intangible about the way he held me in his vice-like spell. I hung my head again and nodded.

'I am sure you realise, Joanna, that what you have just shared with me interests me greatly on more than a professional level. Would you mind if I asked you some questions?'

I nodded feebly.

Adam leaned across the table and lifted my chin until I had no option but to look at him in my embarrassment.

'You're nodding, Joanna. Does that mean yes, you will answer, or yes, you mind answering my questions? I think we both need to be clear on this. Don't you?'

I nodded again, lost inside. Already he controlled me absolutely. The way my insides melted surpassed the experience with Nick a hundredfold. He had staked his claim.

'Joanna!' he snapped kindly, bringing me back to my senses.

'Sorry.' I forced myself to answer him directly and confidently. 'Yes, I do realise that this is more than professional. Yes, I will answer your questions and before you ask, yes, I will be as honest as I know how.'

'Good girl.' There was that toffee again. 'Are you going to meet this group again?'

'I'm not sure really. They have invited me and I have to admit I am very tempted, but I thought it would be best to get this competition thing out of the way first.' Already I wasn't telling the whole truth. What I really meant was that I wanted to get the thing between him and me out of the way first.

'You obviously enjoyed being briefly controlled by Nick. Do you think you would have enjoyed taking that control further?'

'I'm not sure what you mean. This is all so new to me. I longed for more but I have no idea what that implies. I am sure I would have complied with any of his instructions to get the orgasm I needed.'

'I'm sure you would, Joanna, but I believe almost any man or woman would do that. What I want to know is whether your climax was your only goal?'

'I suppose there was more to it than that. Once Nick came into the equation there was, anyway. Up until then all I wanted was as much debauched sex as possible. I wanted to give Rosie as much pleasure as I could and I wanted Mark to fuck me without pause. Then Nick joined us and the way I felt changed. It was as if Nick and I were the only ones there. He locked into my head then almost gave me permission to feel what I was doing and everything I was experiencing took on a new meaning. But still all that mattered was him and his claim that he would make me come.'

'Did you have any doubts that he could carry out his claim?'

'None whatsoever. I felt all along that he didn't take control but rather that I gave it to him willingly.'

All these questions were so exhilarating to me. It was as if I was baring my soul to him. Not for one minute did I want to ask him anything. In a way this was a form of control in itself.

He continued, 'Did you realise that there are many men that would delight in taking just such control of a very beautiful young woman like you?'

I knew that a lot could well hang on my answer to this one simple question. I thought of the best approach and even toyed with the idea of telling him that I longed for him to control me in that way, but I was too scared of rejection. His intentions were still not wholly clear to me.

'I really do hope so, Adam. I've known for a while that certain unorthodox situations make me excited when other girls would get annoyed, but I've never experienced the truth of it until now. What I'm trying to say is that what happened to me with Nick and the way I feel now answering your questions is so right for me. This is who I am.'

'Does it excite you when I ask you intimate questions?'

'Yes.' I swallowed nervously, awaiting his next question.

'In what way are you excited? I want you to describe to me how you feel.'

I burned with shame but managed to answer him. I revelled in the shame and humiliation he was subjecting me to.

'Sexually. Your questions are exciting me sexually.'

'Tell me, Joanna. Describe to me how your body is responding to my questioning of you.'

I looked up at him then, straight into his eyes. I had to know just why he was doing this to me. Never before had I felt so completely helpless and I had to know his motives. I had already lost my will and my control, but even more powerful was my real fear of losing my soul to him. I just had to know why. His eyes smouldered as he waited for my answer. However hard he tried – and I knew he was trying – he couldn't hide the glaring fact that he was just as turned on as I was. I glanced down at his crotch and he fidgeted, unable to disguise the powerful bulge that threatened to burst his zip. He smiled confidently, eyes sparkling as he waited, calm now in the sure knowledge that we were on the same wavelength and that I would indeed answer him.

That look gave me the confidence to tell him what he wanted to hear. I knew my face was flaming but I held his gaze. The writer in me evaporated me as I tried to tell him how he made me feel.

'My nipples are hard and my stomach is churning.'

'And?' he persevered.

'And what?' I knew exactly what he was asking but how could I tell him that my shameful pussy was swollen and dripping? I could actually feel the juices from inside me soaking their way through the crotch of my knickers. I could feel my clitoris as if it were being manually manipulated. I was trembling from head to foot.

'OK. I am wet and horny, but then you knew that anyway.'

'What else, Joanna?'

'What else what?' I was getting confused.

'What about in here?' He tapped the side of his temple. 'How do you feel in here?'

'I don't know. My brain is reacting to you as if I have been pre-programmed. I am very scared at how I am reacting but I am more excited than I can begin to describe. I want ... I want ... Oh, God, I don't know what I want but I know I want something so badly I'll scream if I don't get it. I know you can give me what I want even though I don't even know completely what that is. This is really screwing me up, Adam. I don't know whether to run a mile or get on my knees and beg you to touch me.'

'Calm down, Joanna. Now, I know this is all a little scary to you but I want you to do something for me. Would you do that?'

My heart actually crashed in my chest. I felt my pussy weep in response and I knew that this was what I had longed for. I was shaking inside and out by the time he issued the order. I gulped in disbelief at how we had gone from boss and employee to this within the space of half an hour and one conversation. How did he manage to make it sound as if I was the one in control by asking my permission, when we both knew that I was absolutely under his spell? For those few seconds I knew I would do anything he asked.

'Take off your panties, Joanna.' No preliminaries, no doubt in his voice, just a thrilling edge that brooked no argument. I hovered, unsure if I had really heard correctly. He didn't repeat himself, but just waited, watching my discomfort. I writhed and wriggled inside, unable to believe what was happening. It must have been a good minute or two that I struggled with myself, but eventually we both knew that I would obey. I started to get up to go into his private loo but he just chuckled confidently.

'Here, Joanna. Take them off here for me.'

I stayed where I was, standing in front of the chair and across the low table from him. I squirmed my hands up under my tight skirt and, blushing madly, I peeled my black silk knickers down my thighs. I realised very briefly that I was glad I had put on a pretty pair. Bending over I took them from my feet and of course one leg caught on my shoe so I almost stumbled. I then stood again, uncertain about what I was supposed to do with them. I was in awe of his ability to control my thoughts and deeds, and more than a little scared by my ready compliance.

'Thank you, Joanna. You look so delightful when you blush. I think I'll have to encourage that response in you more often. You've demonstrated to me that even

85

though you are a strong-willed independent woman, sexually you are desperate to be dominated and, as you have probably guessed by now, I am very attracted to the submissive in you. I would love to explore you further. It might be confusing for you and I can't promise it will be an easy process, but I can assure you the rewards will be worth it if you persevere. From my experience, the pleasures to be had in a relationship where one longs to be dominated and the other naturally dominates are phenomenal. What do you think?'

I stood in front of him shamefaced with his suggestions buzzing in my brain. I had my scrunched-up knickers in my fist and a trickle of stickiness on my thigh, but I had no hesitation whatsoever when I agreed to his suggestion. In fact I longed for him to do something, anything, and if I had to agree to his proposal to get him to touch me, then that was fine by me. I nodded.

'Say it, Joanna. I need to be sure you know what you're agreeing to.'

'How can I say yes when I don't even know what you intend to do to me, or what this "exploring", as you call it, entails? If I'm totally honest I'm not even sure I know what being submissive means either.'

'Come round here, Joanna.'

I walked around the table and stood trembling beside his chair. I knew that he was about to do something and the anticipation was excruciating torture. I clutched harder onto my damp knickers. Groaning, I waited for him to issue his next instruction to me.

'Pull up your skirt, please.'

'Oh, God, please. No.'

Again he didn't repeat the instruction but just waited for me to obey. I knew then that I should leave, but even though my knees were trembling frantically I wanted more and he knew it. If we had been at the beginning of a normal relationship and he had kissed me or something then tried to get up my skirt, I would probably have jumped at the chance. I hung my head but did as he asked and raised my skirt. The wave of sweet humiliation washed over me as he just looked at my bared pussy, making me realise instantly that he was right. I wanted this badly. From his sitting position his head was almost level with my crotch and I knew he must be able to smell my arousal – I could. He didn't say anything, but just looked at me as if he were considering me for a part in a production. I was glad that I had shaved around my mound for my meeting with Rosie and her chums, and found myself wondering intently what he thought of my pretty pussy.

My pussy is definitely pretty. The soft dark hair isn't too lush nor too sparse, it curls into neat little coils around my clitoris, just framing it. My clit is luckily quite prominent and the pink hood tapers down to my inner labia that peep invitingly through the hair. I wondered just how blatantly my flesh was peeping through my pubic hair now I was so aroused. I realised with embarrassment that the hair would by now be quite wet.

'Open your legs for me, Joanna.'

'Good girl,' he crooned when I obeyed without question, proud now to show off.

'Put your hands on your head.'

I obeyed.

Adam stood up then and moved the table away, leaving a clear space around us. The close proximity of him threw me all over again and I wanted to cry with the anticipation I felt waiting for his next move. He walked around me looking me up and down. He took hold of my shoulders and pushed them back so that my aching breasts thrust out even more. Still the expression on his face hadn't changed from one of enquiry. He stopped his visual examination and stood in front of me. I waited, unable to move.

'Do you think I could make you come easily, Joanna? Do you think that if I touched you now, and slid my inquisitive fingers between your lips to explore your cunt, I could make you come?'

'Yes,' I groaned, thrusting out my pussy towards him.

'Do you think that if I took the juice from your cunt and smeared it around your bottom you would let me invade that tight little hole, too?'

I nodded frantically, having no idea at all if I would like him doing that but having absolute conviction that I'd enjoy him trying.

'Tell me, Joanna.'

'Yes, yes, yes!'

'Does that mean yes, you agree to us progressing to the next step?'

'Oh, yes. Please touch me now,' I begged shamelessly.

I was blissfully aware of him hunkering down in front of me. He pushed his hands between my thighs and encouraged me to spread my legs to their limit, until my muscles pulled. I felt my lips, now puffy with need, separate of their own accord to expose the slippery channel of my pussy. I could feel my copious juices gathering and cooling on my lips as I waited for him to do something other than look at me. Staring at me with such intent was foreplay in its most exquisite form, but I wanted fucking. I groaned my invitation.

The first thing I felt was a delicate brush of his fingers along the groove of my sex from my anus to my clitoris, gently massaging all the tiny nerve endings on the way. I writhed my encouragement. Then, without warning, he pushed his bunched hand right up inside me until his knuckles grazed my clitoris and I almost collapsed at the intensity of my response. My wail filled the room. Immediately Adam withdrew his hand and stood looking at me. I was stunned by not only the noise I had made, but also my acceptance of his decision to stop. I waited without a word, still with my hands on my head and my knickers in my palm. My legs were stretched so far apart I thought I would topple over if he touched me again.

Adam stood, took hold of my trembling hands, and lowered them from their submissive position. He wriggled my skirt back into its position and straightened my clothing as I stood almost comatose, disbelief screaming through my head. I couldn't believe he was going to leave me like this. But it became all too obvious that that was his intention when he turned away and moved towards his desk. He sat and summoned me. I was shaking too much to lower myself into the chair so I stood in front of his desk like a schoolgirl before her headmaster.

'Well done, Joanna. That was a very important lesson you have just learned. You mentioned that you didn't know what submission meant – well, that was it.'

I suppose I was a bit petulant when I answered him. 'What lesson is that then, Adam? That you are going to humiliate me, tease me, and then leave me frustrated every time you see me?'

Adam's face darkened and I knew instinctively that a part of our agreement was that I didn't speak to him in that way. I apologised quickly.

'What you have just begun to learn is that I will control you at all times. You know now that I could give you unbelievable pleasure, don't you?'

I nodded, the memory of how I felt before he had even touched me threatening to overwhelm me.

'Good. You learned that one well then. I think we have been leading up to this for a long time don't you, Joanna?'

I nodded again, unsure if I had the strength to speak.

'I am quite happy to let you carry on with our project for a while. When you have reached the next stage and you have met your next reader, send me your report and I will arrange to see you. Until then, I want you to follow a few simple instructions for me. Will you do that?'

'Do you mean I won't see you again until then?' I babbled, almost in tears.

'Control, Joanna. I want you to show me some control. I want you to pick the next game with someone that will excite me. I want you to shave your cunt for me and don't ever wear knickers in here again, Joanna. Is that clear? Good.' He smiled without even giving me a chance to answer. 'After all, you do want your naughty little cunt to be available to me, don't you?'

Pathetically, my head automatically nodded its agreement. My pussy dribbled its acceptance and my legs trembled violently.

'Off you go, then. I will look forward to your next report.'

There was no doubt that I had been dismissed, so I turned and left the room. I was completely dazed as I made my way back to my office with my knickers still clutched tightly in my hand. The mirror in the lift shocked me with the wicked image that stared back. I reached my chair unable for one second to believe what had just happened. My hand, that had made its way to my crotch with a will of its own, forced me to face what I had just permitted Adam to do to me. Waves of shame and humiliation washed down my spine, prickling my hair roots and turning my stomach as my hand discovered the extent of my compliance. Copious amounts of my sex juices were soaking my pubic hair and my thighs were sticky with it. Never before had I produced quite so much evidence of my excitement. My face was bright red and my flesh felt feverish to the touch. I desperately wanted more. I longed to go back to his office and demand satisfaction, but on the other hand I knew in a way that he was right; this way I would want him like crazy until the next time I was summoned to him. My hand started its frantic work to dispel my hunger before I went mad.

How would I ever find the patience to carry on in this bizarre relationship, I wondered? I had no idea if Adam even thought of us as having a relationship but neither did I care. It didn't really matter to me if he took this seriously or not, or what he wanted from me. All I cared about was that he did want me, and that he continued to want me for whatever freaky reason. Our connection was electric; the way he made me feel just with his interrogation of my feelings and responses stunned me with the intensity of what I was capable of feeling. I decided to attack my next assignment with extra vigour to astound him. I wanted to shock him with my compliance to his instructions.

To exaggerate the way I felt, I rode home on my bike with my knickers off. It was a shame that I had a tight skirt on because I longed to feel the abrasion of the seat on my naked flesh. I thought again of how it would be to have a fixed dildo sticking up from the saddle and I almost got a case of the vapours. I just about managed to get home in one piece and, after a quick tea, I made a trip to the local pharmacy and treated myself to an old-fashioned shaving brush, a wet razor and some shaving cream. I also bought a tube of soothing cream for afterwards then went home to indulge myself.

Just getting the equipment ready was thrilling in itself. I laid out all the implements of my submission to Adam and ran a bowl of hot water. After trying many places I found the most suitable position for my task was sitting on the edge of my dining table with the bowl next to me and my feet up on a chair. I propped my large square mirror against the back of the chair and stripped from the waist down before getting in place. Oh, how debauched I looked with my thighs splayed apart and my naughty pussy so close to the mirror! I leaned back on one hand and just looked for a few moments at the cause of all my helpless obedience.

Flushed and plumped by my constant arousal, my shameless labia poked from the surrounding hair, making the overall picture one of voluptuous lewdness. As I lathered the brush against the stick of shaving soap and then my hair, the foam bubbled deliciously, sending shivers across my flesh. I loved the slippery touch of the brush and didn't want to stop the caressing of the soap across my eager clitoris. The only trouble was I was close to coming so I tried to concentrate on the matter in hand. When my sex bush was completely white and frothy I began the gentle scraping motion that removed the hair. Even the rasping of the razor was good; I enjoyed every second.

As the soggy hair began to drop away I was surprised to see just how rude I looked without it. Before I had even started on the curls around my lips I knew that I would look extremely vulgar. I pushed my clitoris this way and that as I shaved around the hardening nub but it was all too much for me. I just had to finish what I had started so I swirled the softened soapy brush over and over my clit until I was close to the explosion, then pushed the handle end of the brush into my pussy as a makeshift cock. Running my fingertips across my swollen clit was all it took to produce the deliciously shuddery orgasm that shivered through me.

I couldn't take my eyes from my smooth silky mound. I had removed every last crinkly hair and fluffy patch until I was baby soft and exposed. Every crease and fold of sex flesh was blatantly on show, with my inner lips looking much ruder than I would ever have believed possible. They pouted juicily from the plumper outer lips in a very disgusting fashion and I stared in disbelief at the transformation.

Oh, Adam, are you in for a shock when you see just what you've ordered, I thought, as I smoothed my hands over my nakedness. When I went to put my knickers back on I remembered Adam's other instruction and chucked them in the clothes basket; I wanted to know how it would feel to be naked of hair and of knickers. I even pulled the curtains and roamed around my little flat trying to catch sight of myself in every mirror I owned. I left on my blouse but stayed naked from the waist down, realising that these days I was horny all the time. What happened to the time when I would have an orgasm and then forget sex for a while, I asked myself?

Those days were well and truly gone and good riddance to them, I thought as, yet again, I ran my exploring fingers between my legs. Over and over again over the next hour or two I sat in front of a mirror and spread my legs apart to marvel at my present to Adam. It felt like a present to Adam, this nakedness. After all, no one else had seen it, and I had carried out his instructions to create this whorish look. A part of my head knew from that night on that I wanted more than anything to please him and probably obey any instruction he might care to give me. I slept that night with my right hand placed firmly between my thighs and one solitary finger nestled between my continuously sticky labia. My head was filled with acceptance.

7

As you can imagine, I was in a hurry to get the next winner picked as soon as possible. Not once during my meeting with Adam had I managed to take my thoughts from our games, so I hadn't mentioned my letter from Kevin the transvestite. There was no doubt in my mind, however, that Adam would not find Kevin's plight sexy so, remembering his instruction, I looked through the pile again. By this stage I had over fifty requests to sift through, including another anonymous message from the very presumptuous person who thought I should be punished for my sexual endeavours. After my first session with Adam, the thought of being punished took on a rather intriguing attraction for me. I began to add to my repertoire all sorts of fantasies about being spanked, chastised and even, in my darkest hours, about being strung up and whipped for my disgusting misdeeds.

When I read Mac's letter I immediately experienced the same surety I had when I read Rosie's for the first time. I knew that this was the one I wanted the punters to pick. I am ashamed to admit that I would have cheated quite happily to get what I wanted. I believed that Adam would find this game as horny as I did, especially as he had insisted I expose myself to him. Also I had no doubt that Mr Anonymous would enjoy punishing me if I went through with Mac's suggestions.

Joanna, oh Joanna – please let me introduce you to the unrivalled pleasures to be had from exhibitionism. I grant that lots of people get their kicks from showing off but I take this thrilling fantasy one step further. It is not easy to find a partner to share my love of being watched, especially because of the lengths I will go to for a perfect experience. I am older than you at 45, but I can assure you that I am fit and well able to take care of you in more ways than one. You didn't ask for a photo in your article but I am sending one so you can see that I am reasonably attractive and respectable. I promise I have fresh-smelling armpits and clean feet. Put me to the vote, Joanna, and I promise all your readers that I will not let them down.

Hopefully,
Mac

He had such a nice face. OK, he was right in that he wasn't mind-blowingly gorgeous but I found him decidedly attractive with his sparkling eyes and wide mischievous grin. My curiosity was piqued to say the least.

I put my suggestions to the punters along with my article about my meeting with Rosie and Steve and all their mates. Responses flooded in. I was gratified by the encouragement they offered. There were so many varieties of response, from plain rudeness to genuine appreciation. Many readers told me in graphic detail about how they wanked through my article and more than twenty asked for details of the club I visited. I phoned Rosie to ask if they were looking for more members and she was so pleased to hear from me she squealed in that wonderful way she had and begged me to go and stay with them. She told me that everyone had enjoyed my visit and that they were all looking forward to reading about it. She also said that, although she would like to have a replay of my night with them, what she actually wanted was for me to stay with them as a couple for the weekend. I promised that as soon as my workload was sorted out a bit I would take them up on their offer. I longed to tell her she had been right about Adam. I wanted to share my feelings with her – after all, I had felt a bond with her that wasn't purely sexual – but I didn't know how to begin.

I had a distinct lack of close girlfriends and at that very confusing time it would have been good to pour out all my confusions to someone who was obviously a woman of the world, sexually speaking. Two or three times during my conversation with Rosie I attempted to explain but couldn't find a starting point. I suppose I knew that if I responded to Adam in the way I had, and, if Adam wanted to control me in the way he had, then there must be thousands of others who played the same games we did. I wondered just how many girls and women in the world were, at that very moment in time, giving themselves over to sexual submission. I forced my thoughts back to the conversation and promised again to keep in touch and to send the letters I had received to her for her response.

Just as before, the responses to this second challenge came thick and fast. I suppose that now the readers actually believed that I honoured my promises, they were more inclined to put themselves forward. The suggestions for my time were so varied. Of course there were at least 50 per cent who just practised straight sex and thought they could show me how it should be done, but there were also a lot of exciting challenges. My postbag was just about divided in two: half were telling me how they felt about my article and half were offering themselves for the next one.

The popularity of my new article must have made

its rounds because slowly colleagues started to nod to me in the corridors and the office shark suggested in the most sleazy and obnoxious way that, more than anyone else on the planet, he could show me a good time. Yuk!

The letter from Mr Anonymous in response to my article shocked me but thrilled a section of my anatomy that hadn't been used until I'd visited Adam in his office for the first time. There is a section of the stomach that I am sure is put aside for submissives. It's full of that liquid toffee I told you about and it lurches in a way that is almost indescribable at the most unexpected moments. This next letter from Mr Anonymous was just one of those unexpected moments.

I KNOW YOU, JOANNA

After your first article I knew you to be a naughty young lady. Since reading the chronicle of your encounter with the swinging club I now know you to be a very dirty young lady too. Your actions are crying out to be punished, Joanna. I know you well enough from your writing to know that inside you long for the strict discipline that will assuage your rude deeds.

Put this idea to your readers.

I am sure that they will, like me, long to see you punished as you deserve.

I KNOW YOU, JOANNA

The bit that set the toffee swirling was 'strict discipline'. Those words alone told tales of such thrilling scenes. I imagined myself bent over a hard knee with my knickers down. I couldn't even allow myself to think of having my bottom caned because if I did I just went to pieces; the thought of being spanked was bad enough. I tried to put his suggestions aside but it was difficult. He was right. It appeared to me then that far too many men 'knew me', as he put it. Was there something about women who long to be controlled that gives off a smell, or did they have a certain look about them that was a beacon to the Adams of this world? I didn't think so.

I stood in front of the mirror to make a guess at what they saw that I couldn't see, but it was lost on me. I still looked like the same Joanna but I sure as hell didn't feel like her. It was as though part of me now belonged to Adam. I wondered if he felt the same. If he did want actually to possess a part of me then why didn't he want to see me? I was counting the days and, even though I guessed that I had some pretty exciting experiences ahead of me as part of this challenge, I knew I would trade them all for one word from Adam.

It was a little early when I counted the votes for and against me meeting Mac, mainly because I knew from picking out the odd few that he was the readers' favourite. The close runner-up was a group of couples, believe it or not, that did mud wrestling. I suppose there was a certain fascination about it but I had no inclination to take part. I had begun by trying to offer as much diversity as possible and was pleasantly surprised to find that many people liked the ideas. The mud wrestlers came under the 'diverse' category but were not, as far as I was concerned, a possibility. I preferred to contain my sexual stickiness in one area.

The phone call to Mac went well. He was polite and friendly, making me feel at ease instantly. Mac was surprised that he had won as, just like Rosie and Steve had, he'd believed it was all a farce. When he realised that I really did intend to meet him for sex, his whole tone changed to sexually flirtatious and by the time I had made the arrangements and hung up I was very turned on. Mac had preferred not to tell me too much about his special slant on exhibitionism. I was a little more nervous than I had been for my first assignation – I suppose because there really is safety in numbers, but I was looking forward to the new experience. More than anything I was excited about having to relay it to Adam in minute sordid detail. I intended to make sure there were many sordid details.

The night I met Mac was clear, dry and still warm which, as it turned out, was a good thing. He lived in the Midlands so it only took me two hours to get there but sadly it was a bit too chilly to have Baby's top down. I decided that I would take it all one step at a time. I didn't book a room anywhere in case I just wanted to get back home afterwards – I could always change my mind, couldn't I? He was so excited when we met in the agreed pub that I assumed the meeting place was part of the plan but, within a few minutes, he had told me we would be moving on shortly. When Mac finally went to the bar to get me a drink I had the chance to look him over. Already we had established that we got on well by chattering for ten minutes before he realised I might like a drink. He was very hunky with a rugby player look about him. His blond hair flopped over his forehead, which gave him a boyish look that I thought might be cultivated. I didn't care. He was sexy. His large thighs stretched his black chinos and he still had muscles across his chest that pulled at his sweater. That'll do for me, I thought.

When he came back with the drinks he was looking a little sheepish.

'Are you sure you know what you're letting yourself in for? Sorry, but I'm finding it difficult to believe that anyone as beautiful and talented as you would agree to come and have sex with an oldie like me.'

Who was I to disagree with him?

'I think I must be what is called a liberated woman, Mac. I'm sure there is a more modern term for it but the idea is the same. Basically, I enjoy sex and experimenting. Regardless of what you might have read on my page, I wouldn't be doing this if I didn't find you attractive. I could easily have met you in a pub or club one night and if I had decided to sleep with you on that first night I would have had no idea what you had in mind. At least this way I know what you like and you know I must be up for it or I wouldn't be here otherwise. Anyway, my boss makes me do these things,' I said with a grin on my face, smiling to myself at just how true the last bit was. It was lost on Mac.

'Aren't you even bothered about what I've got in mind? I'll be honest with you, Joanna, I don't want to push you into anything unless I'm absolutely sure you're happy with it. What if you're imagining something completely different to what I have in mind and I end up offending you with my slightly more than odd fantasy? I want to avoid any misunderstandings at all costs. Do you want me to explain my thoughts so you can decide if you still want to go with me?'

'Mac. You're worrying far too much. Trust me when I say that I'm excited at the prospect of tonight and have been since I first spoke to you. Have you read my account of my visit to the swinging club?'

'Fuck, yes, it was wonderful. The thought that you actually did those things just so that you could relay how it all felt to your readers was just so amazingly, staggeringly sensational. You really do my head in, Joanna. I still can't believe that anyone like you really exists. So often I've tentatively suggested exhibitionism to past girlfriends only to be treated like a raving pervert. Perhaps I am a raving pervert? What do you think?'

I bent close so that I could whisper straight into Mac's ear. I knew he could smell my perfume and that my breath would tickle the hairs on the side of his face. I went for full impact.

'I hate to disillusion you, but I'm actually doing this for me. There's nothing I want more at the moment than for you to blow me away with your game and if you choose to think I'm doing this for the readers then go ahead. Surely, though, it will be even more exciting if you acknowledge that the readers are an after-thought. Perhaps we are both perverts, Mac. I couldn't give a shit what others would label us; I can't wait for you to explain to me how we are going to expose ourselves. Are you going to ask me to open my legs here so that the other customers can see my shaved and very wet pussy?' I put my lips on his ear and added in the best husky whisper I could muster, 'I haven't got any knickers on either, so I'm ready for anything.'

Mac groaned deeply in the back of his throat and almost whimpered his reply. 'Oh, fuck it. You horny bitch. Let's do it.' He grabbed my hand and, leaving our drinks half empty on the table, he dragged me outside. I was a little disappointed that I wasn't expected to show myself in the pub but intrigued to find out what he had in mind. Mac led me to his Land Rover, helped me into the passenger seat and then got behind the wheel. He started the engine and, without saying another word, drove through the city streets heading toward his secret destination. His eyes kept straying to my legs in their dark stockings. The sheen of the mesh glinted in the lights, giving my legs an almost dreamy quality. I had decided to wear my black leather skirt and jacket and it was obvious that Mac approved. The slinky white blouse that gaped open at my throat showed an inch or two of the curve of my breasts, but by that time I didn't care. I revelled in his image of me, committing everything he did and said to memory for my next meeting with Adam.

Mac groaned with an almost pained expression as he looked over at my legs for probably the twentieth time. He licked his lips in a desperate way and I gloried in his obvious desperation. I shifted in my seat and re-crossed my legs in such an offhand way I'm sure Mac thought it was an unconscious movement, but that was far from the truth. I was doing everything in my power to excite him further. It was strange how Adam had become a part of my games. Even though Mac hadn't done anything to excite me yet, my instructions from Adam encroached into our space and kept me at fever pitch. I imagined myself standing in front of his desk confessing. I also imagined how Mr Anonymous would probably want to punish me for what I was thinking at that moment, let alone what I intended to do. Mr Anonymous was fascinating me with his reactions to my antics.

When I realised Mac was asking me something I snapped back to the moment. 'Sorry. I didn't mean to ignore you but my mind was off on a fantasy and I didn't hear what you said,' I told him as I laid my hand on his arm.

'I want to touch you so badly. I can't take your words from my thoughts. Are you really sitting here with me without any knickers on and with your ... vagina shaved? I've got to know. What do you call it, by the way?'

'Well, firstly I call it pussy, but I've got to tell you it doesn't look much like a pussy at the moment because it is shaved. Here ... feel. My very excited pussy is as smooth as a piece of silk.' I took his hand off the wheel and placed it between my knees, just above my skirt hem. The rest was up to him. The fact that Mac was so nervous was instantly forgotten when I gave him the invitation to explore further. His hand groped its way up my thighs as he tried to keep his eyes on the road but he didn't do very well, and within just a few seconds he was swerving all over the road.

Just the sensation of his hand slipping up over my stockings was enough to send me into a bit of a tizzy. Shamelessly I let my thighs drop open to show him that I was totally enjoying what he was attempting to do. Again he groaned loudly; this time the noise he made was almost animalistic. His exploring fingers had found what they were looking for. With no preliminaries at all he poked his fingers between my extremely wet and sticky lips and straight into me. This time it was my turn to moan. I did quite a bit of writhing too as his hand continued its adventure. Deep inside me his fingers delved and probed while I wriggled to gain purchase on those delightful intruders. I didn't even notice when he pulled into a lay-by and stopped. I just lay back, enjoying what he was doing. When he took his hand away I went to grab it back but he laughed and pulled my skirt back down to a more decent position. I was devastated, but before I could complain he got out of his side of the car and opened a gate in the hedge, then got back in behind the wheel. Seconds later we were jolting over the ruts in a field, over to the gate at the other side. Still inside the field Mac stopped, got out in the pitch black, and came around to my side, then pulled me out until I was standing beside him.

I felt so wicked standing there with a completely strange man and with no knickers on. I felt a frisson of fear – a heady aphrodisiac indeed. Mac had a comforting way of grabbing my hand that made me feel as if I had known him for years, and he did it now. He pulled me around to the back of the vehicle and took a large blanket from the back. I followed meekly as he led me though a gateway into another field. I can remember so clearly thinking that we wouldn't be doing a lot of exhibiting in such a quiet isolated place. The last house we had passed had been at least a mile or two back.

8

Just as I opened my mouth to ask him about the logistics of this proposed show and tell, the most almighty roaring sound came from the other side of the hedge in front of us. I jumped out of my skin as a train, at least twenty carriages long, thundered past us. It was so close my hair was ruffled. I gasped aloud then laughed as I realised just what he had in mind. Mac was obviously delighted by my acceptance of the obvious and again he grabbed my hand and pulled me through a gap in the hedge in front of us. No more than six feet away, the track passed us and ran on into the distance in each direction.

Mac began to lead me along the side of the track with the gravel crunching underfoot and within three or four minutes the sound of another train broke the silence. We pulled back almost into the hedge as it too thundered past and disappeared into the night. We were so close I could actually see the faces of the passengers in each of the carriages. As each carriage passed us the anonymous faces would stare at us blankly, register what they were seeing and then turn to watch us for as long as they could.

I mentioned to Mac that they appeared to be going slower than most trains and he explained with a grin that just along the track was a sharpish bend so the trains had to slow a little. Just perfect for our purposes.

After the train had passed, Mac took me just a little further down the track until we reached what looked like a small siding. It veered off from the main line but then ran almost parallel for approximately twenty or thirty metres. He turned back to look at me with a smile on his face. Then he moved away from the line and I saw for the first time what he was so pleased about. This part of the line hadn't been used for years. There were tall weeds growing up through the rusty rails and, the best bit of all, there was an old wooden platform on wheels that used to be used by the railway personnel. It instantly reminded me of one I had seen in a St Trinian's film, where a couple of characters bobbed up and down to get it to work.

Mac laid the blanket out on the platform just as another train, the lights creating visibility for our show, passed us. He couldn't have found a better place for us to be on show and I was a little nervous as he climbed on and pulled me up after him.

'Right, you gorgeous thing, you. We've about three and a half minutes before the next train comes past and by then I intend to have you as naked as a jaybird. Stand up.'

I stood as directed and Mac assisted me out of my clothes until he got to my stockings and suspenders; these he decided to leave on. The breeze rippled over my nipples and caused the flesh to crinkle and harden. As Mac lowered my skirt he paused and took a good look at my shaved pussy; he was the first person apart from me to see it. If his reaction was anything to go by I was assured that Adam would be pleased by the finished image. He knelt on the platform at my feet and looked closely at my smooth mound, then bent forward and licked at my clitoris. I cried out with delight at how hot his tongue felt in the cool night air. Like the wanton slut I was becoming I grabbed his hair and pulled his head into my crotch, but he was having none of it.

'Oh no, my lovely. That's far too easy. I have this planned down to the last minute. We only have the time it takes for four trains to pass us. Even if they do call the police it would take them that long to get here from the next town. For the first one, which by the way will be here in about two minutes, I want you to stand as tall as you can, face the train and spread your legs. I want you to stretch your arms as high as you can so you will be almost proclaiming to all the passengers, "Here I am. Look at me." And they will all look.'

I became very excited by his instruction. It was almost as thrilling as Adam's controlling of me. Just as I heard the rumble of the train in the distance I stood tall and forced my legs as far apart as I could, pushed my arms up to the heavens and I yelled like a banshee as the train sped past us. I saw dozens of pale faces through the windows but only one or two saw me in time for me to register their shock. The others either didn't see me or they only saw me in time to react a second or two later. I'm not sure why, but those watchers were even more of a turn on than the ones who stared open mouthed. I felt a bit like I did when Adam made me do something shameful, but appeared to be unaffected by my compliance.

'Stay there. Don't you move a muscle,' Mac shouted as the noise died away. I felt his cool hand thrust itself between my legs and up into my pussy. I ground down onto his hand, prepared to humiliate myself totally if that was what it took to satisfy myself. Already Mac had taken me to fever pitch and I still had no idea what he had in mind for the other three trains. While we waited for the next train he wriggled and prodded my insides, sending me into a frenzy. My legs were already trembling when he snaked his other hand between my thighs and felt for my clit. God, it was shameful! I was stumbling a bit because I found I couldn't stand upright with the delightful things Mac was doing to me. I crouched slightly to give him better access. And I shouted my heat into the night. How abandoned I felt. I was completely exhilarated by his attention.

I was on the brink of coming as the next train passed. I was shaking and sweating, the wetness caused by his exploring fingers trickling down my legs and glinting wetly in the lights from the windows. This time, because I was more aware and was waiting for them, I saw at least thirty people stare open mouthed at my display and I revelled in it. Mac was so right – this was incredible. I realised that Mac had only allowed me to get that close to my climax for the delectation of the viewers because as soon as they had gone he stopped and changed position. Up until that moment he would have been almost invisible behind me but he shucked off his clothes in record time.

'Hmm, done this before, Mac?' I laughed.

'Oh, just a few times.'

Mac's penis was just perfect for playing silhouette games. His extremely rampant weapon stood proudly to attention and thrust outward from his body at an acute angle. It throbbed in time to his rapid pulse and hypnotised me with its beauty. He stood back from me and stroked the length of it sensuously, running his hand over the purple end and sliding it back down the shaft taking the foreskin with it. Without any encouragement I immediately fell to my knees in front of him and he was so right about the timing. As I slid his cock into my more than willing mouth the next train came into view. I didn't even hear this one; I was far too wrapped up in what I was doing. Mac had gently taken hold of my head and was feeding me most generously with hard cock; he slid it slowly into my mouth and then my throat, all the while crooning encouragement.

'Oh fuck, baby. That's it. Let all those people see just how much you want me. More, Joanna. Let me give you more. Christ, I want to fuck you. Can you see them? Every single person on that train can see my cock disappearing into your red hungry mouth. Suck it, sweetheart. They're watching.'

Every word he spoke went straight to my crotch. I opened my throat as best I could and tried my utmost to make him pleased with me. His thick cock slid halfway down until I was almost gagging on the size of him, but still he pleaded.

'Oh God, yes. That is so good. More, Joanna, please!'

I felt the subtle twitching in the shaft that heralds the beginning of ejaculation but, just as the train left our sight, he again pulled away from me.

'You bastard, come back here. I want you back in my mouth.'

'Don't tempt me. I've got to finish this the way I planned. It has taken me days to work this all out to get the maximum pleasure for both of us. Trust me.'

While he said this he was frantically changing position. He stood tall on the platform and I waited to see what he had in mind. I was completely amazed when he picked me up by the hips and hoisted me up until my legs were over his shoulders. He almost roared with the effort it took to get me up there; in fact, I *felt* him grunt with the effort. The breath as it was forced from his lungs with the power of the lift washed over my pussy. I went all shivery with the sheer intensity of hearing the last train in the far distance.

I held frantically onto his head as his mouth opened and lowered until it covered my clitoris – which was begging for attention. He bit gently as the train neared and I knew his arms would break if he didn't put me down soon. It occurred to me that this could be the reason his thighs were so powerful and I thanked the Lord that they were as the lights of the last train came into view around the far bend. For a few more seconds he continued his amazing titillation of my clit but, just as the train drew almost level with us, he gathered one last push of strength and lifted me off his shoulders. He lowered me until I felt his cock, furious at being left out for so long, push its way into me. How he managed to get himself inside me in just one plunge you can probably put down to experience but, by that stage, I didn't care how much practice he'd had. We were side on to the train as it passed and I caught the fleeting glimpse of a man as he gawped out at us. I could tell he couldn't believe his eyes. The shock on his face and the force of Mac's cock as it pounded into me was enough to trigger the climax that we both had worked so hard for. He humped me hard with my legs wrapped around his waist and my arms locked around his neck. I felt his hot sperm spurt uncontrollably into me and begin to trickle, mixed with my juice, down my thighs.

As the haunting whistle of the train filled the night we sunk to the wooden platform, panting and exhausted.

'I can't believe it. That was so fucking brilliant, better than I ever imagined it would be. Are you all right?' Mac asked, but then became quite solicitous when he looked down at me in the faint light from the moon. I had gone completely silent. My breasts were still heaving and my pussy twitched rhythmically, squeezing out the mixture of our liquids. How could I answer him? I was still zinging. I managed to grin manically at him, which seemed to relax him slightly.

'Wow. I don't know what else to say but wow. I knew your ideas excited me but I had no idea just how much I would enjoy it. I'm just a little sad that it was over so quickly, I was just getting to know you, too.' I leaned over and gently took hold of his softening cock, only to find that the second I touched it, it throbbed and grew instantly back to the impressive proportions I had seen earlier. I snuggled into the crook of his arm and shivered slightly as I manipulated him.

'Do you have to be back at any particular time?' Mac asked.

'No, why, what do you have in mind?'

'Will you come back to my place? It's only a mile or two down the road. If you like we could pop back to my local for a quick one on the way. Or have we had too many quick ones already tonight?'

'Why don't we have that quick one at your local and then a very slow one back at yours?' I teased. 'I need to pick up Baby, anyway.'

'No problem. This is what we'll do. Forget the drink, I'll take you back to the car park then you can follow me home in Baby.'

All the way back to the pub Mac kept staring at me from the corner of his eye and running his fingers up my legs. Luckily my stockings had only been snagged in a couple of places so I still looked reasonably decent. I tried to take my mind off what he was doing while I checked my make-up and renewed my lipstick. When we arrived at the pub, Mac obviously changed his mind.

'Let's just have one more before we go back to mine. It's not that I need courage but your legs are sending me to distraction and I've an idea that I think you will enjoy.' I followed him into the bar, excited at the thought of another game. The orgasm I'd had by the track had been good, but I still felt very horny. Mac led me to a darkish corner of the bar and helped me onto a bar stool. It was quite difficult to stay looking decent bearing in mind that I had no knickers on, but I pulled and tugged at my skirt, much to Mac's enjoyment.

During the next half hour we managed to down three drinks each after deciding to leave the cars where they were to be collected in the morning. One or two men passed by us and greeted Mac; they were obviously friends of his. They stared at me and hovered, probably hoping that he would introduce us, but he didn't. He just sat opposite me with his hands trying their best to stay off my knees and failing repeatedly. Occasionally I would cross my legs knowing I was giving him an eyeful and he grinned his encouragement.

'What do you think about this exhibitionism lark, then?' he asked me rather innocently. There was something false about the innocence and I knew instinctively that he was actually asking me a wider question. 'Did you enjoy showing yourself off to hundreds of people?'

'Christ, yes. I honestly thought that nothing could top my experience with Rosie and Steve but what we just did came a very close second. I never dreamed that I could get so turned on just knowing that I was being watched.'

'How would you feel about a more intimate exhibitionism session?' he asked me, all innocence gone now. I squirmed on my stool.

'What did you have in mind? This wine is going to my head and I think I would be up for any devious idea you could come up with.'

'Oh, good, I was hoping you would say that. I think this night is far from over, Joanna. Wait here while I order a taxi.' With that Mac disappeared into the corridor of the pub. I sat and waited at the bar for him to come back and sipped at my drink watching the life play out around me.

My eye caught the inquisitive gaze of a young man sitting along the bar from me. Like me he was perched on a stool but he was swivelled in his seat to stare at my legs. I could tell it was nearing the end of the night because he very blatantly leered at me, licked his lips and nodded in my direction. He called the bartender over and told him to send me a drink. I smiled and nodded my thanks as I shamelessly crossed my legs in full view of him, downed the drink in one, and looked to see if Mac was coming back. There was no sign of him. I felt like a hussy as I climbed down from my stool and walked slowly over to the handsome young man who had bought me the drink. I don't think he was expecting that because the moment I got close enough to see that he was probably no more than eighteen, he muttered something and then almost ran from the pub. I stood still, feeling a little silly, but the bartender said something to me so I turned to ask him to repeat it.

He beckoned me and I leaned over the bar towards him to hear what he had to say. As I bent towards him he cupped his hand behind my head and pulled me nearer. I knew that from the back my skirt would probably be showing off the tops of my stockings but I was too tipsy to care. I wriggled my legs as I leaned right over the wooden bar and he blew me away with his comment.

'You're one very raunchy bird. My mate Mac has told me all about you and if he doesn't treat you right you let me know and I'll show you how a woman like you should be treated.' He was very casual as he spoke, which in itself was exciting but, before I had a chance to answer, I felt a knowing hand slide up the back of my leather skirt and delve between my thighs. I squealed in shameless delight and turned to find Mac standing behind me grinning at the barman.

'You've got no chance, mate. I know exactly what this fabulous young lady needs and I intend to provide exactly that. Come on, sweetheart, our taxi is here.' I shimmied down from the bar, wiggled my fingers at this now rather forlorn-looking man and took Mac's outstretched hand. I felt like a siren as I followed him out into the night and climbed into the back of the car outside. We were still wrapped up in each other as the car started off so it wasn't until we were a mile or two from the pub that I noticed the driver looking at us in his rear-view mirror. The eyes that met mine were bright and twinkly and the smile was more than polite. I looked at Mac only to find him grinning like a loon.

'Don't you worry about him, love. Pretend he isn't there,' Mac cajoled as he took hold of my arm and attempted to pull me over onto his lap. I went willingly, deciding within a second that I had no intention of pretending he wasn't there. I wasn't sure what Mac had in mind but I sat astride his lap with my skirt riding up around my hips as I turned and winked at the driver. Mac and I were in very close proximity, with my breasts crushed against his chest. Without ceremony Mac tugged my blouse from the waistband of my skirt and pulled it over my head. He reached around me and unclipped my bra and threw it onto the seat next to us. Again he groaned with pleasure just as he had by the train track. In an almost involuntary action his hands cupped my large breasts and weighed them in his palms. He leaned forward and took first one then my other nipple deeply into his mouth by sucking hard while squeezing the mounds of flesh. It was so exciting to be on the receiving end. My pussy flooded its response. As he had suggested, the driver was forgotten when I felt his cock hardening underneath me. I ground down onto his bulging groin to show that I wanted more and my mouth took control of his, invading with my tongue and nipping his lips with my teeth. Rosie had taught me that, so I knew just how devastating it felt. Mac obviously agreed; he grabbed hold of my hair and forced his mouth to return the pressure I had started. We were both breathing so hard our snorts filled the confines of the car.

'Oh, please, Mac, fuck me. I really want to feel you inside me,' I whispered urgently under my breath. I didn't care who was watching. In fact, just the knowledge that the cab driver could see us was electric in itself.

Mac needed no second bidding. He unzipped my skirt and pulled it up over my head then fumbled around underneath us until I felt the flesh of his thighs under my naked bottom. I felt like a marionette being manipulated in his strong capable hands. He wriggled about, lifting me and shifting his weight until his trousers were around his ankles. I sat back down and the heat of him made me gasp. His abdomen was hard and boiling hot under me and his cock felt like a pole along the cheeks of my bum. I was grateful for his assistance as I raised myself to guide him in and I was reminded of him lifting me effortlessly on the platform earlier. I manoeuvred my hands between us and took hold of his cock. It throbbed its pleasure as I held it rigid and lowered myself over it. Oh God, it felt so good as he slowly slid inside me right into my depths.

I was half aware of the car slowing down but oblivious to why or to where we were. Mac took my mind off everything as he grabbed hold of the cheeks of my bottom and lifted me cradled in his large hands as I rode him hard. He was choreographing the whole thing by lifting me and then lowering me with just the use of the strength of his arms. I felt completely and wonderfully debauched as I pounded down time and again onto his large cock. I felt a stretching sensation as his hands attempted to dissect me. His manipulative hands pushed apart the cheeks of my bottom, exposing my clenched sphincter muscle to the air, and I howled like an animal. I leaned my hands on the seat either side of his head and pushed my breasts into his face for attention. He obliged immediately by taking as much as he could of my right breast into his mouth and biting quite hard, and then he did the same with the other. I swung my breasts, first one and then the other, for his exquisite attention until their teats were red and throbbing and still I bounced up and down on him. I looked down with delight on the tiny teeth marks covering my breasts and buried Mac's face between them, almost smothering him. I think he would have died a happy man if I had carried on but I couldn't wait to kiss him again. I devoured his mouth. At that moment I would have done anything that he had suggested, I was so unbelievably, disgustingly horny.

All the pounding of my sex down onto his had worked us into quite a frenzy. My clitoris was being bashed with every thrust and I knew without a doubt that Mac couldn't hold on much longer; we were nearing our finale.

'Jim, help us out here,' Mac gasped out. 'This very rude lady needs a little extra to help her on her way.' The seat behind me creaked as I felt the driver's tentative hand slide down my spine and between my widely spread buttocks. I opened my eyes in shock and I stared out into the night through the back window of the car. We were stationary and by the fog on the window had been that way for quite a while. I mewled my response, not only to Mac's horny words but also to the devious fingers that were insinuating their way around Mac's shaft as it drove its way into me. The probing hand gathered some lubrication and found its way back up the crease of my bottom to my anus. Mac must have known what Jim had in mind because he pulled me apart until I felt my skin would tear, but the finger pushing itself into my bottom took all other thoughts away. The sweet delicious sensation as my bottom was invaded for the first time will stay with me for ever. I felt almost faint with the thrill of it all. My head was dizzy as I ground even harder down onto the hand and the cock that filled me to perfection. I truly exploded less than ten seconds after Jim's finger had found its way into my virginal hole. Mac and I collapsed exhausted and Jim started the car without another word.

As we drove in silence through the night I realised, once I had come to, that Mac hadn't climaxed. I snuggled naked into his side and whispered that I was sorry he hadn't come and asked if there was anything I could do to please him.

'You daft thing, you. You were so gone you didn't even notice when I filled you full of sperm while I almost smothered, fighting for breath, in your magnificent tits. It was a dream come true, all of it. I can't believe I lasted as long as I did. I've never had a more fantastic experience. From the first moment in the pub, right up until I saw your face when Jim touched you, it has been a brilliant unreal night. And I swear every man that reads what you write about us will not believe it actually happened.'

'Then I'll have to write it to the best of my ability, won't I?' I answered almost coquettishly.

'Honestly, Joanna, I'll treasure this always. Not every-one gets the chance to fulfil a fantasy but you've done me proud. Thanks.'

'That goes for me, too,' came a voice from the front. 'Now get out, you two, some of us have homes to go to.' I turned and looked at Jim for the first time. He was grinning manically at me so I leaned over and placed a kiss on his cheek. Just as my mouth touched him he quickly moved so I kissed him on the lips and he giggled like a schoolboy.

I was still blushing furiously as Mac let us into his front door, me wrapped in a blanket and him trying desperately to do up his trousers.

Mac was the perfect gentleman. He fussed over me like an old mother hen and helped me into his extremely large navy dressing gown. He made us tea and toast and we curled up on his sofa to talk and eat. I hadn't realised just how hungry I was, so the attention was gratefully received. In the detached aftermath of our very naughty evening we both found it quite unbeliev-able that we had actually done some of the things we had found ourselves doing. Both of us felt comfortable discussing it and as we talked we began to get horny again. I told Mac just how stimulating I found his fantasy and I think he was surprised, not only by the fact that I had carried out the promises in my *Leather and Lace* column, but also by the fact that I had been so abandoned.

'I wish you lived closer to me, Joanna. I would love to have the opportunity to take you out properly, or would that be out of the question?'

'I've got to admit to feeling quite confused,' I tried to explain. 'After I had spent the evening with Rosie and her friends I wished I could go more often and now I've spent such an amazing evening with you I feel tied to you.'

'Hmm, that's an interesting idea. Perhaps I *should* tie you up and then I could keep you here as long as I liked, couldn't I?' With that Mac grabbed hold of my hands and held them in a vice-like grip while he looked into my eyes questioningly. 'In fact, perhaps what I should do is write to you again as someone else and offer a new fantasy. This one would involve having you as my captive for a day or two to do with as I please. How would that grab you? Or what's more to the point, how would it grab your readers?'

'Fuck the readers.' I laughed. 'I love the idea but you don't have to keep me captive. I'll stay voluntarily. Mind you, the captive bit might be fun.' I found myself going off on a fantasy of my own then. How I longed to be a captive of Adam's with all that entailed. I imagined his hands holding mine just as Mac's were and I felt my body flush with heat at the thought. I tried to imagine what Adam would do to me if he did have me captured. I remembered just how devastating his control of me had been and how easily I had allowed him to explore my submission. I blushed when I realised that Mac was still holding my wrists and still looking at me closely.

'What?' he asked. 'Did I stir a memory or something?'

I longed to tell him about Adam just as I had with Rosie, but I didn't know where to start so I fluffed around it.

'I can't believe how adventurous I've become after just two meetings. Neither can I understand how deeply I get involved. After just a few hours with Rosie and Steve I wanted to go and see them and all their friends again. I wanted to meet Rosie by herself to finish what we had started and I also wanted to meet a rather dominant man that took my fancy. He sat in the corner and did a lot of controlling. Since meeting you earlier this evening and finding how well we jelled I could quite happily start a relationship with you if I weren't so busy. I've so enjoyed our time together. Also, I've got to take into account that I'll be spending a lot of my spare time over the next few months doing all sorts of rude things with all sorts of equally rude people and that doesn't make for a good relationship, does it? Don't get me wrong, I'm enjoying every sordid second of it, but I do tend to get a bit too involved.' I looked him right in the eyes and added, 'Anyway, how could I possibly do all the wonderfully disgusting things we've done tonight and not get attached to you? It would be against nature itself.'

Oh, how I love strong men. As soon as I had finished talking, Mac picked me up in his arms as if I weighed nothing and carried me up the stairs to his bedroom. He plonked me down on the bed and began to undress me. I still had the stockings on but he obviously felt that the comfy dressing gown had to go. It was probably the result of the amazing things we had got up to, but as soon as we snuggled under the covers we both admitted that we were knackered. I curled up against Mac's warm flesh and, within minutes, feeling safer and more at home than I had for ages, I fell asleep. I've no idea if Mac lay awake for hours or fell asleep with me but the next thing I knew I woke in a strange bed with the smell of coffee filling my nostrils.

As I heard him tiptoeing down the hallway I remembered his kink and quickly sat on the edge of the bed with a sheet wrapped around me. The second he walked through the doorway I flashed my breasts at him and let my legs drop apart. I knew I was still sticky and a bit smelly from the night before but it all added to the atmosphere as he stood and just stared.

'Oh, fuck, you look so wonderfully abandoned. Would you allow me to take some photos of you? I would love to catch you just like that, with your hair all ruffled from sleep and that little girl grin on your face but with your exceptionally exciting body tantalisingly peeping from the folds of the sheet. I wish you could see just how amazing you look.'

'I don't know what my editor would feel about that, I'm sorry to say. I would love to flaunt myself for you; it would be the ultimate exhibitionism, wouldn't it?' I answered, striking up a pose. 'Apart from that, I know I would be doing it because I'm feeling horny again and I would hate to regret it afterwards. And, much as I like you, Mac, how do I know I could trust you?'

'You would like to, though, would you?'

'God, yes. I can't think of anything more exciting. Well, apart from repeating last night all over again, that is, and I suppose that as it's daylight that's out of the question.'

By the time I had finished what I was saying Mac was rummaging about in his wardrobe and he came out with a very flash looking video camera.

'How's that!'

I had to laugh, he looked so proud of himself as he stood grinning from ear to ear. He was stuttering with excitement as he tried to convince me that he would give me the film to take home. I was shamelessly easy to persuade. I nodded my agreement, increasingly aroused by the prospect of displaying myself for the lens.

'Hmm, just one problem, Joanna, I haven't got a film. How about this?' he asked as he looked at his watch. 'It's opening time. Why don't we get dressed and go down the pub for a drink. We'll pick up a film and come back here for the afternoon and have some fun.'

I was definitely up for it. Not only did it prolong this horny episode with Mac but I would also have the chance to pose in some lurid way without having to face the consequences. I scrabbled from the sheet and gave Mac an eyeful as I grabbed a towel and padded into the bathroom. He looked delighted at my exposure and watched my every move with avid interest.

'That's exquisite, Joanna. I didn't get a chance to see your smoothness last night, well, not properly anyway. I can't wait to see it through the lens. I think we'll have some fun. Don't you?'

'I can't wait.'

I showered as quickly as I could, straightened my blouse and was very thankful that I had worn a leather skirt – no creases. I left off the stockings and suspenders and blushed a little when I realised I had no knickers to put on. Oh well! I walked out of the bathroom and stood with my arms out.

'That's the best I can do.' I had put on a little make-up and combed my hair and, even though I had bare legs and yesterday's shirt on, I knew I looked good. The anticipating sparkle in my eyes helped. I couldn't wait to play with the camera but I was also looking forward to going for a drink with Mac. I wondered if Jim would be there and if he was whether he would comment on the night before.

Again we took a taxi but this time it was genuine and uneventful. We arrived at the pub just as it opened and who should be straightening the chairs inside but Jim. He looked as if butter wouldn't melt in his mouth. He did look me up and down but was very discreet and didn't say a word. Like the night before, we chose the end of the bar that was slightly round a corner from the main body of the room. It afforded us a little privacy and gave Mac a chance to introduce me properly to his friend, the landlord.

'Joanna, I'd like you to meet my good friend and confidant, Jim.'

Jim held out his hand and I went along with the game and put mine out too. Jim took my hand and turned it over until the palm of mine was laying face up in his. He kept his eyes on mine until the last second as he bowed his head and kissed my palm, very softly.

'Joanna, I've heard and read so much about you and I can't tell you how delighted I was to have the chance to be a part of your fun last night. It was absolutely the best night of my life.'

'Goodness, Jim. That's a bit serious,' I giggled, slightly embarrassed by his formality. I had no idea how to respond to all this politeness; after all I could still almost feel his finger exploring my bottom. I wriggled on the stool.

'Knock it off, mate. You're embarrassing her,' Mac stepped in.

'Sorry. I'm only teasing. Seriously though, Jo, I can call you Jo, can't I? I had a ball last night. I could go to my grave a happy man today after that sight I had in my rear-view mirror. And –' he leaned close to my ear '– I had the most amazing wank ever when I got home. And it was all thanks to you. Well, I suppose Mac had a bit to do with it.'

'All I can say is that you were, and are, very welcome, Jim. I rather expect our readers will be grateful to you, too,' I added, in the spirit of his sexy confession. I loved the image of Jim going home and masturbating with the memory of my bottom in his head to trigger his arousal. I loved it a lot. I was getting very horny just talking to these two very sexy men and, although I wanted to go and start the filming, I was enjoying all the naughty dialogue that was developing between us.

While Jim and I had been chatting Mac had been running his hand up and down my naked thigh in a most tantalising way. The sensation as his exploring hand disappeared from view up my skirt was producing shock waves through my crotch. I felt so debauched. It was amazing how in a couple of short months I had gone from the girl who wrote sexy stories because she wasn't getting any to this. Right at that moment I felt that I was getting not only more sex than anyone on the planet but more varied fun than anyone ever had.

When Mac took his exploration one step further and insinuated his fingers between my thighs I frantically looked around the bar but was pleased to find there was no one in view. Mac too had a quick look and when he was satisfied we were safe he moved sideways a little until he was between the door and me and whispered in my ear, 'I can feel that you're desperate for it, Joanna. God, you're a horny bitch. Without even touching your pussy I can feel the heat from you. Your love juice is already wetting my fingers and I can smell your excitement. Don't you think it's time to go?'

I don't think I had ever been that aroused in public before and it was very disconcerting. I knew I had to keep at least part of my mind on what was happening around me but what Mac was doing and what he was saying in my ear was so distracting I lost concentration for long moments at a time. Devastating!

There was quite a scary dividing of my thoughts going on. I was becoming convinced that if Mac ordered me to expose myself to everyone, that I would do exactly what he wanted. There was a pub half full of people going about their usual lunchtime business just a breath away across the bar but it was as if they were on the moon for all the notice we took of them. Then I realised I was thinking about what Adam would do, not what Mac might do. It was Adam that longed to control me, not Mac. I lost it for a few seconds as I wondered what Adam would order me to do in this situation and what Mr Anonymous would dream up as punishment for me for being this bad. It was shocking too to admit to myself that there was a hell of a lot of bad behaviour left in me to discover. And I was revelling in it. I was beginning to recognise the dirty girl inside me just longing to be enticed out to play.

'Hi, sexy bum,' came the sleazy purr from behind me. My eyes had been screwed shut but I quickly snapped my legs together and looked behind me. In my abandonment to Mac I hadn't noticed Jim walk around the bar to stand behind me. His words sent shivery memories down my spine as I remembered thrusting my naked bottom out for the attentions of this stranger. I had no control over my senses as Mac's hand delved between my sex lips and Jim's hands slid their way around my waist. I was like a slice of very submissive meat between the sandwich of two gorgeous men.

'Oh no you don't, you randy old sod. I let you join in last night and that is all you're getting. Bugger off. Joanna and I are going back to mine to create some rather revealing pornography. And you're not invited. Get back to running your pub where you belong.' Mac pulled Jim's hands from around me and for a second or two I felt like a prize in a tug of war. Yet another experience that I knew I would love in the right circumstances.

Just as he had the night before, Mac grabbed my hand and almost dragged me from the pub and I hoped that the outcome would be half as exciting. Jim took it all in good faith and kissed me goodbye, then waved us off. We walked around the shops for a while trying to find the right film for his camera and feared that it would be an impossible task, but eventually perseverance paid off. In the third shop we tried we found a stock of them and Mac enthusiastically bought three films. Wondering how long he thought I was prepared to stay I laughingly pointed out to him that he'd bought twelve hours' worth of filming.

'I'm sure there will be other times,' Mac stated, as if he was convinced of it. 'In fact, I insist there will be other times. I can't possibly let you go after all that we have been through. Who else will I find to carry out all these disgusting ideas I have?'

We walked back to the pub and I climbed into Baby, showing at least enough thigh and crotch to excite me, let alone Mac. I followed him back to his house wondering all the way through the winding country lanes if I was doing the right thing. I knew that if any photos of me got out it could seriously jeopardise my career, but my pussy was throbbing with anticipation. I couldn't wait to start the showing off bit. I had found, not only with Rosie and Steve, but also with Mac that I loved my new career and, far from doing all this to please just Adam, I was in seventh heaven.

When we got back to Mac's house we sat for about an hour having a bite to eat and laughing about Jim's enthusiasm. Mac explained that, far from doing that sort of thing often, he was convinced it was the first time for Jim and he confessed that it was the first time for him too. I was shocked to say the least. I had believed, judging by the expertise he showed, that Mac had been exhibiting himself for years. Knowing that he too was a beginner made me feel much more relaxed about the plan we had for the afternoon. For ages he kept telling me what exposed positions he wanted to photograph me in and explained in minute detail which parts of my anatomy he wanted to capture exposed on film. The conversation had a surreal quality to it but I reacted in all the right ways. I blossomed at his words of encouragement about showing myself. I think at that moment I could have stayed with him for ever. I was really growing to like Mac and his light-hearted approach to sex; it was so far removed from Adam's deadly serious one. Which one excited me most was yet to be seen.

Yes, my relationship with Adam was mind-blowingly thrilling but it was also extremely frustrating. After all, even after months of leading up to our little game all Adam had done to me was tell me to take off my own clothes and then stick his fingers inside me and in less than 24 hours Mac had blown me away with his horny ideas. And we were just about to test another one.

What was the point of even comparing them, I told myself? Even if Mac kept up these sexy games for months, the reaction in my guts wouldn't even touch the surface of how one sentence from Adam managed to annihilate all my resolve. Just the thought of him played havoc with my adrenalin levels.

'Come on then, gorgeous, I've sweet-talked you enough; let's get down to business. To start with I have the perfect picture in my mind of how I want you. Come here.' Mac pulled me to my feet and in his now familiar style dragged me behind him through the patio doors and into the large secluded garden. The layout was very pretty with a sort of pergola made from wood at the bottom, a large shortly cut lawn and a natural looking fishpond with tall reeds and yellow water irises around one end. At the other end there was a shallow ornamental beach made from large slabs of stone that were stacked on top of each other and then sloped down into the water. The pond was surprisingly large for a private garden, taking up almost a quarter of it. There were beautiful vibrant pink water lilies covering the surface that lent an air of the whole scene being staged just for a photo shoot.

'Are you sure you haven't done this a million times before?' I asked him, not caring what the answer was.

'Of course I have, but never with someone as captivating as you. The nearest I've ever managed to my fantasy was with an old girlfriend who encouraged me to buy the camera, but all she wanted was some glamour shots. I remember when I asked her to open her legs she was horrified so I knew that what I have in mind for you would have been out of the question.'

'I am intrigued. What do you want me to do?' By that stage I was ready for anything; my nipples were prickling with arousal and my pussy was starting its familiar pulsing.

'Would you start here at the top of the garden then walk down the path to the pond, bop down to take off your shoes and then walk down the slabs until you are standing in the water? If you can, pretend I'm not here. I am going to follow you while you walk to the pond. When you get into the water try to act naturally and go with the flow. I will probably be whizzing all around you to get the best angles, but try not to take any notice of me. I don't know how far you will feel comfortable going but if you could be brave enough to touch yourself I would be your grateful worshipper for ever. Oh fuck, this is so amazing I can't actually believe it's happening. Look at my hands, they're shaking so hard I can hardly hold the camera!'

I looked over at him and he wasn't kidding; his

hands were shaking so badly the camera was wobbling all over the place, but his sudden vulnerability was an aphrodisiac in itself. I preened like a bird.

'OK. Are you ready to roll?' I asked, as I ran my hands through my hair and checked that my clothes were straight. I licked my lips, mainly because I felt that it was what porno models were supposed to do, and waited a second or two before Mac nodded his head.

Strange how the second I saw the red light on the front of the camera come on I came alive. I stood straighter, I held my head high and stuck out my chin the way Adam liked. Keeping my eyes on the flowers in the pond as if picking them was my sole purpose, I walked slowly and as seductively as I could up to the edge of the tiny beach. The feeling I had as I bent down to take off my shoes was almost surreal. I saw Mac out of the corner of my eye walk around me until he was at the perfect angle to capture my movements. Flirting with the camera was so natural I did it almost automatically. As my hands busied themselves with my shoes I allowed my knees to drop apart slightly and I was gratified by a strangled gasp from Mac.

It was so easy for me to get into the role and tell a story with my actions. I tiptoed into the water and held the hem of my skirt up as if it might get wet; I knew that Mac, who was behind me, now would be able to see at least the lower cheeks of my bottom. I felt the plump mound of my pussy bulge between the gap in my thighs suggestively. It was very exciting exposing myself to him. The night before had been him and me showing off but this was more intimate in a way. I was performing for Mac and oozing as much of my sexuality as I could muster. After a few moments even Mac was forgotten as I bent over in the water to pick a flower. I waded through the shallow pond with my skirt clutched in one hand and the growing bunch of irises in the other, trying to think of my next move. This business was exciting me far more than I thought and I wanted satisfaction.

Poor Mac grunted slightly as I sat on the edge of the pond and then leaned back on one hand in an abandoned sort of a way. He was by then standing on the other side of the water with the camera trained right on me. I looked into the lens, smiled and moved my legs apart. I tried to make it look as if I had been caught out needing a desperate masturbation session mid flower picking. I knew it was a bit silly but Mac didn't appear to care and by this time I really did need to come, so by then it was for real.

In my head I lost Mac somewhere along the way as I ripped off my top and bra, and grasped my breast roughly with one hand. My greed took over. The flowers were dropped and forgotten as my other hand furiously rubbed at my hardening clitoris.

'Fuck, that's horny, Joanna, keep it up. Open your legs further; I want to see right inside you. Come on, baby, that's it.' He almost shouted as I stretched my legs as far apart as I could. 'Yes, yes,' he encouraged.

I got totally carried away by his encouragement and by my exhibitionism; I was in my element sitting there showing all I had to this exceedingly aroused and exciting man. Two endings were vying for attention in my head; should I just go with it and finish myself off or should I entice Mac to come over and fuck me? I have to admit that my hunger took precedence but I told myself it was what he would want anyway – me showing him everything. Briefly I kept up the teasing, but within less than five minutes of self-manipulation I could wait no longer. That's the only trouble with making yourself come; you know what to do *too* well and finish far too quickly. I had read many magazine stories where people told of making their build-up last for hours but I'm sorry to say that I am much too impatient for all that.

I looked straight into the lens again and hoped that I didn't look an idiot as I frantically rubbed in a swirling motion. I could feel the wetness of my excitement and hear the groans from Mac encouraging me on. I could feel the coolish air on my sticky pussy flesh as I stretched my legs as far apart as I could with my toes still in the slightly murky water. Everything began to take shape when I adjusted my movements to include a dip of the fingers into my pussy every three or four swirls; now I was groaning louder than Mac. I was panting hard when the fingers of my other hand, with a life of their own took hold of my nipple and squeezed – hard.

'Fuck, you beautiful rude sexy bitch. Go on, come for me.'

Who was I to argue? Mac's slightly insulting but sexy words spun my head and turned my soaking pussy into the proverbial caldron. I came rather spectacularly even if I do say so myself with my naked thighs twitching and my breasts heaving.

I had no idea how Mac would react to my display or even if it was anywhere near what he had had in mind but it was a bit too late for regrets. I stayed on the edge of the pond trying to regain my composure while Mac switched off the camera and came over to me. For some unknown reason I was more embarrassed than I had been the night before but I was immediately made to feel at ease.

'You really are the most sensational woman I have ever met. That was wonderful.' As Mac raved about how he had enjoyed my performance his hand was absentmindedly playing with the front of his trousers where he was sporting a very healthy hard-on. I raised an eyebrow and gazed purposefully at his crotch.

'Hang on, I've got a brilliant idea!' And with that Mac stacked some bricks up and placed the camera on the raised end of the pond. He posed, showing off as he gauged the range through the viewfinder. When he felt it was perfect he came back, quickly took off his trousers and sat next to me on the ledge. He patted his naked lap and his very impressive cock nodded its agreement.

'I want you to do exactly what you did in the car when Jim was watching.'

Of course, I obliged without a second thought. I straddled his lap and lowered myself down slowly until I felt his knob end nudging between my extremely slippery lips. It was so easy to get to the position we both craved with him right inside me to the hilt. The girth of him stretched me exquisitely and the sheer length of his cock was enough for me to experience its pressure against every wall, filling me totally.

Mac took hold of me under my thighs and raised me like a puppet until his cock threatened to slip out, but I cried out for him to stop. I wriggled and writhed until he lowered me again and my groin could grind again against his. We were like wild animals as we rutted in the garden oblivious to outside influences and unaware of the sight we made through the lens of the voyeur camera.

It only took Mac about thirty deep thrusts to get to boiling point and he grunted in my ear that he couldn't wait any longer, but it didn't matter. Up until Mac had lifted me in his hands I had no inclination for another orgasm but as soon as he played me like a marionette, and then lowered me onto his enormous cock so it could stretch me all ways, I felt the tiny pulses start. I ground down on him shamelessly to gain more purchase and Mac, after seeing my performance a few minutes before, took his hands from under me and grabbed hold of my breast and squeezed. I yelped, but it had the desired effect; not only did it take me to the point where I definitely did want to come again, it spurred Mac on to trickier things.

Oooh, he was so clever – almost a match for Adam. He gripped each of my nipples and raised my heavy breasts until they were dangling in his grasp. The pain was delicious and pushed me into the first throes of orgasm. As I enjoyed the spasms inside my lower half, Mac bucked and thrust underneath me and kept hold of my now tender nipples. My breasts shook with the intensity of Mac coming and sent new shivers down to my crotch. Christ, it was horny.

We both waited until we had calmed a little and then pulled away. The squelchy plop as Mac's softening penis fell away from me took away any embarrassment we felt, leaving us laughing and finally at complete ease with each other.

'Oh, God, look at that, I look awful'. I giggled as I saw my exposed sex for the first time on film.

'Oh, no you don't. Believe me, you don't,' Mac argued with absolute fervour in his voice. 'You look fucking fabulous.' We were sitting back in his lounge almost naked and his glistening cock started twitching all over again.

The sheer exaggerated intensity on Mac's face made me trust that at least for him the film was all he had hoped for. All I could see was a silly look on my face, how huge my boobs were and how very disgusting I was as I made myself come for the camera. I liked the bit where I sat on Mac and thought we looked good together in the pretty setting of the garden. Mac loved the part where I dropped my flowers because I was so horny I just had to play with myself and I could tell that he was happy with everything I had done. We played the film over and over, commenting on each little bit and each single movement we made. It was fun and I felt very happy being there with him.

After we had looked at the whole thing at least ten times we started planning how we would do another one someday. I am slightly ashamed to admit that we were beginning to get excited all over again, examining each sequence and the surrounding areas for possible places our filming could continue another time. My eyes were attracted to a glint in the far hedge, but as soon as I saw it the film had moved on.

'Hang on a minute, I just saw something. Rewind it, Mac.'

'What? What's wrong?'

'I'm not sure, but I saw something in the hedge.'

We rewound the film and sure enough, when we looked closely, we burst out laughing. Jim's face was clearly to be seen sticking out of the hedge at the far bottom of the garden beyond the pond. And when we looked further we caught a glimpse of him later, just as I was sitting on Mac's lap. He was standing well back but visible with his hand cradling his cock and his legs wobbling as he wanked himself silly.

I ended up spending a second night with Mac. This time we took our time over the lovemaking. We played with each other, discovering properly the other's likes and dislikes – not that there were many dislikes to find. I began really to enjoy myself in his company and learned that, apart from exhibitionism, Mac loved to explore. So we explored each other and had a wonderful time. When it was time to go the next morning I really didn't want to. Mac almost begged me to see him again and I was tempted but I knew I might feel differently when I got back to the office and Adam; just because I was going home already I couldn't get the thought of him out of my mind. I tried to imagine what he would do to me this time. I hoped that he would do more of what he had done before. My mind couldn't even imagine what came next, but as I drove away and waved to Mac, I longed to experience it whatever it was. Far from Mac making me long to come back and see him again, he had actually encouraged me to want Adam.

9

When I finally got home after driving for three hours and sitting in endless roadwork jams, I was confused about the way I felt about Mac. I put Baby away in the garage and walked back to my flat. All the way home I had played the events of the last two days over and over in my mind. I had only intended to enjoy the game and move on as I had with Rosie and Steve, but it had turned out differently. I felt that in other circumstances I could have begun a long-term relationship with Mac but, as usual, Adam got in the way.

I sat for most of the evening curled up on my settee thinking about things that had happened over the past months. Yet again I grew rather hot between the legs. I was becoming obsessed with sex. How could I begin to relate the Joanna that had been offered the part of sex pervert extraordinaire, to the Joanna that I was by now? Even thinking about Adam set my mind racing into sordid thoughts. I opened a bottle of wine and managed to polish off the whole lot during my mental acrobatics.

I had begun to attach thoughts of Adam to my inquisitiveness about Mr Anonymous. What the hell was he all about, I asked myself, and how did I really feel about his suggestions? Was I turned on by his proposition and, if so, did I fancy meeting him? The pain Mac had engineered when he gripped hold of my nipples kept leaping into my mind unbidden – I had not only enjoyed it but it had been the catalyst that took me to orgasm. How did that relate to the punishment that Mr Anonymous threatened me with and the way I flooded just at the thought of being chastised? I had no idea what he had in mind to do to me, but I suppose the not knowing was part of the intrigue.

By the time I climbed into bed I was very confused, slightly horny again and anticipating Adam's reaction to my next report. I wondered how he would react to it all.

I eventually dozed off with varied thoughts buzzing around my head: Mac, Jim and my tender nipples; Adam and being made to stand submissively in front of him; Rosie and how I felt between her soft fragrant thighs; and, last but not least, Nick and his finger on my clitoris. I was so ashamed when I woke in the middle of the night actually convulsing in orgasm. It was weird, and another new experience to add to my growing collection.

The confused coward in me took over and I phoned work to say that I would be taking a couple of days away from the office to work from home. It was the first time I had been so cocky about my new position. Usually the most I would do would be to leave early or get in late and say I was finishing an article in the quiet of my own home. The reason for my absence was twofold: firstly, I wanted to have a bit of breathing space to think and secondly, I had decided to buy myself a computer. How easy it would be to write from home I told myself. My computer at work had become invaluable and most importantly I wanted to see what the Internet was all about. I had spent an hour or two of fun with Alex on his but there were private things I wanted to explore that I felt unable to share with him. What better way was there to explore the range of possibilities available?

I was completely unsure of what to get, computer-wise, so I took the opportunity to spend some time with Alex – I had abandoned him a bit since our game in the garden, even though memories of him smacking my bottom were still prominent in my thoughts. When I rang Alex's bell he answered the door with a very bored expression on his face, but brightened up the second he saw it was me. I was flattered and gratified. Being a computer geek, Alex loved the idea of being able to help me choose one and promised that when it arrived he would set it all up and get me onto the amazing World Wide Web.

I curbed my impatience and waited for Alex to get himself showered and dressed. Goodness knows what he had been doing: it was 2.30 p.m. when I knocked on his door and 3.30 p.m. by the time he was ready. I guessed he had still been in bed and found myself wishing I had arrived earlier.

I had to fight hard not to be persuaded to buy a custom-built computer from one of his many university mates, but eventually he believed me when I explained that I was still at the basic stage; I didn't want to play games or play music but just wanted a good word-processing package and the Internet. I couldn't wait to get started.

We chose a middle of the road model with a little more to offer than the basics I had requested but nowhere near as much as Alex wanted for me. The girl assistant in the shop who had spent at least half the time we were in there flirting with Alex was actually very helpful. She listened quite carefully to what I wanted and then once I had chosen she gave me free disks for getting onto the Internet. It was all like a new language to me and made me feel very naïve. The shop was full of kids from the age of eleven or twelve upwards all knowing exactly what they wanted and being able to speak the language fluently. The best aspect of the model I chose was its availability: I was able to take it home with me straight away. So off we trundled, with all the bits I needed all packed into the boot of Alex's car.

Alex set up my smart new toy on the dining table in my lounge. First he told me he couldn't stay and help me play with it because he had a date with the girl from the computer shop. The cheeky devil had chatted her up while I was looking around. I have to admit to being a little peeved, but after I had been shown how to get started on the Net I was raring to go. I made sure he told me everything I needed to know for an evening of discovery, then, pouting a bit for effect, I told him I hoped he would have a good time, hoping inside that he didn't. I know I already had more on my plate on the man-front than I could handle, but there was definitely something a bit special about our relationship and I had begun to rely on his friendship and support.

I explored to begin with but eventually I had to admit what it was I wanted. I was completely and utterly blown away by the response when I put the word 'spanking' into the search engine. Within less than a second or two 13,478 sites were on offer to me all on the subject that was uppermost in my thoughts. Where to start was the burning question and the obvious answer was the first one. So I clicked on the site and sat open-mouthed at the picture that filled my screen. There was a pretty buxom girl sprawled over the lap of a businesslike character who looked a little like Adam. Well, in my eyes he did. Tammy as she was called had apparently upset her master the businessman, and was being punished for her misdemeanours. She lay over his suited knees, helpless in his grasp with her skirt up around her narrow waist and her white schoolgirl knickers lowered in the most provocative way around her upper thighs. Her squashed flesh bulged out around the tight garment, making the sight of her nakedness even sexier if that were possible. Tammy's right leg was raised up in an attempt to protect her bright ruby red bottom from the obviously intense attack it was receiving. Her endeavours however were fruitless and even though it was a still photo I could tell from the colour of her bottom and the tears in her eyes that it wasn't over by a long shot.

I was desperate to find out what happened to the hapless Tammy so I clicked on the next page only to be told that I would have to pay for the privilege. Frustrated and more than a little turned on I tried the next site and the next, filling my hungry brain with pictures and narrative that left my stories for the magazine standing. I played well into the early morning, searching sites that were just as informative and outrageous as the first one I looked at and just as stimulating. When I had become more computer-friendly I began to experiment; I put in the word 'submissive' and yet again was offered a selection of sites that would keep me busy until doomsday. Something raging inside me stopped me actually opening any of them for a minute and I just sat there staring at the site names.

Names like subslut and slave-girl started my chest heaving and the hair on my neck prickling; I was scared to open the sites, anxious about how they would change me. Adam had been abundantly clear on how he saw the dynamics of our blossoming relationship – if you could call it a relationship. He had clearly stated that I was to obey his orders and if I did he would make me feel that knee-trembling ecstasy again. I longed to experiment with it all but even those first few minutes in his control had been more devastating than all the other games I had played put together.

For precious moments I sat and stared at the lists of sites available to me. I ran my cursor down the list, reading the brief description of each one and trying to decide which should be the one to initiate me. I was convinced that once I opened even one site I would never be the same again, and I was right. The site I chose was the tenth on the list and advertised itself as the home of a couple that lived their dominance and submission as a lifestyle. It had never in my wildest imaginings occurred to me that there were people who did the things Adam did to me as a way of life. God, how that thought filled my mind and played havoc with my body. I couldn't let my brain move on to the next function, all I could do was imagine how that would be.

How would it be to get up in the morning and be told how to dress or whether to wash or not, to be left at home while a partner went to work, making promises about what would happen when he got home? Although I had loved every minute of Adam controlling me I wasn't sure how I would feel if I were being controlled every waking moment. I felt it was rather a strange thing to do, to carry what to me was a sexual thing over into everyday life. Would it still feel sexual? Would it be horny to be told what to wear? I remembered how I had felt when Adam ordered me not to wear knickers and knew absolutely that yes, it was sexual. I wriggled in my seat as moisture gathered in the crotch of my knickers – reminding me that I shouldn't have them on at all – and soaked through the material. I had begun by spending every day with no knickers on but found that it became too normal and I wanted to feel special when I took them off. So I decided to wear whatever I liked when I wasn't with Adam and then when I took them off to visit him I would feel much more vulnerable. I liked feeling vulnerable.

The reality of that site far exceeded anything I could make up, let alone envisage. Donna and her Master lived my dream every day. She had given up work to enable them to indulge in their combined fantasy full time. Some days when Donna's Master went off to work he would lock her into a purpose-built dungeon in the cellar of their house and Donna would have to stay there until he got home. Sometimes he would chain her to the bed and he had been known to truss her up like a Sunday roast and leave her for hours while he pottered about doing other things. He would go shopping, or work in his shed while poor Donna lay helpless and horny waiting and wondering what her Master had in store for her when he deigned to return.

I was angry on Donna's behalf but almost deliriously excited by the images on the screen. There was no way Donna was against her treatment and she appeared far from the halfwit I would have expected her to be to put up with his treatment of her. I longed to be in her shoes if only for a day. Adam had only whetted my appetite by his manipulation of me and I wanted to discover everything I was capable of experiencing.

Donna and her lifestyle were apparently not unusual. It seemed from the pages of sites dedicated to the subject of submission and dominance available all over the world, that thousands of couples were stimulating each other with awe-inspiring creativity.

Mortified by the fact that, even with my history of writing what I called pervy stories, I had had no idea of the games people play, I left the World Wide Web and went to my solitary bed. It was 5 a.m. and just beginning to get light. I lay in the semi dark and imagined myself tied up and waiting for Adam to come and have his evil way with me. I pictured him walking through the door and looking me over as though I was a slab of meat, examining every inch of my restrained body.

In one evening I had fuelled the subjects of many, many more stories. My readers had a treat in store for them. Also, I couldn't wait to get started on the account of my session with Mac. The sooner I had it finished the sooner I could submit it to Adam and then, with a bit of luck, submit to Adam. It had been ages since our first get-together and I wondered if he thought about me as much as I thought about him. Somehow I doubted it.

Mac and I were so easy to write about. I had decided somewhere along the way that I would just write about our experience by the train track and leave the rest as an intimate memory. Every second was still so lucid in my mind even after all the new thoughts that filled it from the Internet. I could still feel how it felt to be lifted up in the air naked, with my legs wrapped around his head while he kissed my bare pussy. The memory of that magical moment was swamped by the realisation that, even though I had lived with my smooth sex for days, Adam still hadn't seen it. I wondered how he would react. I had kept my pussy shaved as ordered and the routine of taking off the new growth in the shower every morning had become habitual. The image of my smooth pink shiny skin in the mirror with my noticeably darker bits clearly on show had stopped shocking me with their display. I had actually grown to like the image I portrayed of the sexual adventurer I was rapidly becoming.

Even though there was a side of me that revelled in my submission to Adam, away from him I had strong dominant characteristics. I wanted to control what happened between him and me but then let him take over when I was there in front of him. I had a brilliant idea. I was well aware that the parts I left out of my story about my meeting with Rosie and Steve were the instigation of what came after, so I hatched a plan. When I finished writing my extremely detailed description of my antics with Mac I just hinted that something exciting had happened in the car on the way back to his. I hoped the lack of explicit details might incite Adam the way it had the first time. I described how I had bent forward over Mac and how the cabby could see my naked exposed bottom and how he had turned out to be Mac's mate. That'll get him going, I thought as I finished the piece. I was very pleased with the finished article and then had another brainwave. I e-mailed it to him from home.

I sent the article as an attachment but in my message I explained innocently that I thought it might be a good thing to keep the punters in a state of excitement and that I hoped he agreed. I signed off the e-mail by telling Adam that I hoped my experiences had lived up to his expectations of me. It took courage for me to do this because there was a small element of suspicion in my mind that he would revert back to the unfathomable boss that he had been originally. Because he had stayed so cool about the whole thing I wondered if he would carry on as if nothing had happened. I didn't have to wait long to find out.

When I returned to work I felt that I had been away for weeks; there were piles of post on my desk. I switched on my PC and while I waited for it to load I ran through the envelopes. When my computer had opened to tell me that there were twelve e-mails for me to sift through I could no longer concentrate on anything else. My eyes scanned the sending addresses making my stomach lurch at the site of Adam's name and I quickly clicked on it:

Joanna

Thank you for submitting your latest work to me. You have excelled yourself. Well done. There are one or two things I would like to discuss with you before I OK it for print.

I have scheduled a meeting between us this afternoon at 2. If you are unable to attend perhaps you would let me know.

Adam

I couldn't believe that he had managed to get the word 'submitting' into his e-mail and it thrilled me to the core. Perhaps it was a sign I told myself – I hoped so. I read it over and over trying to read other messages into it but then had to admit there weren't any. The arrogant tone of Adam's message had a way of exciting me beyond belief. I don't know why – perhaps it reminded me of the detached way he had manipulated me the last time we met.

My thoughts see-sawed uncontrollably. One minute I wondered if he'd even given me another thought since the time I had last been in his office, then I would be convinced he was orchestrating the whole thing, even down to the way his formal words overwhelmed me. It seemed that whatever way he behaved he had the power to lure me helplessly forward.

It was still only 9.30 so I had hours to wait, but I decided to take my knickers off there and then to prepare myself mentally and physically for what might happen. I thought that if I was aroused when I went in to see him I might convey that to him and it might prompt him into action. Well, that was what I hoped.

I shut my office door and slipped my knickers off and tucked them away in my bag, noting that already they were damp. Smiling to myself I tried to remember the last time they had been totally dry.

Within five minutes I was happily reading letter after letter suggesting all kinds of games I might like to play. Essentially I wanted to experience everything that was on offer but I had to weed out the silly ones and the ones that I knew were too much for our readers.

It was becoming increasingly more difficult to whittle my postbag down to the two or three we had room to offer the readers. This time it was even more difficult, I suppose because I was more open to some of the bizarre ones. I was enjoying the way that I was able to manipulate which one won. At first I had been worried that I would be pressured into carrying out propositions that I had no desire for but luckily that hadn't happened. I found that all I had to do was choose an offer that was well written and stimulating and couple it with others that were bland, and lo and behold the readers did the rest for me.

As with my other postbags, one or two letters stood out from the dross. Adam had promised to leave me to get on with it and had kept his promise, so I was at liberty to indulge myself. One particular letter buzzed through my head until I wanted to scream. I couldn't get it out of my mind long enough even to take the others seriously. It was written so cleverly and provocatively I just had to respond. I pushed all the others aside – the rubbish into the bin, the possibles to one side of my desk and the contenders to the other.

Dear Joanna

My twin brother and I surprisingly have the same fantasy. Imagine yourself walking along a quiet lane in the dark on your own, when suddenly two men who have planned the perfect scenario set upon you to satisfy their own base urges. If we have read you right your heart is already pounding.

We have checked the dictionary's description of the word 'rape' and feel we must clarify our proposal. The dictionary says, *the act or crime of having sexual intercourse with a woman without her consent, either by using force or by fraudulent means.*

Our proposal is to take out a small part of one word from that description and offer you the rest as a possibility for your next adventure. Imagine this, Joanna – take out the 'out' from without and instantly the prospect becomes awesome.

We have read over and over again about surveys of women's fantasies; many of them fantasise about forced sex. However, it is not so acceptable for a man to admit to having those urges.

We accept that for you the risk of trusting us will be great so we have enclosed full details about us; our home address and our business address – please feel free to check us out. We are hoping that if you are the girl we think you are you will find that risk thrilling, not frightening.

This is our proposal: come to a circuit session at our gym. We will not even acknowledge you. We will treat you like all our other customers with courtesy and respect and you will have no idea what is going to happen or when it will happen. We would like you to come to three sessions. That will give us the element of surprise and will hopefully build your anticipation to the highest possible level. We already know how we will be feeling.

We have discussed this at great length and feel from what we have read and what we already know about women that we have worked out the most thrilling scenario for all of us.

Well, Joanna, are you up for it? If you are, and if your readers choose our proposal, we would like you to book a session with us for three consecutive nights and we will handle the rest. You don't need to warn us, we will know it is you and the surprise will add to the experience for us.

We cannot tell you how honoured we would be if you chose us and how exhilarated we will be the second we see your name in our appointments book.

Till then!

Tony and Jack Mayhew

With the mind-blowing letter was a business card that advertised a gym called Fresh Start, with its main appeal being that it catered for beginners and experienced fitness fanatics alike. The letter was written in large bold neat handwriting and its message stabbed me in the crotch with its images.

It was a bit worrying to find that even the punters were reading me well enough to know that sort of thing about me and I began to wonder if, at the end of all this, I would have to move away. After all, I would have one hell of a reputation.

I dissected the letter and reread the card over and over, trying to imagine not only what they were like but also what it would feel like to be in exactly that scenario. I guessed that if it was carried out well, a consensual forced sex game could indeed be the fantasy of thousands of red-blooded modern women. If my postbag was anything to judge women by, then some would trade anything to be in my shoes, especially if there were no consequences.

Thinking of consequences, I remembered my date

with Adam and looked at my watch. I had been engrossed in my letters for hours. It was lunchtime and if I was to be on time for Adam I knew I had to grab something to eat quickly. I dashed down to the canteen and picked up a sandwich, completely unsure if I had the stomach to eat it. I was so wound up about what was going to happen when I closed the door behind me in Adam's office that my stomach was churning. I took the sandwich back to my little office and sat at my desk nibbling on it and sipping half-heartedly at the bottle of water I had bought. I was still reading the letter from Tony and Jack with my hand between my thighs when it was time to go. I straightened myself up and got a tissue out of my bag to wipe myself with – I had been so turned on over the past hours that I was sticky with heat.

10

I knocked at Adam's door with the usual trepidation, but also with excitement buzzing in my head. Adam's PA wasn't at her desk, which in itself was unusual, but I didn't really think much of it. I waited for at least ten interminable seconds before he opened the door. I told myself it was an auspicious omen that he had not just shouted his invite. He grinned his strange knowing grin and stepped back to let me pass and then stunned me for a second when he turned the key in the lock.

I don't know how he managed to throw me every time but he did it again. After locking the door he just carried on as if things were normal. He directed me to the coffee table and sat opposite me, staring at me all the time. Talk about mind games. He had a way of looking deep inside me and I always felt like shouting *'What?'* I didn't though, I just sat and waited while he picked up my printed e-mail and looked as if he were reading it through. Every so often he would stop and look up at me as if he had either read something that he didn't believe or something that surprised him. It was awful just sitting there waiting for him to speak, but delicious in a devastating sort of way. Anticipation – he was a master of it.

'Well, well, well, Joanna. It seems we are progressing at a rate of knots,' Adam said after he had apparently finished the torture and decided to put me out of my misery. 'This Mac gives the impression of being an inventive sort of a chap. Did you enjoy yourself as much as you say? Or have the details been embellished for my benefit, or perhaps even the punters'?'

Adam looked me straight in the eye. He tried to look detached but I was beginning to know his face and the look he was giving me said 'please tell me it is true'. You would expect a prospective lover – and that was how I saw him – to beg it to be a lie, but this was new territory for me; the world of submission and domination where none of the rules appeared to apply. None of the rules I was used to, that is.

I had gained a little courage by his unguarded moment so I challenged his question boldly. 'Every word of it is true.'

'Even down to the kneeling at his feet in the light from the train windows?' he asked, hanging on my every word.

I remembered how it had felt to kneel on the hard floor with Mac's glorious cock sliding its way down my throat to the exquisite encouragement of his crooning, telling me how wonderful I was. I blushed my answer and I have no doubt Adam knew I was remembering.

'Tell me about his cock, Joanna.'

I stuttered, unsure of what he wanted. Again he had managed to throw me – this question was the last thing I had expected. I decided to try in my own way to blow him away with my answer, and mustered all of my creative vocabulary skills in my response.

'In the light from the train, Mac's majestic cock thrust out from his body proudly, desperate for attention. I had no option but to throw myself at his feet and worship it. I longed to take it into my mouth and savour it. And that's just what I did. The warmth of his velvet flesh slid easily . . .'

Adam interrupted me by laughing. 'You delight me, Joanna. Every time I think I am getting to know you,

you surprise me yet again. There's a feisty little strumpet inside you that I am going to relish encouraging. I like the fact that you fight against me but still keep coming back for more. I sometimes perceive a battle raging inside you; you are torn between telling me to get lost and falling on to your knees in front of me. Is my evaluation of you correct?'

Correct? He had read my innermost thoughts – the ones I still didn't admit to myself. Was I ever to get the upper hand? Every time I thought I had thrown him he would destroy me with one sentence. He had done it again.

I nodded because that was the only option open to me; I was speechless.

'Good. Now perhaps we can move on. Can you remember the instructions I gave you last time I saw you?'

I nodded again, the heat flooding through my body.

'Don't just nod at me, Joanna. Half the pleasure for me is to hear you admit that you have obeyed me. You have obeyed me haven't you, Joanna?' The total unquestionable control was back in his voice and my stomach was churning with molten toffee.

'Yes, Adam, I did obey you and follow your instructions.' I knew I sounded a little stroppy; I was annoyed with myself for complying so readily. I was also ashamed that the knowledge of my eagerness to comply was a large ingredient in my rapid arousal. Already I was desperate for him and we had only exchanged about three sentences.

'Show me.'

Those two simple words were not enough to give me permission to do what he asked. He hadn't actually told me what he wanted me to do. Did he want me to stand and display myself as I had before, or would he be satisfied with just a flash as I sat here on the chair? He sat back and relaxed, watching the battle going on in my head. I was ready to cry at the pressure those words had created in me. I thought if I waited long enough he would explain in greater detail, but of course he didn't. Why would he, he was so obviously enjoying my acute discomfort? He waited and I squirmed until I couldn't bear the tension any longer and like a coward chose the easier option, knowing deep down that he wanted me to display my nakedness. I stayed in exactly the position I was in and raised my skirt.

'Tut, tut.' Adam shook his head and waited again, still not giving me any further encouragement. As had happened before, it was almost my anger that propelled me to my feet. I stood with my legs slightly apart and raised my skirt, knowing full well the depraved sight I must make. I felt the cool air hit my hot flesh, making me whimper with my hunger for attention. Adam, true to form, just studied me for what seemed like minutes and then crooked his finger at me. I was far too eager to get around the table to him. When I was standing in front of him with my legs trembling he managed to demolish me again.

I was stunned as Adam leaned forward and put a pencil on the floor in front of me. He told me to place one foot on it and I did as he asked. Then he put another pencil feet away from the first and explained that he wanted me to stretch as far towards it with my other foot as I was able. If I managed to touch it he would reward me. I tried to stretch my legs that far apart, cringing at the image of how I must look to him, but determined to succeed. Adam just sat and watched my futile tries, knowing, I am sure, that I could never do it; they were far too far apart. While I was still pushing my legs to their limit, Adam stood up and took a large white handkerchief out of his pocket, spun it around until it was a loose sausage shape and tied it around my eyes.

Now I was trembling all over. The darkness enveloped me and dragged me towards acceptance of the inevitable – my submission. I was almost delirious with hunger and I hadn't even been touched. The electric shock of his first contact with my flesh zapped its way around my nervous system. I sobbed my desperate need. His gentle hand smoothed over the stretched flesh of my mound and worked its way downward, over the silken engorged flesh until he reached my pussy. He slid two fingers between my labia and moved them apart until I knew my hole was open and on show for him to see.

I jumped out of my skin when his mouth touched mine; his soft dry lips nibbling and exploring mine. He whispered for me to stay perfectly still while he ravaged my mouth. His fingers were still holding me open, not moving, just exposing me while he kissed me long and hard. I thought I would collapse with the intensity of feelings, but as soon as the sparkles dashed behind my eyelids he would stop and wait for me to calm down. I longed to put my arms up and hold him, to rip off the blindfold and see him, but I sunk into my submission and obeyed.

While Adam's mouth devoured mine and while I couldn't verbally complain unless I pulled away from the rapture I was experiencing, Adam firmly took hold of my sex and squeezed the whole of it in his fist. An exquisite throbbing sensation started up just behind my clitoris, suffusing my lower half in greedy heat. I longed for conventional sex; for him to throw me on the floor and fuck the living daylights out of me, but I also wanted to see the range of feeling he could produce in me.

He gripped me by my pussy tightly then led me like a willing lamb to the slaughter, through the darkness, across the wooden floor and then left me standing alone. I had no idea if I was at his desk or by the soft chairs that we had sat in earlier; all I knew was the darkness, the smell of him and the burning fire in my belly. When I felt him guiding me and pushing me forward from behind with his body, I let the motion take me where he wanted me to go. Hardness against the front of my thighs pushed me forwards from the waist up, so I went with it and bent forward. I knew then that I was bending over the desk. He took hold of my upper arms and pushed them forward until I was gripping the far side of the desk desperately, wondering what he would do to me.

He leaned his torso along the full length of me and slipped his hands up my back under my shirt until he encountered my bra. With one brief flick of his fingers I felt my breasts fall forward and his hands cup them firmly. It's a good job I was partly lying down because the strength in my legs completely failed me then; I was shaking violently. Adam leaned against my behind and ground his obvious erection against my bottom and I returned the pressure, trying to push into him more. He stood and the devastating anticipation of what was to come next forced a ragged moan from my parched throat.

'Open your legs again for me, Joanna. Show me that pretty cunt of yours.' I almost jumped to obey; after all, I wanted him to touch me more than anything. Adam flipped my skirt up over my back and I felt the cool air caress my limbs as he put one foot between mine and pushed my legs even further apart.

His hand ran down the crease of my sex from my buttocks to my clitoris and then my naked mound. He massaged gently on the way, exciting every nerve. He manipulated my clitoris with his now slippery hand and then ran it back to my bottom; I wriggled brazenly, wanting him to do his worst. I think I actually wanted him to spank me, but he had other ideas. His inquisitive fingers again separated the flesh of my pussy to expose me and then I felt them slide smoothly inside me. He explored inside me for a second or two, sending shock waves through my crotch. Just as I leaped toward my climax he removed them slowly and sensuously. His slippery fingers gripped hold and tugged gently on my sex-lips. It was devastatingly rude and I revelled in the feelings of abandonment. All shame had passed and I actually wanted him to degrade me so I wriggled my bottom in encouragement. Silly me – I should have just let him carry on, he clearly knew exactly how to send me crazy.

I shrieked and started to jump up in reaction to the persistent finger that probed at my bottom, but Adam pushed me back down again.

'Oh no you don't, Joanna, stay exactly where you are, I haven't finished with you yet. I have waited too long for you to frustrate me now. I will have you, so relax and enjoy.'

His encouraging words went some way towards allowing me to relax, but I was so shocked at what he was doing. I felt as if he was experimenting with me; doing all the rude things he could come up with to test my reactions. My reactions were clearly exactly what he wanted, because his voice crooned in the background. His pleasure was evident as his finger pushed its way inside my tight puckered hole. My sphincter muscle spasmed as he explored his goal – my bum. This was unbelievable. Here I was lying over my boss's desk with my legs spread wide and his fingers partying in my bottom. I wickedly thrust back to let him know I was enjoying it; in fact I knew that if he didn't stop soon I would come and probably drip on his plush carpet. I couldn't believe I had taken to the violation of my last stronghold quite so easily. Jim's single digit had been bad enough.

'Relax, Joanna; do you want more?'

I moaned my consent.

He pushed his fingers in to the hilt and asked the question again.

'Yes!' I shrieked.

I felt him line up behind me and heard his zip open. I gasped, a little scared at his intent but far too near to my orgasm to protest. His hot cock nudged against my bottom and I involuntarily clenched my cheeks together. Adam slapped my bottom hard and the breath whooshed from my lungs, the heat pulsated through my bottom and I let him in. Adam's hands that had excited me to distraction grasped hold of the cheeks of my bottom and pulled them apart until I felt my entrance give up the struggle and relax.

Adam leaned along my back again until his mouth was as close to my ear as possible and he shattered me with his words.

'Joanna?'

A shiver ran down my spine as I mumbled, 'Mmm?'

'I am going to fuck you so hard. I am going to ram my cock inside you as far as it will go. I will know I have done enough when I hear you scream with pleasure. When you scream, Joanna, you will be mine. Do you understand what that means?'

True to form I muttered my answer, completely lost in the tantalising pressure prodding at my most delicate hole. His words had been controlled and almost sinister in their inflection but I thrilled to the core. I thought I was incapable of answering lucidly but he pushed for the reply he needed.

'Do you understand, Joanna?'

'Yes!' I shouted as the force of his power over me threatened to overwhelm me finally.

Adam slid his rock-hard cock into my pussy, as far as he could. Just as I responded and started gyrating back onto him, he removed it and slid the length of it up the channel of my sex and ran it over the tiny quivering hole that was completely on display for him. The hard end became slimy with my secretions and therefore slid and slipped about in the soft heat of my sex and the crease of my bottom. I don't know which I wanted more; for him to keep it where it was in my pussy where I felt it belonged, or in my bottom where my muscles were clenching and releasing in a frantic invitation. I could feel my tight sphincter muscle screwing shut as he approached and then relax as I concentrated on my other opening. He kept this up until I wanted to scream, but I was buggered if I would give in to his instructions that easily.

Eventually, when I was so frantic for him to penetrate me properly and he had obviously either decided that I was ready or that he couldn't wait any longer, he slowed his motions until his cock paused at the entrance to my bottom. His hand made its way to my clitoris to keep me on the boil and God, how it worked. I truly was at screaming point; I just had to have him.

He had played me so well. I was desperate to be full and to feel him inside me and I would have let him do anything to me, anything at all, and he knew it.

Adam pressed himself into me just far enough to whet my appetite and I groaned my encouragement and acceptance. His hands stroked my back as his crooning increased to questions.

'Are you ready now, Joanna?'

'Yes,' I cried.

'Are you ready to be mine?'

'Yes.' This time I was almost sobbing.

'Again,' he ordered.

'Yes. Yes. Yes!' I screamed loudly. Yes, I understand that I am yours. Yes, I want you. Yes. I *was* screaming now, screaming like a banshee, and it did the trick. Adam rammed up against me, his cock forcing its way into my vulnerable bottom. Instead of fucking me like he would have done if he were buried that far in my pussy, he kept his cock in as far as it would go and just pushed against me and then released the pressure. What sublime torture it was to have him finally inside and not just teasing me. His cock was buried so deep inside me, my poor bottom thought it would tear apart, but of course it didn't. I relaxed and welcomed him in, encouraging him to push me to my limits.

His almost brutal thrusts into my bottom, his almost violent hands crushing my cheeks, my breasts flattened against the desk and his complete control raged through my head and spun me in the darkness. It was true, I was his – his for the taking.

We flopped down onto the desk as our orgasms ran into each other. I felt Adam's hot sperm pump forcefully deep inside my anus as he almost tore the spasms from my belly.

* * *

I longed for Adam to hold me after our shattering game but he made me kneel at his feet. It didn't feel anything like it had when I had knelt for Mac, this was a head thing. Humbled by the intensity of my feelings I bowed my head and waited to see what else he wanted of me. At least he hadn't just sent me out the way he had the last time I had been in his office. He just looked at me in a benign sort of way – the way you would look at a puppy that worships you. I was very confused and I am sure Adam could feel that. His next move was in response to my obvious emotion.

'Do you have any idea what you have agreed to let yourself in for by saying you are mine? Do you really want what I am offering or were you just intrigued by me and wanted a good fuck? Because if that was all you wanted that is OK too.'

Still kneeling at his feet with him sitting comfortably next to me in a chair, I felt more at ease and content than I could ever remember. I thought hard about his question because he was deadly serious when he asked it. I had no idea what part of me his behaviour was aiming at, only that I had responded deep inside to the way he treated me. I had longed for him to use me. I suppose that the fact that I had almost hero-worshipped him from the first time I saw him was a contributing factor. With other men I could be free and have fun, but I craved Adam's control like a drug. I answered carefully.

'I don't care what I am letting myself in for or how much or how little is on offer. I want this. I don't even know how I feel at the moment. I do know I will still be me when I walk outside the door; I will still want to carry on with my life as it is and my career as it is and the project that started all this, just as it is. If this thing with you is going to change all that then I don't know any more. The truth is, Adam, you have bewildered me beyond my comprehension, but I have never felt the intensity of what I just experienced, neither did I know it was possible to feel that way.'

During my little speech Adam had pulled me up from the floor and onto his lap. I snuggled into his jacket; shocked to notice that he still had it on after all he had put me through. Cradled in his arms I knew yet again that I would be able to deny him nothing. He undoubtedly needed to test my level of commitment because, as he talked to me, his hand snaked its way up my skirt and into the humid place between my thighs. He made me keep talking and kept asking me questions as his hand explored my folds and crevasses, exciting me again to fever pitch.

I kept gasping and stopping, but he was relentless. While his fingers were doing their utmost to excite me, and succeeding extremely well, he made me continue talking. Depraved – that's how it felt to be having a normal conversation with this man while his manipulative fingers probed and poked their way inside me.

'Open your blouse, Joanna.' His fingers kept busy as he spoke.

I obeyed his instruction and bared my breasts for him. My bra was still up around my chest and my weighty breasts pushed from the opening and stared him in the face.

'Perfect. Are they sensitive, Joanna? Do your breasts like attention as much as this dirty little cunt of yours?' His fingers gently nipped my clitoris and I groaned my reply. My legs were splayed shamelessly open and my skirt was up around my waist.

'Answer me, Joanna.'

'Yes,' I croaked.

'Good. I know many diabolical games I could play

with these very beautiful, sensitive tits of yours. Would you like that, Joanna? Would you like me to devise some games for your tits?'

I hated the way that he made me say all the most embarrassing things he could think of and at the same time I was deeply uncomfortable at the abundance of my sexy dribblings that were oozing onto his exploring hand, but those feelings were humiliating in the most exquisite sense imaginable.

'Would you?' he repeated with a grin in his voice.

I nodded and, for once, he accepted that as my answer.

'Sit on the edge of the table, Joanna.' He pushed aside the papers and cleared a space just in front of him. Without second bidding, and eager for more attention, I moved in front of him and sat as instructed on the edge of the coffee table. He scooted forward in his seat until he was so close I could just about feel his knees against mine.

'Good girl.' I swelled with pride at those two simple words. 'Now, I want you to open your legs so I can see that pretty cunt properly. After all, you did shave it for me and I haven't had a chance to look at it properly yet, have I?' I knew he didn't particularly want an answer to that question; it was more of the humiliation factor and it worked. I felt waves of pleasure wash over me as he took hold of my knees and persuaded my legs to separate. He kept gently pushing them until my pussy was completely open and exposed. My bare bottom was hot on the cool of the table and I felt Adam's sperm dribbling from me.

'Keep them spread like that until I tell you otherwise. There's a good girl.'

After his hands left my knees they took hold of my blouse and stripped it from my shoulders and then my bra joined it on the chair behind him. All I had left on was my skirt, but that afforded me no protection whatsoever, it was bunched around my waist. My breasts jutted out, the nipples eager and hard when I leaned back on my hands to support my trembling.

'Now look at me, Joanna. I want you to look right in my eyes without moving. Whatever I do and however you feel, keep your legs spread apart like that and your eyes on mine.'

I met his piercing gaze. The look he had in his eyes was unfathomable; it was part arousal, part control and part excitement, but more than anything else I could see curiosity and questioning. He was testing my reactions and filing away my responses like a scientist. I swelled inside with a need to please him.

Oh God, the touch of his hands on my breasts was more intense than full sex with anyone else. The anticipation had been so great that when he took my nipples between thumbs and forefingers I thought I would faint. My legs automatically began to shut, but his knee pushed them apart again and I groaned. In fact I was moaning so audibly by the time he started rolling my nipples and tugging on them that he actually told me to be silent. It was impossible, but he evidently wanted to control me further because he stopped what he was doing until I did shut up.

I learned my lesson quickly and easily. If I made a noise he stopped but if I was quiet I got the attention I craved. I was quiet. My juices ran openly from my pussy and I no longer cared. All I cared about was whether Adam would allow me to orgasm. My clitoris was really tingling, begging for the final assistance, but he denied me any stimulation apart from the wonderful tugging my nipples were getting. My breasts rose and fell at his administrations but my eyes were locked onto his. I saw his pupils dilate and soften when I pleaded with him to make me come, but he just smiled and carried on.

I was panting raggedly and supporting myself completely on my arms as I tried to stretch my legs even further apart to entice him, but he kept smiling and teasing. I wanted to scream or roar like an animal, to shout that he was being unfair putting me through this torture. But I knew my pleas would just encourage him into more diabolical acts, so I rode the waves of pleasure that threatened to engulf me.

'Please, Adam?'

'What, Joanna? What do you want?' he queried, still playing with my nipples and forcing me into the pathetic pleading heap I was becoming.

'Please make me come.' I lowered my gaze as I begged.

'Look at me,' he snapped.

My eyes flew back to his in case he stopped but all he did was nod.

I moaned at what he was suggesting. I knew without a doubt that he was giving me permission to make myself come. How could I do anything as embarrassing as that, sitting here with my eyeballs locked onto his with him watching every reaction? It had been bad enough with Alex but it was so different then, with us both sharing the pleasure. Adam was just observing me. Yes, he was getting pleasure from the watching but it was him controlling all my actions and responses.

Tentatively I leaned over onto just one hand and put the other between my legs. I was mortified at how open and soaking wet I was. Adam loved it when I squirmed. By this stage I had no choice but to look at him; my eyes were cemented onto his. I had no choice but to stroke my clitoris until I came; I knew I would explode if I didn't. I had no choice but to obey him. Just as he had predicted, I was his to command.

My body convulsed into a writhing mass; my breasts and lower body jerking in spasms as the waves of ecstasy destroyed any last doubts I had. Until the day he said he didn't want me any more and regardless of whatever he chose to do to me, or order me to do for him, I belonged to Adam.

11

Our relationship was going to be out of the ordinary, but that was OK – I liked to be a bit different. All I cared about was that Adam wanted me. He had shown that he did in his own strange way, after I had exploded sitting on the table with my legs spread shamelessly apart. We discussed how things would be and I discovered that it would be not so much what we both thought would work best, but more a case of Adam telling me how things would be.

He told me how precise his needs were and explained that he had given up trying to have what most of us would call a normal relationship, accepting that it was too late to change. He told me that he wanted me to carry on with my life and wait for his call. He also told me that he had been searching for years for someone who would respond to his control in the way I had.

'I know this will be very peculiar for you to begin with, Joanna,' he said, 'but I want you to know that every second you're wanting me and I'm refusing you I am complete. Knowing you are out there somewhere, carrying out my instructions, whether it be fucking someone else or just waiting for my invitation, will be perfection. You are perfection, Joanna. You're my perfection. Already I know you so well. Inside you there is an animal lurking, a sexually decadent beast just as there is in me. We have no need for convention or morals. We just want to experience everything our minds and bodies can offer. Most people wouldn't understand us but we understand each other perfectly. Don't we?'

He was so right. He did already know me so well. It was as if he had climbed inside my soul. Even though I hadn't been searching for Adam's sexuality specifically, I knew I had been looking for something.

'Oh, there are so many things I want you to experience. I intend to explore you until I am absolutely familiar with your body, and the way it reacts to me. Then I will control you completely. Go home now, Joanna. Have your fun at your next scenario and write me a worthy story. I will call you when I am ready for you again. Until then I want you to try another exercise for me.'

I couldn't wait to hear what it was. I was scared but exhilarated too. The anticipation of what he might ask of me had climbed to monumental proportions in my list of what was important. It was then that I knew without a doubt that, if this carried on, I could easily become a junkie to sex – Adam's kind of sex. I could possibly end up enjoying a lifestyle relationship like Donna.

Adam walked over to his desk and fumbled around for a few seconds. When he returned he had in his hand two chrome pegs that he used to hold his papers together. He took hold of my hand and opened it palm upward, placed the pegs in it and closed my fingers around them.

Even that he did in a way that shattered me. It was the precise way he took my hand and the way he curled my fingers so intimately that did it.

'Wear them for me, Joanna. Put them on your delectable nipples for a few minutes each day and when I see you again I will test you. I want you to be able to wear them for half an hour. When you have mastered that I have other plans for them and you.' As he said those devastating words his hand slipped between my thighs and stroked my still tingling clit. Shocked at what he was implying, but obviously aroused by it, my traitorous sex oozed again.

I was learning fast. Every time I got comfortable with something Adam said or did he would move the goal posts. As soon as I accepted his words or behaviour he would push me further. It was frustrating because it meant I was in a constant state of excruciating anticipation. Sweet anticipation that is; the most mind-blowing anticipation possible. Sexual anticipation – and I was thriving on it.

I left his office; it didn't occur to me to argue or cajole. What I really wanted to do was stay and get to know him and, if I'm honest, play some more. I had become entirely insatiable. I've always been impatient, but where Adam was concerned my impatience took on mammoth proportions. I didn't want to have to wait until he summoned me again, but neither did I want to relinquish the way that waiting made me feel. It was clear as crystal to us both that I would wait, for as long as it took. Even if I didn't see Adam for months I would never give up hope of him summoning me to him again.

As I made my way back to my office I realised that it was way past closing time and the offices along the corridor from mine were empty, giving the building an eerie feel. How could I let my session with Adam take on such importance? After all, I had spent an exceptionally good time with Rosie and Steve, and Mac had been an unbelievable turn-on. Alex had too, in his own way – he had excited me to distraction. But Adam was different. For me Adam was so different the rest paled into insignificance. It was as if the others had only been there to show me just how adventurous I could be and to exaggerate how I wanted to experiment.

I had thought that I wanted lots of different styles of sex, if you can call sexual preferences styles, but since leaving Adam's office, I accepted that I needed to come to terms with the fact that I was definitely a submissive woman. To the likes of Adam I was anyway. Adam had thrilled me in a way I hadn't thought possible and, in a way, he had me spellbound. If I had my way I would still be in his office, even if it meant just kneeling as I had before, waiting for his next whim. What on earth had come over me?

I sat at my desk, loath to go home. If I went home it would mean breaking the feeble ties I had with Adam. At least while we were still in the same building there was a chance that he'd come to see me, or phone me. But of course he didn't. I suppose I knew deep down that he wouldn't. I might get my kicks from waiting and anticipating Adam's next move but Adam's need was to make me wait. It was sheer torment.

As I sat thinking I remembered the pegs still clutched in my palm and uncurled my hand to look at this latest ploy of Adam's to keep me in a state of anticipation. It was working so well. Mesmerised by the tiny shiny chrome pegs, I tried for the first time to imagine how they would feel attached to my nipples. Obviously I knew they would hurt but I had a feeling the pain would be luscious. I had certainly liked it when Adam had slapped my bottom and that had hurt. Also, I loved the idea of being spanked and I knew that would hurt in a strange sort of way. Perhaps now was the time to get in touch with Mr Anonymous? I guessed that my recollections of any sexual encounter would excite Adam. My thoughts turned back to the pegs and I knew I couldn't wait.

My door was closed and the other offices were empty anyway, so I knew I was safe to experiment. By the time I had exposed my breasts, my hands were shaking badly so it was hard to hold the peg open and line its jaws up with my hardened nipple. I took a few deep breaths and steadied my breast with one hand. I lowered the open end of the peg into place but I was too frightened to let it go. My nipple was swelling with arousal and I could feel the coldness of the chrome closing round it. I took a deep breath and let the tension in my fingertips relax.

At first, as the jaws closed, the sensation was exquisite, sending waves of delicate tremors through me. But as I relaxed and let my fingers relinquish control completely, the tight crushing pain almost crashed through my upper torso. I think I actually cried out, so it was a good thing I was alone. I don't know how to describe the pain as it washed over me. It was certainly thrilling and totally sexual. The knowledge that Adam had instructed me to carry out this torment helped of course. I began to believe that I would be able to tolerate anything if Adam was the instigator and it pleased him for me to comply.

I would have thought that the pain would increase as the peg stayed on, but the reverse happened; as I relaxed into the pain it began to diminish and change. Did I dare to let go of it though? I wanted to put the other one on too but actually letting go was a scary thought. If my hands had been shaking before, now they were more or less uncontrollable.

My hand tentatively relaxed to see what happened and it wasn't as bad as I had thought. The pain didn't increase so I picked up the other peg and, quite courageously I like to think, put it on my other nipple without a pause.

Forcing myself not to touch the pretty chrome pegs that bobbed on the ends of my breasts, I put my hands underneath my thighs in an attempt to trap them. It only just worked; I was breathing in short ragged gasps to absorb the pain from the second peg that was now in place, while the first just tingled and throbbed. I knew that all I had to do was wait for a few more seconds and the pain from the second peg would transform itself as the first had, but it was all I could do not to take them off.

I decided to count to ten and if the pain still hadn't abated I would give up. Closing my eyes I started to count. I thought of Adam and his mad instructions while the weight from the pegs pulled downward wonderfully, deadening the pain.

'Good girl.' Adam's voice invaded my thoughts and my eyes flew open.

He was standing in front of my desk with the widest grin on his face I had ever seen. I hadn't heard a thing; he had managed to walk into my office without me noticing even a change in the air. Up until that moment the most response I had ever seen from him was his unfathomable grin that had left me confused on more than one occasion. But this was unmistakable. Adam was so pleased with himself he was almost laughing. I went to take the pegs off, ashamed that he had caught me being so rude, but he told me to stop.

'Come here, Joanna.'

Without questioning his instructions for even a brief second I stood up and walked around the table. The pegs jiggled about, tugging painfully on my tender breasts. My heart rate increased instantly and the pain immediately changed to exquisite pleasure. I thrust my chest out to him shamelessly and he laughed out loud.

'You are such a barefaced hussy, Joanna. How did I

know that you would be so greedy even after the magnificent orgasm you had not more than ten minutes ago, that you would come back here and have to play? Put your hands on your head.'

I stretched my arms up as directed and my breasts rose with them, adding to the intensity of the pegs. Adam touched them gently and I gasped from deep within at the feeling his touch created. Adam caressed the globes of flesh and jiggled the pegs until I was gasping with every ragged breath. I could feel wetness on my thighs.

'Walk up and down for me, Joanna. You look so beautiful with my gifts dangling from your superb breasts. Parade yourself for me. I can almost feel what you are experiencing. I can read every sensation from your face. You are feeling confused about how much you want to obey me and tormented because a small part of you still would like to tell me to fuck off. I know you are feeling the perfect mix of pleasure that is almost counterbalanced by the hurt but not quite. But even that is bewildering you. Am I right?'

I groaned my agreement of his appraisal of the diabolical situation I found myself in. I was all those things he said and more. However much the pegs were squashing my crushed nipples I had to keep them on because Adam was still giving me attention. I would do anything for him not to stop. Already I was desperate to come; the reaction my body had to his control was phenomenal. An hour ago I would have had to be told twice at least, but now I almost immediately started walking the few paces from where he stood to the far wall and back again. It didn't occur to me to take my hands down, so I walked as I was, waiting for his next instruction.

Every time I turned and walked past him again he

would reach out and touch the pegs. He didn't do it to hurt me, just to emphasise my feelings, and it worked. Every time I knew he was going to do it I held my breath anticipating the delicious humiliation, and each time it came and ran down my spine like molten lava I shuddered but grew in stature. I was proud that I was pleasing him; I don't know why. I began almost to strut. I thrust my breasts out to show them at their best, but it was obviously not what he wanted.

The next time I went to pass Adam and expected the gentle knocking, he took hold of both pegs and held me in place. He turned me around until I was standing in front of him again and kept hold of them. All he did was fiddle with the pegs, but the effect it had was incredible. The intensity of my reaction was shocking to me and, I like to think, to him too. I trembled violently as the intense spasms of sensation kicked though my body. I almost collapsed onto the floor as he jiggled and dragged my breasts this way and that. Funny, but I still kept my hands on my head. I must have been learning his ways.

Adam kept up the onslaught until my breasts and nipples were screaming with pain, and my pussy was screaming even harder for attention.

'Oh, fuck. What are you doing to me? I've never felt anything like this . . .'

'Shhh!' Adam smiled quietly almost to himself and one of his hands left my breast and wormed its way between my thighs. He tutted loudly when he found my river of juice and chuckled to himself as his fingers delved into it. His fingers massaged my sopping wet clit for no more than ten seconds before the contractions shuddered through me. As soon as he knew I was in the throes his hand again took up the peg that was gripping my nipple. My breasts were lifted high as the thrilling spasms racked my weakening body. I longed to collapse on the floor but his unremitting encouragement forced me up onto my toes. I thought the tremors of my crashing orgasm would never stop but, of course, eventually they did.

As I came down from paradise he tenderly let me return to a natural standing position and, within two seconds and while I was still throbbing in places I had never throbbed before, he left the room. As he left he turned, grinned and said, 'Hmm! Very good, Joanna. I think we are going to enjoy each other very much.' He turned to go and then remembered something else.

'Perhaps you had better increase the half an hour to an hour, otherwise it won't be a challenge to a naughty little slut like you, will it?''

I stumbled back onto the edge of my desk to recover. My clothes were all over the place, my legs were still trembling and my clitoris was throbbing and spasming still as if my orgasm was reluctant to abate. The sweat was sticking my hair to my scalp and I knew that I must look like the slut Adam had called me. I smiled to myself and whispered, 'You ain't seen nothing yet, Mr Jacamann.' I carefully removed the pegs, sending fresh shivers though my breasts, and tidied myself up before I left for home. I took my knickers out of my bag and slipped them back on; the trickle of wetness on my inner thighs was enough to prompt me into a shiver of shame. It didn't last long; soon I was riding my bike home enthusiastically with the saddle clutched between my legs, grinding up into my tired pussy.

12

Exhaustion completely incapacitated me after I got home. I dropped onto my bed tied up in knots about the way Adam had made me feel. How could I allay my fears about the roller coaster of emotions he had put me through? Up until Adam, OK, I had been a little naïve, but at least I knew who I was. Now I was totally screwed up about what I felt and how I could cope with the mixture of relationships that were scattered through my life.

Even the magical games I was playing with the punters were enough to send me into utter turmoil about my sexuality and whether I should be doing all those rude things with people I didn't know. While I was doing the unspeakably vulgar acts with a variety of men and women, I didn't care a jot about what was right and wrong, but in my bed at night it all felt just a little sordid. Each specific game, if I thought about it individually, was not the one that made me ashamed. Rosie and Steve had blown me away. Mac had not only blown me away but wormed his way a little into my heart too. Actually, so had Rosie, if the truth were known. So ... when I analysed all the separate experiences I'd had, none of them actually shamed me at all, so I put the whole thing down to my perception of what society expects of single women.

I had no one to answer to so I put all worries aside and thought about my next encounter. This game would take on a whole new meaning. The image of being forced had for me, like many other women, fuelled many a fantasy. Of course the actual horror of true rape didn't even come into it, but the desire to be taken by a man or men of my choice was a mainstay in most of my masturbation sessions. I suppose that was why Adam managed to pick me so cleverly. There is clearly an ingredient in my make-up that shrieks at a dominant man, 'here I am, control me'.

I lay wide awake for what seemed like hours, just running over and over in my head what was happening in my life and at the end of all the soul searching I decided to get on with it and stop worrying. I was loving every minute of my encounters for Joanna's Journal, so why upset things? Why rock the boat? And, as for Adam, I don't think that at that stage I could have stopped if I'd tried. The added attraction of knowing that Adam would get a kick from hearing me relaying my experience to him added to the overall thrill of the unknown.

Joanna's Journal had actually become my excuse for trying any sexual fantasy I liked, so who was I to put a spanner in the works? What I was finding was that with every new episode, others would present themselves to me. When I played with Rosie and Steve, all I could think of afterwards was having a one on one with Rosie or testing my reactions to more of Nick's control. When I was with Mac all I could think of afterwards was how it would be to have had Mac and his mate Jim in a more comfortable environment. I would have taken great pleasure in taking them both to bed and experimenting together. I didn't doubt that the outcome would have been very interesting indeed.

Already, after my treatment at the hands of Adam that afternoon, I was imagining more. I wondered what it would be like if he instructed me to pleasure another man in his presence, or another woman come to that. I then drifted off into a fantasy where Adam sat on a high throne and on his lap sat Rosie. He beckoned me up the long run of stairs, up to the dais on which the throne sat. He then held Rosie back in his arms and told her to open her legs and hold her pussy open for me to lick. He actually held her legs back and open and then watched in complete fascination as I sucked, nibbled and licked Rosie to a shuddering climax. Occasionally, when I elicited an especially loud groan from Rosie, Adam would pat me on the head like a dog and tell me what a good girl I was.

My whole life had changed. I had never been particularly gregarious but lately I had become totally isolated in my job and Adam. I didn't really mind because that was all I could think of at the time and I revelled in my fantasies. I found that no sooner did one experience finish than I wanted a new one to start. I didn't actually want to have to wait for the readers of *Leather and Lace* to digest all my suggestions and choose whom I was to see. I was becoming insatiable. Even as I lay on the bed recovering from my meeting with Adam, and while my nipples still tingled from the pegs, I was moving onto my next game and I knew it had to be the twins.

What a perfectly exquisite turn-on it was to imagine two identical men and how it would be having them both at the same time. I wondered what they looked like and if they had ever even partly tried their fantasy. I actually wanted to meet them that minute but as usual I was being greedy and knew I had to be patient and wait until the readers of Joanna's Journal picked them. There would still be ages to wait but I had to accept that and try to get on with things.

Lying on the bed with Adam still in my thoughts and the twins vying for supremacy, I made one rather unsporting decision; I was going to see the twins even if they weren't chosen. I was going to cheat if I had to. So far all I'd done was make sure that when I wanted one particular party to be picked, like Rosie or Mac, I'd weighted the attraction of that one and put it with a group of boring, ordinary offers and it had worked a treat. But this time I would cheat if that was what it took for me to have my own way. I didn't really feel very guilty at all. Anyway, the people who read Joanna's Journal would still get a racy, stimulating piece to read, so what was the difference? I managed to convince myself.

My mind drifted to the Internet and all the fun I'd had on it so I thought I would spend a couple of hours trying to enter a chat room. I had attempted it before but hadn't quite got it right. I'd had at least a dozen men with very dodgy nicknames like Jungle Warrior and Red Eye clamouring to 'talk' to me, but I had been unable to find the way to 'talk' back to them. I grabbed a sandwich and a cup of tea and sat at my computer. Quite excited at the thought of talking to someone I had never met, I logged on and, after an hour of trial and error, I finally got the hang of it.

What fun it was to sit there in my own sitting room with my feet still in comfy slippers having decidedly rude conversations with strangers. I was astonished to discover just how readily people will talk about their most intimate sexual fantasies without even knowing what each other looked like. I found after a while that I didn't mind either. I found a chat room on a site for people in sub/dom relationships, hoping I might get some insight into what made Adam tick. Oh, how right I was. I had to make up a name, so I called myself Sub-chik, which was a bit of a play on the spelling because apparently there was already someone else with the name spelled correctly. That put me off a little but I soon got over it and signed in. All I said was that I was a woman who had recently found out that I was sexually submissive and I thought it would be good to talk to other like-minded people who could answer my queries. Within seconds my screen was like the Blackpool illuminations.

'Sub-chik, let me dominate you. I could make you crawl.'

'Kneel for me now, Sub-chik, I am your Master.'

'Slut, I am your new Master and I will punish you severely if you don't immediately agree to serve me.'

There were at least twenty or so messages that followed along those lines and completely put me off. I couldn't think why they thought I might even consider their suggestions. But, just as I was giving up hope of finding someone I could just chat to I noticed one that stood apart from the others in its simplicity.

'I'm a dominant man. My name is Controller. How can I help you, Sub-chik?'

Just his name thrilled me to the core and after he had explained to me how to do it we moved to a private room where we could chat away and not be disturbed by the others who had been a bit daunting for me.

It was time-consuming typing one line and then waiting for a reply, but it was easily learned and I cottoned on fast.

'Thanks for being ordinary, and not like the others,' I typed, to break the ice.

'I don't think I have ever been called ordinary before, but go ahead, Sub-chik, how can I help you?'

'I have just had a very exciting experience with a man that I now know to be dominant. It was a little scary but also extremely exhilarating. I can't begin to imagine what he will ask of me next.'

'What did he do to you this time that made you scared, and what was it that scared you?'

'This is really embarrassing.'

'Don't be silly, Sub-chik. You are never going to have to meet me so you can say anything. Come on, be brave and tell me what he did to you.'

'Well, he made me put pegs on myself and told me that I had to wear them for a few minutes every day until I could suffer the pain for half an hour.'

'Where did he make you put them?'

'On my nipples.'

'That thought is very stimulating for me, Sub-chik. How did that make you feel?'

Before I even had a chance to answer that one, another sentence came through, breaking our rhythm and showing to me just how eager Controller was getting. 'Did you like it?'

I got a little braver knowing that my words were thrilling him and, after pausing for a second or two, I answered.

'It hurt at first but as soon as I got used to it the pain turned into pleasure and yes, I did enjoy it. What I want to know is what is likely to come next?'

'First I would love you to describe your tits to me so I can imagine them with pegs on. Were they garden pegs?'

'Big, I'm afraid. I wear a double E cup and the pegs were little chrome ones that are used as paper clips.' I carried on explaining, and knowing that I was turning him on was also turning me on. 'They tugged downward on my crushed nipples and jiggled about when he made me walk across the room. What do you think he will make me do next?'

'Well, sweetheart, if it was me I would bind your tits until they stick out and the pegs are almost forced off your tender nipples and the flesh of your tits bulges around the rope. Then I would push a large dildo into your sexy cunt and another fat one up your arse. Then I'd tie them in place with a crotch rope. When those toys are in place I would put a large penis gag in your mouth until your jaws were forced apart and your mouth was stuffed full, tie your hands behind your back and pull you across my hard knees. Then, Sub-chik, can you guess what I would do next?'

'?????' That was all I could manage. I was palpitating crazily.

'I would spank you, Sub-chik, to within an inch of your life. However much you sobbed and pleaded. However much you begged, I would paddle away until your arse cheeks with the crotch rope dissecting them were purple.'

'Oh, Christ. Sorry, Controller, I've got to go. There is someone at my door.'

I came out of the site immediately, petrified by the things he had told me, but as usual aroused beyond belief about the thought of a spanking. Even with the threat of it being more than I could stand it still delighted me. The suggestions he had made shocked me more than I can say and I had to try really hard even to imagine what he was describing. I had no idea what a crotch rope was but I would have loved to find out; the idea of it was wonderful. How could you bind breasts? And ... why was it so electrifying when he referred to my breasts as tits? He had also called my pussy by the C-word and that thrilled me too, just as it had when Adam had used the same forbidden word. I tried to visualise what I would look like with a dildo in each of my orifices and a hot purple bottom where it had been soundly spanked. I shook my head to clear the thoughts raging through my brain.

Only minutes later I sat curled up on the sofa with the computer switched off and memories of Mr Anonymous's words running through my mind, causing yet more oozing from places that Controller wanted to stuff full of dildos. It appeared that Mr Anonymous was destined to flit through my thoughts every time any type of spanking or punishment was mentioned. I was more than intrigued to know if the punishment he threatened would be as harsh as the ones suggested by my friend on the Internet. I wished I hadn't come out of the site so readily. I knew in retrospect that, regardless of what he was saying, he couldn't ever carry out his threats unless I consented. So I could have played with him awhile. Oh well, I put it behind me and for the millionth time I toyed with the idea of giving Mr Anonymous a ring just to see what he was about.

I had started keeping his brief letters apart from the rest; there were four now and they all sent the same message – 'I know you, Joanna'. I read them over and over, trying to gain more information, but his promises still elated me however familiar his words became or how well I could recite them. I even found the sentence, 'I know you, Joanna' playing repeatedly through my brain like a stuck record.

Don't be stupid, Joanna, I told myself, you know exactly what he is wanting and unless you definitely want to experiment with spanking then I suggest you leave him to those submissive women who know that's what they want.

One of the things that confused me was the way Mr Anonymous had become the spokesman in my mind for all the men in my life who enjoyed controlling me. There was Adam with his serious domination, Mac who liked to choreograph every move we made; that was a sort of control wasn't it? There was also Alex who had slapped my bottom and Mr Anonymous had become the voice of them all. Just the circumstance of his being anonymous made him almost fictitious, so I could apportion his suggestions to all and sundry.

Over the following days I just went through the motions of daily life, trying to be as normal as possible. All I wanted to do was go and hammer on Adam's door and beg him to do something. Can you see how bizarre it all was? I didn't even have a clue what it was he might do to me but I wanted it anyway. I realised that he might actually want to perform all the diabolical acts that Controller had gleefully explained. And the pegs were just the first innocent stepping stone. Perhaps that was the sort of thing that all dominants do. Would I want Adam to be in command of me to that extent? Would I trust him enough to let him take control totally? What if he did gag me as Controller had suggested and I hated what he did while I was helpless? What would I do? I would just have to accept his decisions and suffer his choice of game without even being able to say, 'hey that hurts' or 'no, please don't do that'.

I am utterly mortified to admit that even at that early stage, all of the above thrilled me in the most fantastic manner. I didn't care what he chose to put me through as long as I didn't have to wait too long for it. By the second week it was clear that Adam was going to keep to his word and that I wouldn't see him again until after I had seen the twins.

As instructed, I had practised with the pegs and could proudly strut around my place for hours with them on. To begin with they would sting but after only a few minutes they had the desired effect of arousing me and making me think of Adam; not that I didn't think of him all the time anyway. Occasionally I would remember what he had said as I'd left, about putting them somewhere else. The only place I could think of was my pussy and I was almost convinced that he wouldn't mean that. I wasn't quite sure though, so I sat in front of my mirror one day and looked closely at my silky shaven mound. I pulled on each crinkly fold and tried to pluck up courage to put on the pegs. I thought that if I did it before I met Adam again it would be a lot easier, but I couldn't pluck up what it took to carry it out. I couldn't let go.

The mirror in my bedroom became a regular stopping place for me. I would pace up and down with my breasts dangling and bouncing as I walked. The wicked little pegs would jerk about with a life of their own as I swished from one room to another. I would sit and watch telly with them on but every few minutes I just had to go into the bedroom to have a look. Of course I could see them by looking down, but the only way I could even imagine how I looked to Adam was to use a mirror. I would touch them and gently flick them to illicit shivery shudders of delight through my whole body.

When I sat in front of my mirror on a hard-backed chair it was all I could do to keep my hands off myself. I could quite happily masturbate ten times a day, but I found that the more I did the more horny I became, so I tried to ration myself. The little pegs did their dirty work though and I would succumb at least three times daily. When I woke up in the morning I would lie in bed and think naughty thoughts and that was hopeless. Then as soon as I came home after working on rude letters and horny stories all day that was impossible.

By the time I went to bed I had usually had my practice with the pegs and sat in front of the mirror, so what could I do but indulge?

Anyway, as you can see, I spent weeks just thinking, working and doing sex until it was time to count the results of the issue that offered the twins as a potential game for me. I didn't need to worry about cheating – by this time I was getting bags of post but there were more votes for the boys than there were for all the others put together. Yet again I was to have what I wanted.

13

'Hi, could I book a block of sessions in your gym please? I am a beginner, so I would need to be shown the ropes.' The phone call was surprisingly easy.

'Sure. When would you like to come? I can offer you afternoons or evenings.' The voice on the other end was male and velvety. I wondered if it was one of the twins.

'Well, I'm staying in your area for a few days and I need to shape up a bit. I have heard you are the place to go. Early evening would probably be best. Do you have vacancies for Monday, Tuesday and Wednesday next week?'

'Uh huh. We can do Monday and Tuesday at seven p.m. for an hour and Wednesday at eight p.m. Would they be OK?'

'Excellent, thanks.'

'Could I take your name please?'

'Mmm, it's Joanna Anderson.' There wasn't a pause or so much as a minute inflection in his voice as he confirmed the booking and said they would be looking forward to seeing me. Again I wondered if that had been one of them.

I decided that I just had to take Baby. What better way to pose at a gym than to arrive in a soft-top sports car? I just hoped it wouldn't be too chilly. The gym was in Southend on Sea so I had to decide which would be best. I could either drive there each night or prevail on the generosity of Jacamann Publishing yet again and rent a room in a hotel somewhere.

Because I was practically the boss's mistress I thought I should at least stay somewhere nice, so I phoned the local Tourist Board and they put me onto a hotel that they assured me would be perfect for my needs. I threw caution to the wind and ordered a room with its own private bathroom and a small lounge. I was informed it was a suite but I thought I would reserve judgement. I was also told it had a view of the sea but again I took this with a pinch of salt.

I spent the Saturday before I was due to go shopping for some clothes for the workout. It was not the easiest thing in the world to find an outfit that would travel well from the gym to the scene the twins were planning, but the choice I made after hours of searching was just the right combination. I even bought some new very expensive trainers, wondering if I could claim on expenses. I was certainly going to try.

When I got home after an exhausting but fun few hours, I tried on all my purchases. A cropped pair of leggings in black shiny Lycra topped by a sort of G-string that went over the top of the leggings and cut right up my bottom, pulling the tight Lycra over my cheeks. The G-string was white and came as a set with a tiny crop top that forced my breasts into the spotlight and accentuated my nipples. Since I had been training my nipples with the pegs, they had taken on a life of their own and were erect, from the moment my mind focused in the morning until I dropped into sleep at night. I added the white Nike footwear and a pair of sports socks which showed off the tan I had. I was quite proud of the way I looked and yet again got prematurely excited. I was becoming insatiable. I tried to commit to memory how I felt, as I stood prepared for the game, so I could tell Adam.

Monday finally arrived as Mondays tend to do, and

Baby and I made the short journey to Southend in an hour and a half. The sun was shining, making the day even more perfect if that were possible. The A130 was the only fly in the ointment as I sang to the radio. Bumper to bumper traffic as far as I could see only slightly dampened my spirits. I was even more wound up for this game than I had been for the others, I suppose because now Adam was a part of it too. I couldn't decide then, two hours before my appointment, which aspect was more stimulating – the twins or Adam.

I had done the hotel an injustice. Not only was it very pleasant but there really was a view of the sea, and a breathtaking one too. Their other claim had been well founded too; the bedroom was large and airy with a king-size bed, the shower room was small but absolutely functional and the sitting room was pretty and intimate, with chintzy easy chairs and a mismatching sofa, a small television in the corner with a coffee-making area next to it. All in all it was a suitable abode for anything that might happen later. I had no idea how the men planned to set up the abduction or even if there was to be an abduction, but I couldn't wait to find out. The only part of the whole thing that was a put-off was the possibility that it might not happen that night. And even that, if I am honest, was a turn-on anyway. I just felt that after having Adam make me wait for his attention, waiting for this too would be far too much to bear.

I showered early and took all the time I wanted to get ready, sitting on the edge of the sink to shave my pussy baby-soft. Just to look at the bare rude flesh between my thighs was enough to set me dribbling. I massaged moisturiser into my skin after shaving and let the soothing cream soak in. I finished off by misting a fine spray of Clinique Elixir over my exceedingly hungry body.

The tightness of the Lycra and the way it accentuated the hairless crevice between my legs was rather embarrassing. If I looked carefully I could make out the gradual bulge of my pussy and even the slight nub of my clitoris. I found myself hoping that I didn't get too turned on in the gym; the puffiness of arousal would make things impossible to ignore. Then I remembered just how wet I had been getting lately with all this submission and dreaded what the evening would bring.

After finding out the directions to the gym from the friendly hotel receptionist I left and climbed into Baby. It took me about ten minutes to drive across town and I arrived with minutes to spare, parked Baby in a safe place and, shaking at the knees, entered the foyer. It looked just like every gym I had ever seen on television, with clean bright areas for sitting and waiting. I announced myself at the desk and was told to go along the green corridor and I would be met at the other end.

'I think you're booked with Jack. He is running a little late tonight, so please make yourself at home and start a warm-up. There are a couple of girls already here who'll show you what to do. Jack will be with you as soon as possible. Oh, and Miss Anderson? He sends his apologies.' I quaked badly as I walked down the long corridor. On either side were doors that led to saunas, steam rooms, changing rooms and staff areas. At the end of the corridor ahead of me I could see the looming shapes of equipment through double swing doors. The doors reminded me of the ones that lead into operating theatres and that didn't help my nerves one iota.

'Hi, you must be Joanna,' said a female instructor brightly. 'Welcome. We are just about to start if you would like to join us. Right, ladies, walking on the spot please.' Still there was no sign of anyone acting suspiciously. The pretty girl's lilac leotard put mine to shame. She led the group of four through a basic warmup routine. I took the opportunity to have a look around me and found that again there was nothing out of the ordinary – just a regular gym with what appeared to be regular clients.

Sophie the instructor, with her tight perfect body, started stretching high above her head. We copied her moves tentatively. 'Come on, ladies, I'm sure you can do better than that.'

I was puffing and panting by the end of the ten-minute warm-up. Sophie had pushed us really hard and we were all glowing like beacons; it was most unsexy. There was still no sign of Jack as I continued the obligatory bends and stretches, acutely aware of the sight I must look from behind, with my legs spread apart, my arms dangling down to my toes, rocking from one side to the other. I could feel the tight string of my G-string cutting tightly between my cheeks and wondered if Jack and his brother were somewhere watching. I hoped so. I hoped they could see just how my breasts thrust forward when I did a particular stretch that Sophie seemed keen on.

There I was with my legs spread apart again, my arms behind me with the palms flat on the base of my spine. I knew there must be damp patches under my arms and probably in other awful places, but we were all in the same boat, even Sophie.

'Come on, ladies, push those elbows and shoulders back. You should be able to feel your breasts lift if you are doing it correctly. Now is not the time to be shy. Can you feel what is happening to your breasts, girls?'

I mumbled a 'yes'. Anyone would think I was talking to Adam. Just as the other girls moaned in sympathy with each other, the double doors opened. Oh yes. I just knew that had to be Jack. The other girls and Sophie preened before this god. Stomachs were pulled in tight and buttocks squeezed. He was at least six foot. His body was exactly how you would imagine the owner of a gym's to be. A few too many pumped-up muscles for me but superbly fit and bronzed. He strode across the room knowing that every eye was on him. He grinned, baring sparkling white teeth and winked in our direction. Oh dear – that was a bit over the top, I thought. He was starting to look like a Thunderbird. Once that thought had reared its ugly head I was unable to think of anything else.

This posing Adonis was wearing a very brief pair of tight Lycra shorts and not much else. On closer inspection his chest was actually so big that his nipples looked as if they had been stuck on as an afterthought, and I began to be seriously disappointed. He even ran his hands sensuously over his glistening torso. I tried so hard just to see the aesthetic beauty of this man that every other girl present noticeably adored and craved, but once I had noticed how shallow he appeared to be it was impossible. I was half expecting him to lick his lips like a porn star. He even stood in front of us while we were still warming up and started massaging his massive thigh muscles. By that stage I wished I could crawl away.

'Pack it in, John. You do this every week. Leave us alone to get on. How can you expect my ladies to concentrate with you showing off in front of them?'

John! His name was John, not Jack. Thank God for that. I don't know what I would have done if he had been Jack. It would have been the first time I had refused to comply with my brief.

John sauntered sensuously away over to the other

side of the room and we moved to the equipment. There were so many exciting bits of equipment to try. A couple of the girls started on the running machines and got into a gossipy conversation about John. One of the others asked Sophie to help her with thigh curls. This amazing piece of apparatus called for the user to lie down on her stomach on a bench that was shaped to make the bottom stick right up in the air, while a bar was lifted and lowered by the feet. It was rude and sensuous. I suppose if I had come just to work out it would have been easier, but all these bodies and suggestive movements were sending me crazy – a powerful foreplay to something that might not even happen tonight.

I stood hypnotised as Sophie helped her to use the piece properly. I could only stand and watch helplessly, trying not to picture what an adventurous man could do with her body in that position. What I could do with her in that position even; she was a very fit attractive girl. It wasn't easy and I lost myself for a second or two in the rhythm of her contortions and the image of her pleasing bottom.

''Ello love, you must be Joanna.'

I spun around to face the man who broke through my lurid thoughts. He was grinning his welcome. His extremely cheeky grin and knowing green eyes told me immediately that this was indeed Jack. As he put his hand out to shake mine I had the chance to look at him properly and, even though his outward appearance, with his crew cut and broken tooth, didn't stand a chance against the torso of John, this man was pure animal. He looked a tad like an East End villain with a rugged craggy face and hard solid body. I even think his nose might have been broken at one time. The overall picture was one of a sexy man with a slightly mean streak. He looked forbidding. The type of man that would make your mother cringe inside but also makes every hot-blooded woman cringe in a different way.

'Jack,' he offered, as he looked me up and down. 'Shall we get started?'

Jack put a friendly arm over my shoulder and walked me past the other girls who were busily chatting and straining, over to a short bench.

'Sit astride this, love, and I'll show you what to do. This exercise is extremely good for the chest muscles.' Jack looked blatantly at my chest muscles and the heat of my embarrassment spread from my chest, up my neck to my face. After I had sat down with my inner thighs stretched apart over the width of the bench, he helped me to place my forearms behind two large leather cushions that were attached to vertical metal bars. A chest press, he called it.

'OK, it's easy. All you have to do is push your elbows towards each other.'

This had to be the most vulnerable position imaginable. My arms were trapped behind the pads that in turn not only pushed my breasts out but also left them helpless to protect themselves. My nipples were unashamedly popping out behind the soft material of my crop top, begging for attention.

Jack stood to the side of me, adjusting the weights that determined how easy it was for me to push the bars towards each other. His hard torso was bare from the waist up. His legs were encased in a classy pair of joggers that clung probably more than was necessary and emphasised a swelling in the crotch area. Casually leaning against the side of my defenceless breast he managed without any visible movement to surrep-titiously brush against it. I moaned softly to show him what he was doing to me but he totally ignored my attempt to change the status quo. Knowing I should go along with what he had described as his fantasy, I pretended that this was just a visit to the gym with a hunky trainer. It was difficult not to show how much I was enjoying the lead-in to this most electrifying of games.

'OK, babe, try that. That should do the trick. Just pull your arms together gently and let your legs relax.'

He did it again; as he mentioned my legs he looked pointedly at them, concentrating on the growing damp patch in my crotch. He smiled right at me then, showing his slightly crooked teeth that did nothing at all to diminish his attributes. I don't know to this day just what it was that Jack had that other men don't – perhaps it was his sheer arrogance. He didn't need to preen and strut in front of women; his natural confidence was a magnet. Without the pretty looks or the massive body of John, the beefcake poser, he managed to exude all the temptation that I, for one, found absolutely irresistible. I wanted him to fuck me there and then.

One of my feet was turning inward and instead of telling me, which would probably have been adequate, Jack, while standing the opposite side of the bench, bent over my legs and straightened my foot. His head was within six inches of my crotch. He paused in that position and audibly breathed in through his nose. My poor stomach somersaulted in reaction to this provocation. I didn't know how long I could continue pretending I was just a normal customer if he kept up this barrage of suggestive behaviour. I was desperate now. I even began to suspect that Jack was enjoying toying with me, in which case he would probably not make a move on the first night. How could I possibly wait and go through all this again tomorrow, not knowing if it would be then either? I was annoyed with myself for agreeing to book three sessions.

Jack sat on the other end of my bench facing me and watched my breasts tighten and lift with each movement I made. I pushed myself to the limit until my arms were shaking with tension and the sweat was running down my face in rivulets, but still he encouraged and watched.

'That's it, girlie. Show me what you're made of. Come on, shove that chest out. Ten more, Joanna.' Panting with exertion I kept up the pace of close and open that had us both hypnotised. My pussy was tingling and hot and of course sticky with sweat and other more disgusting secretions. Jack loved it. He put his large hands on my knees and gently pushed my legs further apart, almost shouting at me now to carry on with the chest exercise. I was desperate to move up a notch but he was clear in his treatment of me that he intended to do this his way. Seven, eight, nine, ten, my head screamed.

'Jack, I can't do any more,' I croaked, as I almost collapsed with exhaustion. My chest was heaving and my tongue was sticking to the roof of my mouth. Jack gently helped me to take my arms from behind the pads; I was too knackered to move.

'Gutsy. I like that in a woman. You did well, love; perhaps you should call it a day now. After all, we don't want you to be too tired, do we?' It was the first time Jack had made any allusion to our agreement and it sent a shiver down my spine. I carefully got off the bench wondering if I should try something else or call it a day. I hoped that Jack would make it clear what he had in mind but all he did was ask if I wanted to have a go at the toning tables. He assured me that they were gentler than the chest press. I followed him to a room off the gym, watching his tight hard bum as he walked. No one appeared to take any notice of us as we disappeared. As yet I hadn't seen any sign of Jack's brother and yet again I wondered if they were identical.

The room was bathed in a soft pink light that turned the peculiar contraptions into strange shapes. Jack led me over to a padded table that looked on the surface to be like a massage table, but when he asked me to lie on it I noticed that it was indeed very different. The half of the bed that was under my bottom and legs was split down the middle. I couldn't think why it would be in two separate halves – I am so stupid sometimes. I was sitting up examining the strange gap when Jack took hold of my shoulders and pushed me down onto the pillow area. His hands were firm and warm on my shoulders. The bed was quite comfortable but, before I even had time to think, Jack had switched on a motor close to my head and the leg sections began to move.

The top half of the bed stayed where it was with my torso lying on it comfortably, but my legs were being moved apart as if the bed had a will of its own. Or Jack's will, perhaps. To start with the movement was almost imperceptible but within two or three minutes the movement became quicker and my legs were scissoring apart at the rate of one second each direction. Jack observed my movements in a rather detached way and I have to say that it was even hornier than if he had been leering. I felt as if he knew exactly what all this was doing to me and all he had to do was wait and I would be ready; a bit like waiting for a cake to cook – you've mixed it with all the right ingredients, put it in the oven and all you have to do is wait for it to bake.

I began to notice that, with each opening of the legs of my bed, the gap was widening. The muscles at the top of my thighs were being stretched further and further apart until it almost became unbearable, especially coupled with the stirrings in my stomach. Just as I wanted to bawl that I was cooked and ready, Jack stopped the machine. He must have done this many times before because, with the skill of a practised man, he stopped it with my legs at their widest.

'Ouch!' I cried. My thighs were screaming.

'Shhh,' Jack coaxed. He moved around the bed and walked casually between my stretched legs, right up close to me until his hardened cock, which was now clearly visible through his joggers, pushed against my wet crotch. The jolt of his touch shot through me, sending me into a shameful ragged breath display. I couldn't help myself. If only I could just rip my clothes off and let him take me there and then. But, as usual, I let Jack call all the shots. I lay back and tried to let myself just enjoy whatever he chose to do. What girl wouldn't? I wanted him to rip off my clothes and shove his cock so far in me I choked on it. I imagined him taking hold of the gusset of my leggings and tearing them apart, displaying my naked pussy and tearing into me regardless of the fact that I am begging him to stop. As if I would be begging him to do anything but fuck me.

Before that thought could take momentum I heard the door open, and walking towards us was a replica of Jack. Captivated I turned my head towards him to watch as he approached the table. My fantasy was complete. For the life of me I couldn't remember his name, but it didn't matter. This clone had a gold hoop earring and a gold tooth where Jack's was broken. My God, even their dental history was the same. He walked around the bed until he was standing behind my head. When I looked up I could see him watching Jack, fascinated by what he was doing. They grinned at each other and the gold tooth flashed in the pink light. They actually nodded to each other as if to start the session and everything took on a surreal quality. Even though I could still hear the low murmurs from the other side of the door, we were in a cocoon of mutual desire.

Gold Tooth took hold of the shoulders of my top and pulled them sharply down until they were around the tops of my arms, trapping them in place and pushing my breasts even further out. He stared appreciatively for a few moments then grabbed hold of them with a vice-like grip while Jack pulled aside the G-string that was cutting between my swollen sexlips. His finger probed and pushed its way inside me, taking the material of my leggings with it. My body arched wantonly upward, begging for deeper penetration and more attention to my breasts. I was desperate now and whimpering under my breath.

'Come on, you bastards. Fuck me if you are going to.'

My voice had become guttural and my pleadings sheer vulgarity as I begged for more. Jack and Gold Tooth worked their magic on me until I was a writhing mass of limbs and orifices beseeching them to stick it in me. To stick anything in me.

They stopped! Everything they were doing from the fingers that now were opening me, and the hands that manipulated my quivering breasts, stopped. I was speechless. Almost in tears with frustration, I shouted at both of them to stop fucking around.

'If you are going to do it, then for Christ's sake do it!' I goaded them, hoping it would spur them on. They laughed. It wasn't a cruel laugh, more of a 'we are calling the shots' laugh.

'You haven't got a chance, love. Do you think we've waited all this time for you to tempt us now with your sopping crotch and your incredible fucking tits? That's not the way it works, girlie. Run along home now and come back tomorrow as planned. It won't harm any of us to wait a bit longer. Trust me, love, when you have the Mayhew brothers, you will know you have been had and *we* will do the taking. Isn't that right, Tony?'

'Too right, mate! Trust us, babe, you'll never forget your meeting with the Mayhew brothers.' While he spoke, Tony's fingers strayed back to my body and began lazily to stroke my face. His crotch was so close to my head I could smell his maleness and yet again I shamelessly groaned and arched toward him. Tony gripped hold of my jaw and moved around the head of the toning table until he was standing next to me. Jack just watched, obviously amused by the proceedings, and that excited me even more.

'Open it, babe. Open your mouth for me,' Tony coaxed, while his fingers worked at separating my jaws. I was up for anything and relaxed my grip. As my mouth fell open Tony did the last thing I expected. I hoped he was going to put his cock in – the position was perfect. I wondered if he was going to kiss me and I imagined it would be hard and a little brutal. I would like that. I lay there waiting with my mouth straining open until he gently ran his forefinger around my softened lips. My tongue instantly darted out to welcome it and both of my tormenters chuckled at my eagerness.

'Whoa, whoa, baby. Wait for it.' With that his finger delved in my mouth and I sucked on it hard, grateful for at least something to feast my attentions on.

Tony removed his finger and my mouth gaped and hunted upward like a drowning fish trying to get it back.

'Relax and do as you're told. Open your mouth.' There was an underlying threat in Tony's voice, but it only sent a thrill through my bones. Was I ever only going to meet men that wanted to control me? Or did I attract them? Maybe all men had that streak in them and something in *me* encouraged it to surface. Of course, I obeyed at once. Letting my mouth relax as he had instructed I waited to see what he had in mind. Tony's finger again entered my mouth and toyed with my tongue. It swirled around the interior of my mouth, playing cat and mouse with my tongue. The experience was so teasing and enticing. Tony's other hand still kept hold of my jaw, so I was unable either to resist or encourage when he began to move his finger in and out in a fucking motion. I swear it was as arousing as being fucked.

Jack began to tease my other end and I thought I would explode. His clenched fist was grinding against the material strained across my pussy. I tried to draw my legs together but Jack had other ideas. His body was firmly wedged between my spread thighs so I could do nothing but brazenly writhe to show my encouragement, so I did just that.

'Jack, we have 'ere one very dirty girl. I think when we get her tomorrow or the next day we are going to have to show her just what happens to dirty girls, don't you, Tony?

'Fuck it, Tony. Let's do it now. She's gagging for it.'

I groaned even louder and began again to suck on the finger dancing in my mouth.

'No chance! You know what we agreed. We've waited ages for this and I don't intend to fuck up me chance now just because we're all randy.' There was a hint of menace in his voice but that just added to my longing for action. I wanted to be taken so badly. I wanted them to thrust into me and make me scream with the intensity of their assault. The illicit anticipation of being forced was boiling through my veins. There is a certain stage of arousal in me that can only be satisfied by penetration and nothing else comes even a close second. This was one of those moments,

It was as if Jack's word was law. Within seconds Tony and Jack were solicitously helping me off the table and trying to regulate their breathing by taking deep breaths. My legs were like jelly, so Jack swept me up in his arms and carried me through to the shower room. I assume it must have been part of their private chambers because it was small and empty. I hoped I was going to get a rude shower with the pair of them but he just stood me down, handed me a fluffy white towel and left, closing the door behind them. As the door closed, Jack peeped back in and said, 'We'll see you tomorrow night as planned, babe. Don't be late.'

14

I have to say I was gutted. How could they do that, I ranted in my head. I stomped up and down the tiled room in frustration – I was so annoyed that they had left me, after tormenting me relentlessly. I rashly decided that I would not come again. It was OK for Adam to treat me that way because it was part of the games we played, but if I was going to have to take this disappointment with every man I met I needed to change my ways. Where were all the men that met a willing girl like me and just fucked them?

I shakily sat on a chair in an attempt to calm down. My clothes were sticking to my body with sweat and were cooling rapidly; my pussy was still contracting rhythmically with a need for attention. I stripped off and stepped under the scalding water and washed, trying hard not to linger on any of the places the boys had tormented. My breasts felt bloated and heavy with arousal but my pussy was shamelessly swollen and gaping open. The water poured over my flesh, calming me and softening my resolve until I knew that I would turn up the next night, and the next night if I had to. I really did want to fulfil this promise. I was desperate for these slightly dangerous men to do their worst with me, and I didn't give a damn what my readers or Adam thought at the end of it.

It was so disgusting to have to put back on the sticky sweaty clothes I had taken off but I quickly dressed and left the gym. Just as when I had arrived, not one person behaved out of place or looked surprised to see me coming out of the door marked PRIVATE. As I quickly made my way to the exit, the girl behind the desk cheerfully called, 'See you tomorrow, Miss Anderson.'

The evening air chilled on my skin as I climbed, still shaking slightly, into Baby. I left the top up because I still felt in that intimate state that you feel when you are aroused and unsatisfied. I hadn't come down in any way at all. Still angry and frustrated, I drove back to the hotel and parked. As I walked through reception I was relieved to find that there was no one there. It would have been awful to have to face anyone. My hair was still wet from the shower, my clothes looked terrible and I knew that my face was still flushed – whether it was from the shower or the sex I am not sure.

I hurried up the stairs to my rooms, anxious just to get behind closed doors and lick my wounds. I felt shockingly abused already and I had only been to the gym once. My guts were in a knot, tense with disappointment and need, and my limbs felt tired as if I had run miles. I'm not sure why I felt so distressed – probably because my head was confused and my body was more so. Adam ran rings around me and left me devastated by his control and these boys had managed to do the same thing. What I needed was a long soak in the bath, a gentle play with myself accompanied by a fantasy and an early night in a comfy bed. Perhaps I had experimented too much too soon. Only brief months ago I had been a rather naïve girl who wrote about her fantasies to titillate other people. But I had since accepted that it had been my way of getting my kicks. After all, it was far easier than actually having to go out and get sex. Then all this had happened and suddenly I was getting more mind-blowing sex than most people experience in a lifetime.

I unlocked my door but, before I could step into my room, I was grabbed off my feet from behind. The breath whooshed from my lungs and, just as I opened my mouth to scream the place down, a hard hand was clamped over my mouth. Even though I had just been thinking about how angry I was that Jack and Tony hadn't yet acted out the scene, I was terrified. I thought my head would burst with the tension of being unable to scream. The person holding me had one strong arm around my waist from behind and the other tightly over my mouth. He picked me off the floor like a doll and I grunted and squealed, wriggling and wrestling as best I could.

I was carried into the room and the door was slammed behind us. The room was dark; the heavy curtains that were drawn across the windows defused the faint light from the street outside. I could make out the distinct shape of another man in front of the window. He had a ski mask pulled right down over his face with slits for his eyes and mouth and his clothes were dark and forbidding. Even his hands were gloved in black leather. I knew it had to be one of the twins but still I was frightened. The adrenalin was pounding through me and I fought hard. I kicked and wriggled as hard as I could. If I was going to enjoy this I had to know that it was Tony and Jack. I stared at the one in front of me but, apart from the fact that he was about the right height, I couldn't tell for sure it was one of them. I struggled to get my mouth free but the hand was rock solid and I could hardly even grunt.

The man in front of me walked up to me and I could see his eyes through the slits in the hood but still I couldn't tell. I was distraught with anger but, without warning, I felt the flood of my juices start soaking their way through the already wet crotch of my leggings. I truly was ashamed at my reaction but that made it worse. It was the old humiliation thing that always tripped my arousal with Adam.

The man facing me fought to grab hold of my legs but I managed to stay free of him for quite a while, still kicking and fighting for all I was worth. This wasn't what I had thought it would be and I needed to know it was them. Eventually, of course, I tired of kicking and in my weakest moment he grasped hold and I knew I was a step nearer to my fate. He calmly tucked both my legs under one of his arms in a vice-like grip and whipped a length of rope out of his pocket. I squealed again as he wrapped it around my ankles and, less than a minute later, I was almost helpless. The room was clearer now my eyes had become accustomed to the darkness and I stared into his eyes. My fear must have shown because he held my legs still tucked under one arm and with his other hand he smoothed my hair away from my face and cupped his hand on my cheek.

I tried so hard to read his eyes. Was it Jack or Tony? Of course it was. If it wasn't, the situation would be incredibly ironic. I tried to calm down a bit but I couldn't. I had to know. Again I started struggling as best I could. I was like a wild thing. The rope might be holding my legs together but they were still movable and, contrary to what my captor obviously thought, I hadn't given up.

I was carried unceremoniously into the bedroom and dumped on the bed but, before I could draw breath to scream, my adversaries were sitting one on each arm and a piece of soft cloth was being pushed into my mouth. My tongue was depressed by the intrusion and I knew that if I didn't stop them now, once they had gagged me I would have to accept whatever they decided to do to me. Again my treacherous body responded in completely the wrong way. My stomach flipped as partial resolve flooded my stomach.

A scarf was produced by one of these men and tied around the packing in my mouth. My eyes frantically swept from one to the other of them, searching for any sign that they had been invited, but it was impossible. The only consolation I had was that, clothed like that all in black with masks covering their faces, they did look identical. I just wished one of them would speak because I knew that their voices would give them away. The rough East End accent that had been a little intimidating in the gym earlier would be like a gift now. A gift that would allow me to relax and enjoy what was happening to me.

My wrists were tied together and then to the headboard of the bed, then both men moved confidently to my lower half. They now each had both hands free to do their worst. Still I kicked as best I could but it was very difficult with my upper half restrained and my legs tied together. Still, I was damned if I would let them think they had won. They sat either side of me on the end of the bed and as I struggled futilely to see what was happening, each took hold of an ankle. The rope was untied and they just sat there for long seconds holding me still. Both of them looked at my face as they slowly began to spread my legs apart. It was just like earlier in the gym but this time I had no choice.

I was so torn. Anger still surged through me but it was impossible not to notice what was happening to me; my whole sex-starved body was fighting not to strain upward and thrust myself towards them. I longed just to give in and let it happen but that little niggle about their identity would not shut up and each time it reared its head I had to fight. When they relaxed a bit, assuming that I was conceding, I kicked out and got my bottom half free. It was a bit of a hopeless attempt because they immediately caught my legs again and this time held them tighter. I felt the G-string tightening up my crotch as my legs separated. Neither of my captors was even breathing hard; they were so in control of the situation it was awe-inspiring. I loved the sensation as my legs parted and I secretly groaned as my ankles were tied to the legs of the bed. I was staked out for the taking and I wondered what they intended to subject me to. I knew without a doubt that it would be bordering on aggressive because of the matter of fact way they had treated me so far. The way I had been grabbed left me in no doubt that even if these two men were Jack and Tony they still meant business. I thrilled insanely at that prospect.

My eyes almost popped out of my head as I saw one of them standing over me with a knife. My nostrils flared with terror as I kept telling myself not to be silly, it was only Jack and Tony. The reasoning in my head argued that, even if it was them, I didn't really know them, either. For all I knew they were capable of anything.

The man with the knife climbed on the bed and sat astride me. All my senses told me he wasn't going to harm me; there was nothing threatening in his manner and as he climbed on me he was careful not to squash anything. But my heart crashed wildly through a few beats as the knife was lowered to my chest. The fabric of my top was lifted and held taut as the knife sawed through the Lycra. My bra was next and I noticed that I wasn't the only one holding my breath expectantly as my breasts tumbled free from the confines of the garment.

An audible groan from the man sitting on my chest helped to ease my fears as he wriggled down until he was sitting across my hips. The other man took hold of the waistband of my G-string and held it away from my torso as the knife did its work yet again. My pussy was pounding now as the G-string cut deeply in the channel of my sex and then popped loose. All that covered me now were my leggings and the man sitting astride me. I couldn't wait for him to start on the leggings. I longed to be naked and at their disposal.

The man with the knife slipped off me and sat like the other one again on the edge of the bed. They both gazed at my breasts and, from what I could tell, enjoyed what they saw. The one who had watched as the other cut away my clothes reached out and flicked one of my erect nipples. The frisson of pain zipped through me as I shuddered and groaned in surprise. My nipple instantly crinkled and sprung to attention. He leaned over to the other and did the same. The feeling was exquisite tingling pain. I growled through my gag like an animal and desperately tried to grab a breath through my nose. His hand then began to knock my breasts from one side to the other. The feeling was sexual but it also made me feel very silly, as if they were mocking me. I hated that feeling but was unable to respond with anything but grunts and snorts. My eyes must have glared at him because his unnerving gaze took on a twinkling quality that showed his amusement at the situation. His hands kept up their teasing, rocking my breasts and alternately flicking the nipples. The shame flooded my sex as my breathing speeded up.

I must have looked quite desperate to them after that because the other one stroked my nipples gently – I think to allay my fears. It only lasted a second or two before they snapped back into their planned agenda. One stayed by my side and the other got off the bed, stretched and walked around the end. I could only see him if I struggled to raise my head but they must have wanted me to be able to anticipate their moves because the watcher on the bed placed a folded pillow under my head. I watched mesmerised as the one at the bottom of the bed leaned forward and grabbed a bunch of material from the crotch of my leggings. He pulled it away from my pussy and poked the knife through the soaking wet material. The bastard tutted loudly, deliberately humiliating me as he pulled the blade towards him, pulling the crotch of my leggings away from me in the process. For an eternity the material held and just kept pulling but eventually the point of the knife burst through and shone in the dim light. I gasped into my gag. And the weaker one of the two groaned yet again.

I thought he was going to cut off my leggings, but as soon as he had made a hole he stopped and put the knife back on the floor. I breathed a sigh of relief. I closed my eyes for a second or two, trying to relax now the knife was out of the picture, but they flew open again almost immediately when I felt his finger delving into the hole and probing my pussy. The other man just watched as his partner pushed and twirled his finger insistently into and out of my hole. All other thoughts were brushed aside as he poked and prodded his way into me with that single relentless finger. I ground my hips against him and pushed upward as best I could, all the while trying to read his eyes, but it was impossible.

I had to have more. Just one finger was teasing at its extreme but my encouragement appeared to fall on deaf ears. Even tied up and with a gag in my mouth I was verbal and made it obvious I had to have more. He began to poke harder and faster and I began to realise I had nothing to do with his actions. He was doing this because he wanted to and to gauge my reaction, and not because it was exciting me, and I knew it. Another finger joined the first and again I arched up towards them but again he pushed me too far, until the intrusion became almost abrasive. I tried to turn away but they held me in position so he could continue. He pushed his bunched fingers hard into my tender hole at least ten more times until I shook my head and he heard my muffled cries. He stopped.

The other man scooted up the bed until he was sitting next to my head and his hands began the soft caressing of my breasts and nipples he had started earlier. I responded admirably, the pounding forgotten. Just as the warmth of his attentions soothed me, the fingers returned and began their thrusting again. I can't say it hurt but it was harder than I would have chosen, so again I protested. He stopped but so did the hands on my breasts. We played like that until the attentions to my breasts became so important that I accepted the slight discomfort of the fingers driving their way right up inside me and let myself go. As soon as I accepted their control it was as if my insides blossomed outward and, instantly, his fingers were not enough.

I pushed downward onto the fingers that had become my ticket to orgasm and thrust my breasts up for more attention. One of the men chuckled. I grasped at the sound to try and recognise it but it sounded totally alien so my fear slammed back into the present. This time the fear became a part of the arousal and I begged with my body for more. They kindly obliged. The man at my breasts took hold of my nipples between thumb and forefinger and shook them gently while the man with the hand made a fist and forced it into my disgustingly dripping pussy. I was incorrigible as I groaned and strained toward heaven. The hand inside me began jabbing motions that excited the fear in me and took me to the first level of orgasm and I hovered there revelling in my situation. The fingers tightened on my nipples, sending shivers of pain through me as the hand pushed inside and stayed as deep as it could, stretching my lips apart and forcing itself against my straining clitoris.

Deep inside me the fingers of the invading hand began to spread until I felt I would split open but as soon as I had the image in my head of his hand opening to fill me, I crashed into my climax, my body pumping with the spasms.

I was only given a moment or two to relax and regain my equilibrium before my captors started to untie me. Even on the down slope of my crashing orgasm I was still excited enough to be anticipating what they intended to do to me next. One pair of hands fumbled excitedly with the knots as the other pulled off my tattered leggings. I was naked but my captors were still fully dressed, right down to the ski masks. These two men were so large and powerful that I felt helpless and thoroughly intimidated as they climbed on to the bed with me. They kept hold of an arm and a leg each so I was still spread open and available. Perhaps it was designed to keep me hot and it worked. My naked pussy, oozing its hot sticky fluid shamelessly down my thighs and over the hands that held me, still tingled from its previous attention.

A little bit of me wished they would remove the gag so I could join in properly and tell them how I was enjoying myself, but the fact that they left it in place to silence me added the tremors of fear that threatened to send me crazy. My head tried frantically to understand what they were setting up when one of the men laid on his back on the bed and the other pushed me on top of him. As I obliged and began to climb aboard it was made clear that they wanted me on top of him but on my back. What could I do but comply with their wishes? It was rather a horny place to be anyway.

As I lay on his hard body I heard him unzip himself. Then I felt the solidity of his cock nudging between my thighs from behind. It felt exquisite, all hot and solid and probing. I was pleasantly surprised to notice that the cock that thrust at my bottom was a size he could be proud of. It nestled intrusively between the cheeks of my bottom, mixing with my wetness and sliding up and down the slippery groove. I remembered how it felt to have my bum fucked by Adam and wondered if that was what they had in mind. I was so glad I had already been initiated.

I was wrong. The body under me wriggled a little until his cock was pushing its way into my pussy and he grabbed my arms behind my back and pushed me up into a sitting position. As I rose up straddling him his cock buried itself so far in me I could feel it jabbing against my cervix. I sat there impaled on his stiff cock while the other one stood next to the bed and stripped off, leaving only the ski mask in place. I am sure if he had realised just how beautiful he looked he would have posed but all he did was shuck off his things as quickly as he could.

Wow! He was outstanding. His magnificent cock stood proud and erect, bobbing to his pulse beat. He automatically took it into his hand and stroked its length, sending shivers of wanting through my veins. His huge balls lifted and fell as he ran his hand the length of the shaft. His eyes took in my nakedness, for it was blatantly on show for him and his mate. My arms were almost painfully wrenched behind my back, which forced my breasts forward. Their flesh was rosy from the teasing, and my nipples were rock-hard and more prominent than I had ever known them to be.

I sat proudly upright as the cock inside me jerked in response to my clenched muscles. I was grinning as best I could at the man before me while my muscles tucked high within my pussy contracted and released rhythmically. The body beneath me began to buck in time to my game as the man in front of me stroked faster. I snorted through my gag and stared at his cock, at the blue veins that threatened to burst with excitement, trying to convey to him that I wanted him in my mouth. Without a second thought, and before the man under me could protest, I had been lifted bodily from the bed, off the shaft of hard flesh that filled me. I was stood on my trembling legs in front of him and I immediately grabbed for his cock, but my hand was slapped away.

As soon as the other man got off the bed they had a silent conversation with a few gestures and the odd mumble that told me nothing. At the end of it I was pushed on my back across the width of the bed and immediately the naked body fell on top of me and, forcing my legs apart, ripped into me. Yet again I showed my pleasure by grunting aloud and arching my body, boldly shoving my groin up to him in invitation. He rammed into me, bashing his torso down on mine repeatedly while the other walked around the bed and took his clothes off too, again leaving the ski mask in place.

He stood over me with his cock, still tacky from me, waving over my face. The man pounding into me shoved me across the bed until my head was hanging over the side and the other one carefully removed my gag. I knew what was coming and I mewled with pleasure as the cloth was pulled from my mouth, releasing me for the next stage. My mouth gaped open, desperate to become an active part of this fucking. My head was cradled as the smooth warm knob prodded its way between my lips. I hungrily grasped with my mouth, sucking it deep into my throat. With every hard thrust into my pussy I jerked my head upward on the cock that filled my mouth. I could smell myself on his pubic hair and that sent me wild with delighted disgust. I couldn't believe I was actually doing this; lying here starkers with two strangers, one buried so far up me that I was being jerked with every thrust and one with his cock so far down my throat that I thought I would suffocate if he wasn't careful.

The mingled smell of us filled the room and our audible enjoyment raised the hair on my scalp. We pounded ruthlessly at each other, each of us desperate for our own release. But just as had happened before, the man fucking me pulled out and dragged me back down the bed and joined me. He lay flat on his back, still with the black ski mask hiding his face, and pulled me until I was sitting astride him with his cock finding its own way in this time. It slipped up my hole as if it was made to be there. I rode him hard. Pounding up and down on his hips to gain the best depth possible, I was insatiable. My hands were spread wide on his chest as I bumped up and down, grinding my pussy into his crotch and then rising until it almost slipped out.

I realised in a soft moment between thrusts that his mate had climbed onto the bed behind me. He too was astride the legs that I sat on and his chest was crushed against my back. His hands snaked around in front of me and, as I bounced, he held my hips to control the rhythm. The hands of the man that I sat on grabbed hold of my breasts and gripped them hard. I gasped with the intensity of the hold he had me in but secretly revelled in the dangerous sizzle that zapped through me.

I was pushed forward from behind until I was lying over the face of the man that filled me so exquisitely. I went with it and was surprised when the slit in the ski mask parted to reveal a mouth that latched onto mine with a vengeance. An insistent tongue darted in and out of my mouth as the lips crushed mine. Still his hands gripped and held me in place.

When I felt a pressure between my buttocks my instinct was to get up and I tried helplessly. Because of the position I was in, my cheeks were forced open and one of my abductors obviously intended to make the most of the opportunity. He gripped hold of my bottom cheeks and pulled them apart until I could feel my sphincter muscle give up its hold. I was open and could do nothing about it. My breasts were still in the vice-like hold that kept me face down on the man fucking me, keeping me in place for what came next.

I was stunned when I felt the second cock trying to drive its way into me. Surely there would be no room for this second invader? I pulled my mouth away from the passionate kiss and began to protest but, with no warning, I felt the soggy cloth from earlier shoved back in my mouth and my arms pulled again behind my back. My arms were tied behind by back with the rope that had restrained me earlier, and again I was shoved forward until I lay helplessly on the chest of the man underneath me.

I was in a sandwich, helpless and full up, with another intruder attempting to force his way in beside the first. I was frightened this time and wondered what they would do when they found it was impossible. I tried in vain to spit out the gag but the position I was in made it impossible. The pushing into my rear increased and I felt my bum give way a little, but there was no way a cock that size could possibly find its way in.

The man behind me ran his hand between his partner and me and slid his finger into my pussy beside the cock. It was such a strange sensation and I wriggled brazenly. His wet finger was removed from the sopping caldron and drove its way into my bottom. I screeched as the two invaders met and rubbed side by side in my twin openings. The fingers searched about, leaving a slick covering for his purpose so, when the finger was removed, I held my breath.

The man under me stayed stock-still as the cock at my anus tried for a second time to push its way into me, and this time he took it more slowly. Centimetre by centimetre it forced its entrance, stretching me wide open and filling the restricted space to its limit and beyond. Everything in me accommodated the pair of intruders. My pussy enveloped the cock that sat quietly waiting for its cue. My anus bloomed outward, inviting and persuading its assailant to violate its depths. My bruised breasts drowned in their human restraints. I lay on the chest underneath me, vulnerable and too weak to resist as the pair of cocks pushed together to enlarge the entrances into my body. My head was nestled in the crook of his neck and I could smell a spicy aftershave mixed with sweat and sex – what an intoxicating mix!

I kept trying to push my hands down to protect my tender opening but they were too well restrained and my hole was pulled further apart. The head of his cock finally made it. I was full to bursting and all he had in was the bulbous head. I panted shallowly to accommodate this new intrusion and slowly it wormed its insidious way further into me, alongside the other in my pussy.

For a few seconds we all sat as still as we could to allow the intense experience to wash over us. We were a sweaty heap of joined bodies. First the man under me carefully began to thrust his cock in and out, past the bulk of the cock in my anus. Then the second one joined in and I had the courage to push back gently onto him. That was the final ingredient needed. I was stuffed full to the point of bursting with two bodies encasing me. My rocking motion gained speed until all three of us found a rhythm that suited us. I am surprised I didn't tear open as these two rampantly horny men drove themselves to fulfil their fantasies. They were raping me with my consent. Each of us was getting what we wanted. I knew deep down that they were indeed Jack and Tony but I could kid myself that they were strangers to give myself an even more forbidden thrill. The twins, if their hard-ons were anything to go on, were in their element. A couple of times I had fought their advances, but they had forced me to carry on and that was how they got their kicks.

We drove ourselves until the sweat was dripping off us and the room was filled with groans and moans of pure sexual abandonment. Jack and Tony pulverised my poor tender lower regions but I gave as good as I got by ramming myself onto them and rocking back and forth to gain maximum penetration. It seemed impossible to believe that only seconds before I had been convinced that my orifices would split into each other if they carried on with their assault.

I felt the beginnings of a climax rumble around my stomach like the fluttering of a drunken moth and I encouraged it. I clenched my holes around the cocks that filled them and crushed my clitoris down onto the groin of the man beneath me and that not only did the trick for me but he grunted and sped up. The cocks tore into me in response to my tightening. The sounds of our desperation filled the room in a manic dance of sound that assailed my ears and heightened my encouragement to begging proportions. I had to come . . . now.

When the gorgeous man clutching my breasts centred his special treatment on my sensitised nipples I knew I was snorting in a most shameful fashion but I didn't care. He squeezed and pulled until I knew I couldn't help but come. We pounded together until first the man behind me collapsed and I felt his seed erupt into me. Then my spasms took over and I rode the softening cock in my bum and the rock-hard cock in my pussy until my needs too softened. I sat more upright as the cock in my bottom plopped out and I rode furiously until the one inside me swelled ready to come. I actually felt every boiling hot spurt as it pumped me full.

As the pleasure of orgasm filled his eyes, the man between my legs ripped off his ski mask and grabbed my face between his hands. Jack pulled the cloth from my mouth and replaced it with his mouth and kissed me thoroughly as Tony fell beside us on the bed.

We all lay in a row, speechless for at least five minutes. Jack was curled into my side with his fingers lazily playing with my breast while Tony lay on his back the other side of me with his hand caressing my hairless mound, paddling in the mixture of my juice and Jack's that dribbled from my still gaping pussy. Tony's sperm trickled between the tingling cheeks of my bottom while my muscles unsuccessfully tried to return to normal. It seemed as though I could still feel the hard length of cock shafting me and I knew I would for a long time to come. I still had the rope around my arms and the experience of being a helpless maiden was still fresh in my mind as they titillated me.

I felt that as soon as the rope holding me was removed we would all revert to the people we were, but they didn't remove it. They carried on with their game until my unashamedly corrupt body began reluctantly to respond. They pinched and probed and examined until once more I was writhing. Tony spread my legs and intimately examined my bits and pieces, much to my mortification, while Jack continued his onslaught of my nipples. He squeezed them and pulled them, he nipped them then sucked them until I was undoubtedly going to orgasm yet again. Tony exposed the tip of my clitoris and dove between my legs to taste my wares.

My stomach somersaulted as the heat of his wet mouth latched onto my sex and the pull on my nipples increased. I exploded into a gut-wrenching climax that strained my insides and pounded through my head.

'No! No! No more. Please, no more. I can't take any more.' I was almost sobbing as I lay with my legs still apart around Tony and my breasts heaving. I tried to roll over away from their meddling hands but they wouldn't allow it. They held me in place and Tony began again to suck on my pussy. My oversensitive clitoris responded against my wishes and the pleasure lurched yet again through my guts. Even while my head screamed 'NO', my sex-lips were swelling anew and my juices were flowing into his hungry mouth. Tony slurped and sucked loudly, rekindling the pounding of blood to his penis.

Jack, meanwhile, had taken my breast and cupped it between both of his hands and I watched mesmerised as he lowered his head to the burgeoning reddened nipple and gripped it with his teeth. As Tony pushed my poor tired pussy again, Jack bit down. The final orgasm that raged through me was more painful than pleasurable but still my insatiable body bucked its response and still my pussy flooded its invite.

I collapsed, completely exhausted. Jack and Tony knelt over me and wanked until their equally tired cocks spat their fluid. They rose above me in all their arrogant glory with their groins stuck out until they were almost touching across my waiting body and they rightly looked proud of themselves. Jack aimed for my face and his spurts landed on my cheek and my lips. A stray one landed in my hair, which made him grin, but Tony aimed at my pussy, hitting my clit with enviable accuracy. The rest of their come sprayed over me in globs.

We had all had enough. Not one word was spoken as Tony undid my bonds and Jack retrieved the blankets from the floor where they had fallen. I languidly rubbed the sticky fluid into my skin, massaging my breasts and limbs with the stuff.

We snuggled up together and I have no idea who fell asleep first but I suppose it must have been me because the next thing I knew I was waking up in an empty bed. I was actually quite glad they had gone. It saved the embarrassment of having to face them after all the unbelievably sordid things we had done the night before. As I was stretching my tired limbs and trying to wake there was a knock on the door.

I grabbed my robe and, slipping it on, opened the door. There was a trolley full of breakfast, newspapers and a large bouquet of flowers outside my door. My hand flew to my head as I remembered Jack's aim from the night before but there was no one to see the state I was in so I wheeled it in and gorged myself on a full breakfast, tea and toast. I read the papers surrounded by discarded clothing, ski masks and bits of rope and then turned to the pretty flowers. Tucked right down inside was a card that said: *You* are *a very dirty girl, Joanna, and we will be forever grateful for it.*

Heat flushed my face and other parts of my anatomy that should have still been comatose. I buried my face in the flowers and began to formulate my article. I thought I could start with just those words.

15

On the journey home from Southend on Sea with the flowers on the back seat and a lingering heat in my crotch, I vaguely formulated my article. I knew that I wanted to blow Adam away and of course encourage him to do wicked things to me. I was getting a taste for the more exotic side of sex. It was at that stage that I accepted the fact that this was me and I would not be going back to the Joanna that I had been before Joanna's Journal. I had almost forgotten how it felt to be that Joanna, how it felt to be abstinent.

As before after Mac and Rosie, I decided to take some time off to get back into the swing of things. I had a curious detached feeling that was difficult to understand or shake off. These games were affecting me more than I liked to admit. These days all I wanted to do was have sex; my every waking thought was filled with sex of every description. It was all I could think of. I reread the stories I had written only months before in the copies of *Leather and Lace* that I kept at home and was surprised to realise how naïve they were. Not any more. Now I knew more than most women discover in a lifetime and I was enjoying myself immensely.

I longed to experiment further, to try every suggestion that had been put to me. I wanted to meet the transvestite that had written begging me to meet him and I wondered what it would be like to play with a man dressed as a woman. There were so many others. The girl who got her kicks peeing over anyone who would allow it, the couple who were into heavy S & M and, of course, Mr Anonymous who had plagued my brain since his first letter suggesting that I deserved to be punished. So often his words had invaded what I was doing; even when I was with Adam my thoughts strayed to him occasionally. Perhaps now was the time for me to meet him. I knew undoubtedly that it was time for me to experience the dubious pleasures of being chastised, punished, spanked or disciplined. It didn't matter which word was used, they all sent tremors of anticipation down my back. I felt that all these provocative words were invented for just the likes of me. I even found myself wondering if I should be punished for all the immoral things I had done and all the things I had allowed to be done to me. Perhaps if I were punished I could put aside all my negative thoughts and just enjoy what was becoming a truly exciting hobby. Mr Anonymous said over and over again, 'I know you, Joanna,' and I was beginning to believe that he did. I wasn't at all sure that I knew myself though. Not completely, anyway.

The concept of being punished for what was in truth an extremely thrilling sequence of events was mystifying to say the least. There was a slightly hidden part of me that was somewhat ashamed of what I was getting up to. After all, no female is brought up to believe that the level of sexual experiment I was indulging in was acceptable. Every mother through history has hoped deep down that her daughter would grow up to be good and wholesome and I am sure my mother was no different. But in this modern world things were different, so where did Joanna's Journal fit into that ideal? Whichever way I turned and twisted the subject, I was always left with the slight tinge of guilt that racked my secret thoughts when I lay in bed at night.

The night I returned from my game with Jack and his twin I was more tortured than ever about the ethics of what I was getting up to. It seemed that the more I enjoyed a session the more I felt guilty. After looking long and hard at the events of the past, it shocked me to have to face the fact that the ruder I was with a punter the more I enjoyed the experience and hence the more guilty I felt. And the guiltier I felt the more I believed punishment was the only answer. Then the more I thought about punishment the more I craved sinful explorative encounters. Oh hell! What turmoil I was in. That day I decided to contact Mr Anonymous.

I retrieved the letters that Mr Anonymous had sent so far and each and every one of them managed to arouse me with curiosity that threatened to take over my waking thoughts. I really had become obsessed with the image of being spanked. I longed to be chastised and wondered how he would do it if I agreed to meet him. I wondered what he would be like. Would he be nice or a bully? Would he be young or old? There didn't appear to be any age restrictions on that type of sexuality according to the websites that I'd trawled through. The only trend that I noticed time and time again was that older men emerged as the most likely perpetrator. I thought hard about it and agreed that if I could choose, it would have to be an older man that initiated me into the depths and pleasures of chastisement.

All the men I had met over the past few months had at some time either slapped my bottom or gone a little bit further like Jack and Tony and briefly spanked me. Everyone involved had enjoyed the experience, especially me, so I sat and pored over the last letter he had sent which had arrived just before I left for Southend. I had begun to notice that his invitations didn't only come after one of my articles any more. They were regular and insistent.

I know you, Joanna.

This cannot wait much longer. You are spiralling out of control and need to be shown your destiny. Only punishment can pacify your demons. You should be face down over a hard and unforgiving knee where you will be educated in the extremes you crave.

Ring me now, Joanna

What should I do? I was tempted to ring and see what he was all about. I had gone past the stage where I felt I could only meet someone if the punters chose that person. I was hooked on these games and the magazine had become irrelevant. Adam was still in the forefront of my thoughts so I knew I must get on with my article. I knew he wouldn't even consider seeing me again until I had sent him my article. As I said, I was becoming insatiable.

I picked up the phone and waited at least three times over until the peep blasted my ear telling me I had waited too long before dialling. Eventually I plucked up the courage required and dialled the mobile number. It rang at least eight times and, and just as I was about to give up, the message cut in: 'I am sorry there is no one available ... blah blah blah'.

I quickly hung up. I was shaking like a leaf, petrified at what I had done. Why was this one scarier than the others I wondered? Perhaps it was because I had decided not to let the magazine or Adam know about it. And I was nervous that I might find out something about myself that I was perhaps not ready for. I took a few deep breaths and decided that an answer phone was actually perfect. I could leave a message and wouldn't have to talk to him straight away. I dialled again.

'Hi, my name is Joanna. I'm from *Leather and Lace* magazine. I received all your letters and thought perhaps we could discuss them. Would you be kind enough to ring me back and we can take it from there.' I knew it sounded stilted but thought that would be safer. That way if I thought he sounded like a creep I could just tell him he hadn't been chosen and to stop writing. Whatever way it went I would at least get a chance to suss him out. I also sent him my e-mail address in case he felt happier using that. I would enjoy having a correspondence with him if nothing else. Then perhaps I could find out what it was that was tormenting me.

I put him out of my mind, slightly disappointed that I wasn't going to get to talk to him tonight, but my article for Adam took over and filled my thoughts. I really wanted him to be energised by what I wrote so I put everything I had into it. I described in minute detail each drop of sweat and each forced degradation. I even added just how thrilling that degradation was for me. I lingered on the parts where I felt I was being controlled the way he controlled me, hoping to titillate his fancy and persuade him that he needed to see me right away.

The piece that emerged was a bit longer than normal but I hoped he would be able to squeeze it in and I desperately hoped the extra words reeled him in. I longed to be under his spell again. Being with Jack and Tony had only whet my appetite for more. I wanted to explore further, right into my deepest fantasies, but with Adam this time. I wanted him to summon me. The waiting was devastating.

I e-mailed my piece to him and waited for three days. Still I didn't go into the office but waited around the flat hoping he would either come and see me or at least acknowledge receipt. He did neither, so I reverted to watching videos and pigging out. I played every one of my old films and laughed myself raw yet again over my series of Blackadder tapes. Audrey Hepburn made me cry and Bridget Jones excited me afresh when she flirted with and then fucked her boss. How alike we were, Bridget and I. I sat for hours with chocolates on my lap and the remote control in my hand. The days almost dragged into each other. I drank too much wine and stumbled to bed on more than one occasion.

After the third day, when I was just beginning to think I would never hear anything, I had an e-mail from Mr Anonymous.

Joanna,
I am glad you have seen the error of your ways. We will meet soon and you will embrace your punishment. Wait to hear from me and prepare yourself.
I know you well, Joanna.

What on earth did he mean? Prepare myself? How could I prepare myself for him when I didn't even know who he was or what he had in mind? I ran his words through my thoughts, allowing them to thrill me over and over again. It was as if I had made a connection with him, just because I had left a message and he had responded.

I was slightly annoyed at his firmness but, as with Adam, that firmness became my downfall. I obeyed Adam and waited but now I was waiting for Mr Anonymous to summon me too. How could a rampant desperate girl like me end up waiting on two separate men who insisted they wanted her but she had to wait? It wasn't fair. It was the weekend and, although I tried to lighten my mood by doing totally unrelated things, I did sulk rather. I moped about still in my nightclothes until Sunday lunchtime. I kept switching on the computer, hoping to have received a message, but the screen was full of crap messages from porn channels that tried to entice me in. Their drivel was lost on me. I wanted the real thing and only that would do.

The phone ringing almost came as a surprise; I had so retreated into my little life. I rushed to it but was instantly disappointed to hear a woman's voice.

'Hi, Jo, it's Rosie.'

'Oh, hi, Rosie. How are you?' I was instantly alert and thrilled that she had broken my train of thought.

'Well . . .' She hesitated. 'I'm sort of in your area, and I know it's a bit of an imposition but I wondered if you were free. I will understand –' I cut her off sharply.

'Of course I'm free and I would love to see you. It's ages since, well you know what I mean.' I was rather embarrassed.

'I'm actually just leaving my mum's in east London, so I could be with you in an hour or so. Would that be all right?'

'Absolutely. Let me give you my address.' I reeled off my address and a few directions then zoomed about the place like a mad thing tidying and cleaning. I had no idea if Rosie was visiting as a friend or a potential lover and I found that I didn't really mind which it was. I dressed carefully though, just in case it turned out to be the latter, and I gave away my preference when I perfumed my body. I wondered what Rosie would make of my shaved pubes. If it got that far. When I looked in the mirror I knew that I looked good, from the tight jeans to the soft silky blouse that showed the lace of my bra and the swell of my breasts as they attempted to bulge over the top. I brushed my hair until the red glints shone and added a little subtle make-up.

'Rosie. I'm so glad you came. Come in.' I stepped back to invite her into my cosy living room and, taking her coat, pushed her in the direction of the sofa. She appeared extremely shy about something and I wondered what it was she had to say. I tried to flush her out but while I made the tea and pottered about putting her coat away she sat almost speechless just answering in monotone single syllable words.

'Hey, what's wrong?' I encouraged when I was finally sitting beside her. I gazed again in awe at her sensuous mouth. Already my resolve just to be friends, if that was what she wanted, was abandoned. Just as the first time I met her I was hypnotised by her lips and perfect teeth. She smiled timidly and the radiance lit up her face. God, I fancied this woman.

'I can't get you out of my mind, Jo. I have tried and tried but you are in my thoughts every day. I want you again. When we met last time I hated having to share you. Don't get me wrong, I absolutely enjoyed everything, but it was actually my first time with a woman. Steve was gobsmacked when I let you do what you did to me. I had always said that I was only interested in either watching both sexes or indulging with just men, but I didn't want you to think we were country hicks so I let myself go. You were so sophisticated, all I could think of was that a well-known sex goddess was between my thighs. And, incidentally I'm very glad I did.' By this time she was more relaxed and apparently enjoying herself. I couldn't help it, I laughed out loud.

'If only you knew, you silly. I'd never done anything like that at all. My only experience was from writing and fantasising and until I met you lot I was practically virginal so to speak – well, on the pervy front I was anyway. And, I'm far from well known. I think you'll find that your group were the only ones who really knew about me. The rest of the punters, until I started Joanna's Journal that is, just saw me as the person who wrote the words they got off to.' I looked into her cornflower-blue eyes and added, 'Until I met you, Rosie, I'd always wondered what it would be like to be with a woman but had never imagined I would ever get the opportunity to experience the amazing feelings that you awoke in me. I loved the softness of your skin and the musky, flowery smell of you.' I knew I was blushing and could feel the heat suffusing my neck. 'You tasted heavenly and I didn't actually want to leave. I wish in retrospect that we'd met first, just the two of us.'

Rosie sat and stared at my face speechless, probably at how much I had changed since the day I visited her and her swinging group. To me it seemed like a lifetime ago. She took my hand and we held the gaze for a silent minute or two, each of us searching the other's face. As if in a trance we moved towards each other still with our eyes locked on. Only for a fleeting second did I wonder just what Rosie hoped to get out of this. I knew that for me it would be a very beautiful interlude while I waited for my fate – be it Adam or Mr Anonymous.

Rosie's mouth tasted of mint. Her dainty tongue darted into my mouth to tease and tantalise. I was instantly horny with a hunger for something sweet, something feminine, far away from the rutting of the twins and the controlling nature of Adam. Rosie didn't let me down. She took over the show after gently pushing me back into the cushions.

'Oh no you don't. This time it's my turn. You had your chance when you were in my house, this is all for me. Just lie back and enjoy.'

We hadn't even finished our tea and she had been in my house no longer than ten minutes before she had me stripped off and spreadeagled, half on and half off the sofa. As she divested me of my jeans and knickers, she delighted me by gasping at my shaven pussy. She stared and gaped blatantly as she stroked the smooth silky skin. Her fingers brushed the tip of my clitoris and I moaned shamelessly but she just giggled. As she explored me I explained how Adam had ordered me to shave. Rosie was fascinated by our relationship and asked more questions. While her inquisitive fingers prodded and examined my wet folds she asked what other orders he had given me.

It was difficult to talk and not gasp with her fingers exploring me intimately, but I did the best I could. I wanted her to carry on and my descriptions were obviously arousing her to experiment further. And I liked her experimenting on me. I told her about the little chrome pegs and Rosie insisted that I went to get them. I was loath to leave her but quickly trotted to the table where I had left them. I had been keeping my promise to Adam and already was able to wear a peg on each nipple for ten minutes or so. Even though the initial fear and pain had diminished, the pegs still made my stomach flutter with shivers of pain. It seemed strange to be handing them over to Rosie and I wondered yet again what she had in mind.

Rosie pulled me to the edge of the sofa and she dropped onto the floor between my legs. My bare pussy was stretched wide in front of her face and the luscious humiliation washed over me. I forgot the pegs for the next few minutes as her delightful tongue played with my sex. She dipped it hotly between my sticky sex-lips then ran it the length of my slit until it grazed my clitoris, sending me into a frenzy. I just let my legs drop as wide apart as I could, totally abandoned now. I would have let her do anything. I did let her do anything!

Rosie's hands ran up and down my legs as her mouth danced over my pussy. It was so obvious that she was a woman as she pleasured me and I began to believe that I would have known even if I had been unable to see. She worshipped my arousal that manifested itself by oozing drips of my essence to mingle with her saliva. I could see the wetness glistening all over her mouth as she looked up at me, still sucking on my pubis.

I knew Rosie was beginning to hot up the pace when she jabbed her tongue right into me. It was burning and so different from a cock that I squealed with delight. I couldn't believe how different her mouth felt on my shaven crotch. I pushed my body towards her, shamelessly begging for more and, of course, Rosie obliged. She shoved at least two fingers into my pussy and twirled them gently until I was groaning and whining for more. It was when I realised Rosie had removed her fingers and her mouth that I leaned up to see what was going on. I was shocked to see her still sitting in place between my legs but with one of the pegs in her hand, turning it round and around. She held it up to me and grinned.

'What was it Adam said about other places, Jo?'

My stomach lurched with expectation of what she intended to do. I sank back on the cushions and groaned again. I felt Rosie delicately take hold of the plump flesh of my outer labia and then the biting twinges of pain as the peg was released onto it. I panted rapidly to absorb the smarting but relished the intensity. I wriggled my approval when she picked up the other peg and dangled it before my face. She quickly placed the second one and immediately I felt the erotic dragging tug of them.

My clitoris swelled so much I felt its growth as it poked from its sheath. Rosie brushed her fingertip across the sensitive end and I jumped with the sudden intensity of it. Oh, God, it was so electrifying when Rosie picked up on my reactions and slipped the hood of my clit back to reveal the shiny nub of nerve endings. She swirled her fingertip in my juices and then ran it around the hard swelling that my clit had become. I was gripping the cushions of the sofa in response to the power of the feelings she was dragging out of me. Grinding up and down was the only way I could respond; it was as if her fingers were drawing my hips up off the cushions. I was mewling like a demented cat as her finger relentlessly toyed with me and I knew I was swelling more than I believed possible.

'Oh, fuck, Jo. That is so pretty. Look what your clit is doing.'

I leaned up again and saw what she meant. My clitoris that usually stayed quite happily buried in the folds of flesh that protected it had taken on a life of its own. As Rosie gently rubbed it, it grew more. It swelled like a tiny cock and the extreme force of feeling that flooded my body spurred her on.

'Fucking hell. Look at that. Its amazing.'

Rosie bent down and flicked her tongue over the end of my straining clit and the intensity grew. She kept the hood drawn back to expose the sensitive bud and, raising her mouth, took it between her finger and thumb. I was flabbergasted when she began to massage me. I couldn't believe that this sweet feeling was what men had every time they were wanked. I wanted to laugh at the power of my emotions as she carried on until I was gasping and writhing in time to her movements. Just as I knew my orgasm was near, Rosie touched one of the pegs and jiggled it, evoking more additional intensity.

I was grabbing her hair and tilting up to receive

more when Rosie plunged the fingers of the hand that had been drawing me toward my goal right up inside me. There was no resistance whatsoever and her hand slipped in as if on a tidal wave. I didn't need to be ashamed at the volume of juices I was producing because she was a woman too and she knew what she was doing to me. Her fingers pushed the pegs so they crushed me anew but the pain this time was the ultimate pleasure. The biting of the pegs and the coolness of the air on my exposed clit combined to send me crazy for her. I was producing a keening wail that had never been a part of my vocabulary before. Rosie lowered her mouth yet again to burn my cooling clit.

Wow! I don't know how else to describe it. The intense heat of Rosie's mouth as she sucked wantonly on my engorged clitoris, added to the other feelings she was inducing in my lower regions, detonated the powder keg inside me. The wonderful pulsing of my orgasm swelled and retreated at least a dozen times before I came down to earth again.

I lay back on the sofa, wheezing and shaking with the passion she had aroused in me.

'Oh, Rosie, come here.' I wriggled down onto the floor beside this amazingly horny woman and we slotted into a perfect 69 position as if we had spent half our lives there. I dragged her clothes up and a little roughly pulled her knickers to one side to allow access. It was not enough so we scrabbled about to strip her too. Luckily the room was warm enough for us to play our unrehearsed game. It came so naturally to suck and lick and nibble at Rosie's appealing pussy. It was almost like coming home and I settled down to enjoy my turn.

Every time I got Rosie to the point where I knew she would start the bucking motion that would herald her climax, she would pull away and tug on one of my pegs. I yelled over and over as she teased me with the exquisite pleasure of the pain they induced. We rocked like the proverbial two-headed beast and it felt as if our bodies were designed to slot together. My breasts squashed against her warm tummy and my head tucked nicely between her thighs, filling my senses with the pungent aroma of her. While my mouth was busy on her I gripped the cheeks of her bum and dragged them apart to expose her anus. It was right before my eyes – tiny, pink and screwed up with fear. I squirmed further under her to get at her, biting her bottom and pulling her cheeks further apart.

'Argh. Jo. Don't you dare do that.' Rosie tried to worm herself away from my prodding tongue but I knew from experience what she was feeling. Just like me she was probably longing for me to insist but duty-bound as a female to argue that it was disgusting and that I should stop. Of course I didn't stop; I continued to tease the entrance to her tight little hole until she relaxed reluctantly and my tongue grabbed the cue. She surprised me by tasting just as sweet there as she did in her other places that enticed me. A set of insistent teeth bit down onto my pussy, nudging the pegs and sending alarm bells to my nerve endings and I responded automatically. My tongue stabbed into her, past the sphincter muscle and into her tight hot hole. She wriggled deliciously in my grasp and tried to force herself onto my intruding tongue; all sense of disgust had been dispersed with the power of the familiarity of my mouth.

'Oh. Oh. Oh, Christ, that's so good, Jo. Don't stop, whatever you do.'

I had no intension of stopping. I forced her cheeks apart until her pussy gaped wide too and, removing my tongue, relentlessly delighted her with my every nip and dip of the tongue. I slurped shamelessly from one hole to the other until her fluids ran down my face and dripped off my chin. I buried my face in her depths and forced myself into the channel that opened up to encourage me, jabbing and stabbing my fingers and tongue in whichever hole presented itself to my administrations. I truly wanted to violate her sexuality. I wanted to astound her as she had me when she manipulated my clit. It appeared to work. Brief seconds later she gripped my face between her thighs as if her life depended on it and thrashed about, moaning her delight at the strength of the climax that threatened to devastate her.

16

The ping of the computer telling me I had an e-mail
startled us both as we padded naked around the flat.
We had lain for an hour, revelling in our combined
pleasure and discussing how incredible our lovemaking
had been; both of us had reached new heights of
enjoyment that neither had known existed. I ignored
the noise to begin with and we continued our shared
dissection of every move, nibble and suck that had
taken us to the level of enjoyment that now left us
almost humble.

'I had no idea my clit was that big, or that it could
feel so good to be wanked. Perhaps we should have
been born men,' I joked, as I grilled some bacon for
sandwiches. Rosie stood beside me with her hair all
tousled; her mouth had an unconcealed crushed look
about it. She looked wickedly sexy and I hoped I looked
the same to her. I suppose I must have done because
every few moments she would look at me and grin in a
way that made us both flush with embarrassment.

'Aren't you going to have a look then?' she asked,
tossing her head in the direction of the computer that
sat like a sinister eye blinking on the table.

'Nah. There's plenty of time for that. I want to enjoy
you while you are here. Can you stay tonight? I don't
want you to go.'

'I'll have to ring Steve, but I'm sure he won't mind.
Why don't you look at your message while I phone

home? It could be fun. Anyway, I want to see if its from one of your suitors.'

We sat and drank tea curled up on the sofa with the bacon butties perched precariously on our naked laps. It was strange how comfortable I felt just sitting with her. I was acutely aware that I had never felt this easy with any man I had been with and I have to confess I was enjoying it. We rehashed the night I had visited her club and then what we had done earlier and Rosie glowed under my admiring gaze. It seemed we were in awe of each other; our shared experience had shocked us both in its intensity.

'You can't leave it for ever. Go on. I'll phone Steve and you have a look,' Rosie cajoled.

I sat at the table reluctant to break the thread that joined us and clicked 'Mail'.

I KNOW YOU, JOANNA.

And I know what you have been doing, you dirty girl. Come to my house tonight at 8 p.m. Your behaviour over the past few months merits the punishment it will receive. This visit will be in the form of an initiation and will introduce you to the destiny I have pledged to demonstrate to you. It is time to admit that you long to be chastised.

Do not fail me, Joanna. It is too late to back out now.

The heat flashed through my body that still ached from Rosie. I was trembling as she walked over to me, telling me that Steve was quite happy for her to stay with me.

'Steve says I can stay, as long as I tell him all the sordid details when I get home ...' Her voice trailed off when she saw the shock on my face. She hunkered down beside me and asked solicitously what was wrong. I pointed to the screen. My new friend read the words quickly and silently. She whimpered a little when she got to the bit about me needing to atone, just as I had. It was the dirty girl bit that excited me to the point of delirium though. His words, 'I know you, Joanna,' rang more true than anything I had heard before. He did appear to know me as he claimed. He certainly knew how I felt inside. How I felt like a dirty girl but delighted in that fact. He also read my mind when he said that it was time to admit to my ache for punishment.

'What am I going to do, Rosie? Should I go?' I stared at the screen, surprised to find that Mr Anonymous lived only twelve miles from my home. 'It would only take me half an hour to get to him and then I would know, wouldn't I?'

'Know what, my lovely? What is it he knows about you that you haven't told me?'

'Nothing really. It's just that I have this craving for punishment. Every man I have been with has played at spanking me or just teased me about wanting to spank me, but I long for more and he seems to have read my mind. He says he knows me and I really believe he does. If he doesn't know me then he knows, or has known, other women like me. You don't know what I'm like with Adam, Rosie; I am so submissive it scares me a little. I am longing for his every touch to the point where I don't care if that touch is painful or humiliating. I have to have that contact. I just have to have him controlling me. Even knowing that it's because of his control that I am not seeing him is sublimely erotic to me and I have spent the last three weeks or so permanently aroused.

'I would literally do anything for him. I have an idea

that slinks though my mind every now and then that if I am punished for what society saw as my misdeeds then I might be able to move on a bit, or at least to a point where I am not so obsessed with Adam. Does any of that make sense?'

'Not really,' said Rosie, adding to my confusion. 'I have to admit that I would love to experience a thorough spanking, but it's a sexual thing for me. I just know I would get off on the whole raunchy episode. What is it that you think you will get out of it then?'

'I want to be degraded, Rosie. I want to feel humiliation wash through my veins as I subjugate myself in reverence to a dominant man. I don't even know if it is about sex with me or not. I suppose sex must have a lot to do with it because already I am as horny as hell, my breasts ache and my clit is throbbing again.'

Rosie delved her fingers between my thighs and tutted her disgust at the mess she found there. 'He's right you know, you are an exceedingly dirty girl. So what is stopping you? Its obvious you want to go.'

I thought for a moment or two, not sure myself what the true answer was. She was right – I did want to go and had done since his first provocative letter. I told Rosie so and she offered to go with me.

'I could wait outside in the car if that would help. Then at least the dangerous element would be removed. All you would have to do would be to tell him as soon as you walked in that you had a friend with you and that I would be expecting a call on my mobile every hour or so.'

I could think of no other excuses and, to be honest, I didn't want to think of any, so I decided to go. By eight o'clock I was a nervous wreck. I had decided at least ten times that I couldn't go through with it, but there I was outside an enormous mansion house in the country.

The drive was at least a quarter of a mile long with an avenue of poplar trees lending the house a regal air. Massive white pillars that intimidated me, almost to the point of turning round, flanked the front door.

Rosie had stayed at home after all but promised she would wait for my phone calls. I sat outside the gates trying to pluck up courage to go through with it. I was wearing one of my favourite flirty skirts and had bare legs. My tight T-shirt accentuated my big breasts and showed them off to their full advantage. Rosie had told me that I looked like the dirty girl I was but I believed her when she told me I also looked irresistible. That'll do for me, I thought, as I drove up the drive. I parked in front of the house and read the e-mail again to make sure I was at the right place.

I was surprised to see a note pinned to the front door. I tore it off with hands that were shaking almost uncontrollably. It was addressed to me and told me to let myself in and wait in the hall. At least I knew I was in the right place. I followed the instructions with my heart hammering in my chest and all my senses on full alert. The hall was enormous, with a knight's suit of armour standing in one corner and a large refectory table down the centre. Everywhere was dark panelling that gave the whole place an imposing atmosphere. I felt totally out of my depth. I thought afterwards that it was all part of the control thing.

I hovered, tentatively called out 'Hello?' and waited for someone to show themselves. As I waited I looked around. I was delightfully shocked to see a large tapestry hanging on one wall. The scene was suggestively erotic. A man in pale breeches and knee-high riding boots was sitting on an enormous black stallion in front of a large house that looked remarkably like the one I was in. Draped across the horse in front of him was what appeared to be a serving wench with her head dangling and her skirts bunched up around her waist. Her white cotton mop cap was askew and her hands were frantically clutching her red bottom. Her legs were clad in white, above-the-knee stockings held up with red ribbon garters. The 'Master' was casually clutching a riding crop between both hands and grinning down lasciviously at the wench. His eyes rested on the pale flesh that contrasted so obviously with her reddened bottom. My heart thundered but I forced myself to move on, scared that I might miss something.

There were antique frames displaying miniatures down the length of one wall, depicting women in all stages of undress with their furry mounds on display. One particular picture that set my pulses racing was a scene in a Victorian schoolroom where a young girl stood before what looked like a schoolmistress with her hand held out before her, palm up. The tight-lipped mistress with her hair scraped back severely into a bun held a cane just above the girl's palm, ready to strike. The girl's other hand was clutched behind her back and her eyes were wide with fear. Or was it anticipation?

My chest had gone tight with expectancy by the time I discovered the next temptation. I walked to the end of the hall and found groups of antique hardware hanging like trophies on display. A set of stocks, a yoke and an old pair of handcuffs all dangled together to dry my mouth and set me trembling. On the wall above them was a row of punishment implements: a riding crop like the one in the picture; a whip with a long tail and a fluffy little end; a school cane that looked scarily well used and, last but certainly not least, a cat-o'-nine-tails made of pungent leather.

I was intrigued and fascinated by these treasures and totally forgot my reason for being there as I wandered around drinking in the dark atmosphere. I moved over to the long wooden table and noticed a large bronze statue which was at least two feet high. I don't know how I missed her the first time I walked past. She was absolutely exquisite. Every curve and swell was perfectly in proportion as she bent down to touch her toes. Her bare metal breasts dangled provocatively and the sinews down the backs of her long slim thighs were rigid with the strain of her position. Her long flowing hair dragged on the ground, making her look exceptionally helpless. I longed to be in her position. I turned her round and looked behind her. Her pussy was very detailed as it bulged plumply from between her thighs, the inner lips pouting from between the outer lips. I bent closer and touched my finger to the cold metal flesh and half expected it to be wet – mine was. My pulse was thundering now and my head almost ached with the tension of the arousal this was causing. She looked so real. I could almost have believed she was.

'Quite superb, isn't she? That's Matilda.' The voice sent shivers through my veins and I spun round to face him.

'Adam. I er ... I um ... I didn't expect...' I was completely speechless. Adam was the last person I expected and my head was screaming questions. How? When? What?

'Have I shocked you, Joanna? Don't tell me you are surprised. I have nurtured you for months for just this day.' As he talked in his hypnotic way he was moving across the hall to me. All I could do was stare with my mouth hanging open and my hand still on Matilda's pussy; she was still cold to the touch.

'But I don't understand. How did you...' I knew I was stuttering but had no control over my vocal chords. In fact I had no control at all.

By this time Adam was standing in front of me. He took hold of my hand, moving it away from Matilda, and placed it on top of my head. He picked up the other hand that trembled by my side and placed it too on my head and, for some unknown reason, I left them there; it didn't occur to me not to.

Adam began a soft soothing mantra that did little to calm the questions that raced through my brain. 'You have been begging for this for years, Joanna. You were meant to be here with me. If you will allow me I will show you just what you yearn for, what I have been shaping you for. Trust me when I tell you that I know you, Joanna. I have been able to see through your façade to the core of you for months. You are a dirty little girl who is screaming out to be punished for not only her naughty deeds but her thoughts too. And you do have some very dirty thoughts, don't you, Joanna?'

'Yes,' I whispered. My eyes dipped to the floor. The sweet humiliation I craved drizzled down my spine.

'I read your piece about the twins with avid interest. I have also taken into account that this visit was not agreed between us. Is there nothing you wouldn't do to add a new experience to your repertoire? Would you try anything to wallow in your depravity? Be honest with yourself, Joanna.'

My mind scrambled to decide which answer he wanted. But after a few seconds I resigned myself to tell the truth, whether he liked it or not.

'Yes.' It was beyond me to converse with this powerful dominant man. All I was able to manage were monosyllables. My mouth had dried up and I was feeling a little light-headed. I looked once more at Matilda, passive and waiting, and I envied her, her serenity.

'That's my girl. Come here, Joanna.' He held out his

hand to me and I swallowed a sob in the back of my throat. I walked towards him quivering in anticipation of what he intended to do. My head knew really but my body was still in shock. I didn't dare take my hands from my head and he had obviously wanted it that way because his arm curled protectively around my waist and he led me towards a door in the dark panelling.

The room he led me into was a study or library. It was lined with books, row upon row of books. There was a large fireplace that was the focal point of the room. Placed around it were three large leather studded wing-back chairs. Adam manoeuvred me towards the one that was the most worn and sat on it, leaving me standing beside him petrified of what was to come. I fidgeted as he picked up a tomb of a book from the table beside him. He pulled out the red satin marker and opened the page. I have no idea what the book was but the words he read thrilled me.

I stood almost to attention with my hands still on my head and my back ramrod straight as I listened.

' "It is the lot of a submissive woman to adhere to her Master's wishes and to obey at all times. The submissive woman's sole aim in life is to entertain and please her Master, to relish the chance of pleasing him and to subjugate herself before him.

' "If the submissive transgresses it is the duty of her Master to punish as he sees fit.

' "If these conditions are honoured the submissive will be rewarded for her compliance and be fulfilled in her destiny – that of pleasing her Master."

'I think we must start with a clean slate, Joanna. You need to be punished for your wilful behaviour up until now so we can move forward. Do you agree? Will you give me your permission to discipline you for your wantonness?'

I nodded, reduced to a helpless heap in the face of his dominance. If I had thought he was commanding in the office, this was a whole new understanding. There was not one iota of rebellion left in me. He was right – he *did* know me. I was the Joanna he wanted me to be. I was the Joanna I wanted me to be. This was so right.

'Then put yourself over my knee.' He patted his knee in invitation.

I was stunned by the way he had gone right to it and I couldn't respond. I was standing and he was sitting so far below me, I didn't know how I could drape myself prettily over his knee without looking ungainly. I hovered, trying to work out which leg to start with and where to put my hands to take my weight, but the adrenalin pounded through me encouraging me to try. I wanted this so badly.

Adam, true to form, just sat not even looking at me, waiting for me to obey his instructions. I stumbled as I leaned forward but managed eventually to end up lying over his hard knees. I could feel the heat of his body on my tummy where my skirt and top parted company. My breasts were crushed against the edge of the chair and I wriggled to make myself more comfortable. My head was dangling just like Matilda's and my arms were flailing about with no place to go.

'Put your hands on the floor, Joanna, and your toes on the floor too. I want them to stay in those positions until I tell you different. Is that clear?'

I did as he instructed, pushing my limbs to their limit to gain purchase on the floor. It was a bit of a struggle but I loved the helpless position it left me in. My bottom was squarely over his knees and poking up in the most shameful manner. Adam smoothed my skirt and top down to make me tidy and I felt as if the gesture was a little futile with what he had in mind.

He waited and I wondered what for, but as he waited my nerves calmed a little and I began to concentrate on what was to happen. I thought about the words he had read out to me and was overjoyed at their implication. Adam wanted me.

After what seemed like ages, when I had relaxed and he had composed himself, Adam took hold of the hem of my skirt. I felt his warm fingers brush my thighs and I moaned under my breath.

'Shhh!'

I wasn't sure if that was an order or an endearment but I resigned myself to silence just in case.

Adam lifted my skirt until it was lying over my back, exposing my bottom. Just as he did that I remembered the knickers – I wasn't supposed to have any on. Adam tutted deliberately and slowly, making me squirm.

'Stand up.' His order was almost curt. I complied. 'Take them off.'

All the embarrassment that I felt in his office at such instructions was gone and I removed my knickers without a pause, actually ashamed that he had caught me disobeying him.

Adam stood up then and walked around me. I blushed and trembled, waiting for his next move. He stripped off my T-shirt and bra within seconds and left me standing in just my skirt. When Adam took two small chrome pegs out of his pocket I whimpered my response, my legs threatening to buckle. The bite as he placed one on each of my extremely sensitive nipples was sublime and I moaned under my breath.

'Wait there.' What else was I going to do?

Adam returned with the cane that had up until then been a decoration in the great hall. He held it up and placed it between my teeth. The waves of humiliation threatened to engulf me as Adam casually sat down again and patted his knees. The struggle to lie across his knees with the pegs on my nipples and the cane clenched between my teeth was degrading, but even the emotion that accompanied degradation was sweet to me now.

He rolled my skirt until it was neat and tidy, all the while raising my expectation to frantic levels. I squirmed a bit but he ignored my invitation. I knew then just how important his agenda was to him and I had no doubt it would be carried out in a time-honoured fashion that he dictated.

His hand smoothed the skin of my bottom cheeks, running over the globes and down the tightness of my straining thighs, and I had to bite my tongue to stay silent. Anticipation of the impending spank threatened to overwhelm me as I waited for him to start. I had no preconceived idea of how it would feel or how much it would hurt, I just hoped that I would be brave enough to endure it and make Adam proud of me.

The first slap with the flat of his hand landed on my right cheek, sharply and firmly, followed quickly by the same on my left. I felt my flesh jiggle in response and the glow warmed me. Without preamble he continued to rain blows on each of my cheeks and down the back of my thighs until I could feel my skin burning. I was beginning to attempt to move away from the persistent assault but Adam had other ideas. He wrapped his arm over the small of my back and held me tight up against him. I loved the position but the vulnerability was a bit scary. Adam's hand was beginning to hurt as it persistently punished my bottom.

Minutes of this treatment left me weak and confused. I didn't understand what it was supposed to achieve and I began to wonder if he knew me at all. All it was doing was hurting me and I wanted him to stop.

Just when I was ready to complain he paused and ran his hand sensuously over the blazing flesh of my cheeks and thighs and instantly I pushed my bottom up for more. I felt the wetness between my thighs trickle downward. It was a shock to me to have to admit that my traitorous body was responding so admirably. He continued his caressing, dipping his finger briefly in my slit until I was groaning and wriggling again. Adam tutted in response to my groans but with a trace of amusement in his voice.

He began in earnest then, slapping each cheek separately and quite hard. Repeatedly he caught the tender underside of each buttock; that place where the skin is extra sensitive. With each blow the pegs on my nipples jiggled and tugged deliciously. The feelings inside me had cunningly changed as the heat suffused me. I could feel the intimacy of his knees beneath me and the firmness of his hand as it held me in position, and I began to revel in my fate. I gritted my teeth as the blows rained harder but the boiling in my stomach refused to abate; the pain had transformed itself into the most amazing stimulation believable. Each blow now mixed the shiver of pain with the glow of pleasure and I wanted it to continue for ever. I had Adam's full attention; I knew he desired me because I could feel his hardness pressing into my belly. I knew I was pleasing him and I wanted nothing more than that. The words he had spoken earlier began to make sense. I gripped the cane with dear life.

My sole aim at that moment was to entertain and please Adam. As soon as I recognised that, the spanking took on a new meaning and, because of that acceptance on my part, it also became sublime. Each new blow thrilled through me and sent me wild with wanting. I was groaning shamelessly and wriggling my pleasure as the sweat dripped into my hair and my pussy flooded.

I had no idea that I was crying until Adam's hand took on a new tack. The hand that had been holding me in place was needless now and it moved to work its way into my dripping pussy with his wrist snuggled between the cheeks of my bum. The hand that had been remorselessly spanking me worked around the one buried inside me and continued up and down my already smarting flesh. I was yelling inside with the intensity of feelings that ravaged through me as Adam's hands increased the pressure. The spanking hand hit harder and harder but the hand delving inside me explored and filled me to capacity, stretching me wide open and exposing my clitoris that was still sensitive from Rosie's administrations.

He removed his hand from within me and I sobbed with disappointment but I noticed that his other hand had stopped too.

'Open your legs, Joanna. I want to see how excited you are.'

I moaned but did as he instructed without a second thought. I struggled to spread my legs as far apart as possible, after all, the words he had read me told me to obey at all times. My fingers were clutching the rug as he began to tap on my clitoris. Grunting was almost impossible with the cane gripped in my mouth, but I managed it. I spread my legs even further apart, my feet scrabbling to gain purchase. With the flat of his hand he spanked my pussy and the surrounding flesh, occasionally tapping sharply on my aching clit until it was throbbing and inflamed.

'When I say no knickers, I mean no knickers, Joanna. Do you understand?'

I nodded frantically.

Adam's hand went back to its place holding me firmly over his lap while he continued to violate me. It was exquisite torture to be spanked in such a delicate place. I was sobbing openly and begging him not to stop at the same time as struggling to get away from the onslaught. I could have shut my legs to stop it, but I didn't; I longed for him to take me further. He was so clever in his knowledge of me. Each time my movements posed a threat to the proceedings he would soften his smacks until I was writhing and begging for him to continue. He would prod his fingers that were dripping with my juices into whichever orifice was closest at the time and then start up again with the spanking.

I was exhausted. I was desperate to come but desperate too for him never to stop what he was doing. I had come home and never wanted to be anywhere but over his knee, begging for liberation.

'Do I know you, Joanna?'

'Yes,' I screamed.

He carried on tapping and spanking my crotch and dipping his fingers. Every so often he would rain one really hard slap onto my tender bottom, which took my breath away but left me wanting more.

'Do I, Joanna?'

'Yes, yes, yes.'

Adam held me tighter to him and I guessed that a crescendo was imminent. A flash of fear was instantly dispersed when his hand again forced its way inside me and fucked me insistently until yet again I was crying with frustration. He removed his hand and massaged my clit until I felt my orgasm building. I wailed openly, all orders of being quiet forgotten. The cane fell on the floor in front of me and I cowered. But still I pushed my legs as far apart as I could and pushed my bottom up towards him. Adam bent and picked up the cane, tutting in that maddening way he had. He actually sounded delighted that I had failed.

'Shut your legs now, Joanna. I am going to prove to you irrevocably just how well I know you.'

Reluctantly I did as he instructed. I could feel the swollen nub of my clitoris squashed between my inner thighs and I gripped hard.

'Count for me, Joanna. Count each one out loud.'

'One,' I screamed, as the cane landed for the first time and threatened to undo me. It was harder than I would have thought possible but by this time I was already in a place that numbed my pain threshold and turned it to a radiant pleasure.

'Two,' I screamed again.

We carried on like this until I had counted to ten and my pussy was desperate for an end to it. Each cut of the cane thrilled me to the core and sent me even closer to the rapture I craved.

'Are you a dirty girl?'

'Yes.' I was greedy to agree.

He carried on caning me harder, with the questions as punctuation. My whole body was grasping for the catalyst that would spark my orgasm but he continued to keep me hovering between ecstasy and pain.

'Will you obey me in all things, Joanna?'

I had no hesitation as my body began the climb for release. 'Yes'.

Adam placed the cane beside us on the floor and I held my breath for a second.

'I am going to punish you harder, Joanna. I think you deserve a stiffer punishment for all your misdeeds: for Rosie and Steve, for Mac and everyone on the trains and especially for the twins who led you into new areas of debauchery. Oh, and of course for the naughty knickers.'

Each of the names was followed by slaps that took all his strength to administer and left him breathing heavily. It was the first time I had seen him less than in complete control and it elated me. I pressed my body down onto the shape of his hard cock and wriggled and writhed my contentment.

Adam responded to my movements and began to press upward in rocking movements and I knew I had him. For the first time I knew that Adam wanted me just as much as I wanted him. His cock grew beneath me and I longed to show him just how much I worshipped him but I hoped that would come later. I intended to be everything that Adam wanted me to be. I hoped he would want me to carry on my quest for new experiences, but under his control.

I thought he would never allow me to finish but, just as the wailing from my throat became croaky with overuse, he read me perfectly and pushed his fingers yet again into my pussy, wriggling them through the sticky gap at the top of my thighs. I gripped his fingers with everything I had and bucked upward.

He pounded his fingers in and out, forcing me to take the length of them by holding me tightly in place. His knuckles bashed against my crotch as he fucked me remorselessly.

I came then; it was inevitable. It was as predictable as me ending up over his knees. The racking spasms were forced from me, scrunching my guts as they pounded through me, inducing a keening moan from my throat that sounded as if it came from the depths of my soul.

As the throes of my incredible climax softened, Adam

pulled me up onto his lap and into his arms. I curled like a child and purred. Adam looked down into my tear-streaked face and over what was left of my dishevelled clothing.

'Oh yes, Joanna. I think I know you very well. Don't you?'

'Yes, Master,' I whispered.

Visit the Black Lace website at
www.blacklace-books.co.uk

FIND OUT THE LATEST INFORMATION AND TAKE ADVANTAGE OF OUR FANTASTIC FREE BOOK OFFER! ALSO VISIT THE SITE FOR . . .

- All Black Lace titles currently available and how to order online
- Great new offers
- Writers' guidelines
- Author interviews
- An erotica newsletter
- Features
- Cool links

BLACK LACE — THE LEADING IMPRINT OF WOMEN'S SEXY FICTION

TAKING YOUR EROTIC READING PLEASURE TO NEW HORIZONS

BLACK LACE

LOOK OUT FOR THE ALL-NEW BLACK LACE BOOKS – AVAILABLE NOW!

All books priced £6.99 in the UK. Please note publication dates apply to the UK only. For other territories, please contact your retailer.

SATAN'S ANGEL
Melissa MacNeal
ISBN 0 352 33726 5

Feisty young Miss Rosie is lured north during the first wave of the Klondike gold rush. Ending up in a town called Satan, she auditions for the position of the town's most illustrious madam. Her creative ways with chocolate win her a place as the mysterious Devlin's mistress. As his favourite, she becomes the queen of a town where the wildest fantasies become everyday life, but where her devious rival, Venus, rules an underworld of sexual slavery. Caught in this dark vixen's web of deceit, Rosie is then kidnapped by the pistol-packing all-female gang, the KlonDykes and ultimately played as a pawn in a dangerous game of revenge. **Another whip-cracking historical adventure from Ms MacNeal.**

THE INTIMATE EYE
Georgia Angelis
ISBN 0 352 33004 X

In eighteenth-century Gloucestershire, Lady Catherine Balfour is struggling to quell the passions that are surfacing in her at the sight of so many handsome labourers working her land. Then, aspiring artist, Joshua Fox, arrives to paint a portrait of the Balfour family. Fox is about to turn her world upside down. This man, whom she assumes is a mincing fop, is about to seduce every woman in the village – Catherine included. But she has a rival: her wilful daughter Sophie is determined to claim Fox as her own. **This earthy story of rustic passion is a Black Lace special reprint of one of our bestselling historical titles.**

Coming in October

SNOW BLONDE
Astrid Fox
ISBN O 352 33732 X

Lilli Sandström is an archaeologist in her mid-thirties; cool blond
fisherman Arvak Berg is her good-looking lover. But Lilli has had enough
of their tempestuous relationship for the time being so she retreats to
the northern forests of her childhood. There, in the beauty of the
wilderness, she explores and is seduced by a fellow archaeologist, a pair
of bizarre twins, woodcutter Henrik and the glacial but bewitching
Malin. And when she comes across old rune carvings she also begins to
discover evidence of an old, familiar story. *Snow Blonde* **is also an**
unusual, sexy and romantic novel of fierce northern delights.

QUEEN OF THE ROAD
Lois Phoenix
ISBN O 352 33131 1

Private detective Toni Marconi has one golden rule: always mix business
with pleasure. Provided, that is, she can be in charge. When she sets out
on the trail of a missing heiress her friends worry she may have bitten
off more than she can chew. Toni's leads take her to a nightclub on the
edge of the Arizona desert where she meets characters with even
stranger sexual appetites than her own. And then there is 'Red' – the
enigmatic biker who holds a volatile sexual attraction for her. One
thing's for sure, Toni will not give in until she's satisfied, whatever the
consequences. **Macho bikers and horny cops get sleazy with a sassy**
heroine who likes to be in charge.

THE HOUSE IN NEW ORLEANS
Fleur Reynolds
ISBN O 352 32951 3

When Ottilie Duvier inherits the family home in the fashionable Garden district of New Orleans, it's the ideal opportunity to set her life on a different course and flee from her demanding aristocratic English boyfriend. However, Ottilie arrives in New Orleans to find that her inheritance has been leased to one Helmut von Straffen – a decadent German count, known for his notorious Mardi Gras parties. Determined to claim what is rightfully hers, Ottilie challenges von Straffen – but ends up being lured into strange games in steamy locations. **Sultry passions explode in New Orleans' underworld of debauchery.**

Coming in November

NOBLE VICES
Monica Belle
ISBN O 352 33738 9

Annabelle doesn't want to work. She wants to spend her time riding, attending exotic dinner parties and indulging herself in even more exotic sex, at her father's expense. Unfortunately, Daddy has other ideas, and when she writes off his new Jaguar, it is the final straw. Sent to work in the City, Annabelle quickly finds that it is not easy to fit in, especially when what she thinks of as harmless, playful sex turns out to leave most of her new acquaintances in shock. **Naughty, fresh and kinky, this is a very funny tale of a spoilt rich English girl' s fall from grace.**

A MULTITUDE OF SINS
Kit Mason
ISBN O 352 33737 O

This is a collection of short stories from a fresh and talented new writer. Ms Mason explores settings and periods that haven't previously been covered in Black Lace fiction, and her exquisite attention to detail makes for an unusual and highly arousing collection. Female Japanese pearl divers tangle erotically with tentacled creatures of the deep; an Eastern European puppeteer sexually manipulates everyone around her; the English seaside town of Brighton in the 1950s hides a thrilling network of forbidden lusts. **Kit Mason brings a wonderfully imaginative dimension to her writing and this collection of her erotic short stories will dazzle and delight.**

HANDMAIDEN OF PALMYRA
Fleur Reynolds
ISBN O 352 32919 X

Palmyra, 3rd century AD: a lush oasis in the heart of the Syrian desert. The inquisitive, beautiful and fiercely independent Samoya takes her place as apprentice priestess in the temple of Antioch. Decadent bachelor Prince Alif has other ideas. He wants a wife, and sends his equally lascivious sister to bring Samoya to the Bacchanalian wedding feast he is preparing. Samoya embarks on a journey that will alter the course of her life. Before reaching her destination, she is to encounter Marcus, the battle-hardened centurion who will unearth the core of her desires. **Lust in the dust and forbidden fruit in Ms Reynolds' most unusual title for the Black Lace series.**

Black Lace Booklist

Information is correct at time of printing. To avoid disappointment check availability before ordering. Go to www.blacklace-books.co.uk. All books are priced £6.99 unless another price is given.

BLACK LACE BOOKS WITH A CONTEMPORARY SETTING

☐ THE TOP OF HER GAME Emma Holly	ISBN 0 352 33337 5	£5.99
☐ IN THE FLESH Emma Holly	ISBN 0 352 33498 3	£5.99
☐ A PRIVATE VIEW Crystalle Valentino	ISBN 0 352 33308 1	£5.99
☐ SHAMELESS Stella Black	ISBN 0 352 33485 1	£5.99
☐ INTENSE BLUE Lyn Wood	ISBN 0 352 33496 7	£5.99
☐ THE NAKED TRUTH Natasha Rostova	ISBN 0 352 33497 5	£5.99
☐ ANIMAL PASSIONS Martine Marquand	ISBN 0 352 33499 1	£5.99
☐ A SPORTING CHANCE Susie Raymond	ISBN 0 352 33501 7	£5.99
☐ TAKING LIBERTIES Susie Raymond	ISBN 0 352 33357 X	£5.99
☐ A SCANDALOUS AFFAIR Holly Graham	ISBN 0 352 33523 8	£5.99
☐ THE NAKED FLAME Crystalle Valentino	ISBN 0 352 33528 9	£5.99
☐ CRASH COURSE Juliet Hastings	ISBN 0 352 33018 X	£5.99
☐ ON THE EDGE Laura Hamilton	ISBN 0 352 33534 3	£5.99
☐ LURED BY LUST Tania Picarda	ISBN 0 352 33533 5	£5.99
☐ THE HOTTEST PLACE Tabitha Flyte	ISBN 0 352 33536 X	£5.99
☐ THE NINETY DAYS OF GENEVIEVE Lucinda Carrington	ISBN 0 352 33070 8	£5.99
☐ EARTHY DELIGHTS Tesni Morgan	ISBN 0 352 33548 3	£5.99
☐ MAN HUNT Cathleen Ross	ISBN 0 352 33583 1	
☐ MÉNAGE Emma Holly	ISBN 0 352 33231 X	
☐ DREAMING SPIRES Juliet Hastings	ISBN 0 352 33584 X	
☐ THE TRANSFORMATION Natasha Rostova	ISBN 0 352 33311 1	
☐ STELLA DOES HOLLYWOOD Stella Black	ISBN 0 352 33588 2	
☐ SIN.NET Helena Ravenscroft	ISBN 0 352 33598 X	
☐ HOTBED Portia Da Costa	ISBN 0 352 33614 5	
☐ TWO WEEKS IN TANGIER Annabel Lee	ISBN 0 352 33599 8	
☐ HIGHLAND FLING Jane Justine	ISBN 0 352 33616 1	

To find out the latest information about Black Lace titles, check out the website: www.blacklace-books.co.uk or send for a booklist with complete synopses by writing to:

Black Lace Booklist, Virgin Books Ltd
Thames Wharf Studios
Rainville Road
London W6 9HA

Please include an SAE of decent size. Please note only British stamps are valid.

Our privacy policy
We will not disclose information you supply us to any other parties. We will not disclose any information which identifies you personally to any person without your express consent.

From time to time we may send out information about Black Lace books and special offers. Please tick here if you do <u>not</u> wish to receive Black Lace information. ❏

Please send me the books I have ticked above.

Name ....

Address ....

....

....

....

Post Code ....

Send to: Cash Sales, Black Lace Books, Thames Wharf Studios, Rainville Road, London W6 9HA.

US customers: for prices and details of how to order books for delivery by mail, call 1-800-343-4499.

Please enclose a cheque or postal order, made payable to Virgin Books Ltd, to the value of the books you have ordered plus postage and packing costs as follows:

UK and BFPO – £1.00 for the first book, 50p for each subsequent book.

Overseas (including Republic of Ireland) – £2.00 for the first book, £1.00 for each subsequent book.

If you would prefer to pay by VISA, ACCESS/MASTERCARD, DINERS CLUB, AMEX or SWITCH, please write your card number and expiry date here:

....

Signature ....

Please allow up to 28 days for delivery.